*For fans who follow Annette, and are interested in the series time line, this book takes place after Bitcoin Bluz and before Dixie Bluz*

*My passion for cars has moved beyond my career, as a Ford Motor field operations employee and subsequent Automotive Dealer Consulting specialist. My editor wife and our children suffered the slings and arrows of multiple relocations during my automotive profession. Germantown was one of our favorite places to live. My passion for cars has become their passion as well.*

*I would like to acknowledge the contributions of Marilyn Emmett, my editor, and the contributions of Lou and Julie Aronica for their good eyes on my work.*

# Mustang Bluz

# By: Patrick W. Emmett

- <u>Scam</u>: A common and informal term for a dishonest scheme.
- <u>Swindle</u>: A more formal term for cheating someone out of money or something else of value.
- <u>Deception</u>: A broader term encompassing any act of misleading someone, whether it involves a trick or a more elaborate scheme.
- <u>Fraud</u>: A more serious form of deception, often involving illegal activities.
- <u>Trick</u>: A simple act of deception, often involving a clever ruse.
- <u>Hoax</u>: A deliberate deception, often involving a fabricated story or event.
- <u>Grift</u>: A term often used for con artistry, where someone gains something by deceiving others, often by exploiting their trust.

## Characters:

- **Wolf LeDuc** – Owner of LeDuc and Johnson Automotive Consulting
- **Annette Dupart** – Employee of her cousin Wolf as a CPA. She is sometimes a contract employee for the FBI due to sharpshooting skills
- **Roger the Dog** – Wolf's Golden Retriever
- **Chick Farrell** – Wolfs' friend and Owner of Reliant Security and former FBI employee.
- **Clarence Smith** aka The Black Fox – Works for Chick and is a friend of Wolf and Annette
- **Connie Strong** – Office Manager for LeDuc and Johnson
- **Ezra Johnson** and wife Lavon –Johnson of LeDuc and Johnson
- **Stony & Sarah Carter** – Stony is a LeDuc & Johnson new hire
- **Frank Carlson** and **Tony Morrison** – LeDuc & Johnson Employees
- **Hop Dickerson** – FBI Cybercrimes Manager and Annette's love interest
- **Florence Sallaz** – FBI Field Agent assigned to Hop
- **Steve Williams** – Murdered salesman at Global Classic Vehicles
- **Connor Franklin** – General Manager of Global Classic Vehicles
- **Detective Mace Robertson** – Olathe Police
- **Detective Cory Sanders** – Olathe Police
- **Mark Dvorak** – Murder suspect
- **Clay Bonner** – Accomplice to Dvorak
- **Charles (Karel) Jensen** (aka Perry Sanchez) aka many names
- **Brenda Jensen** - Charles Wife and mastermind of the con set-up
- **Albert Jensen** – aka Cal Marsh, Son of Charles and Brenda
- **Eline Jensen** - aka Rita Simpson, daughter to Charles and Brenda
- **Dirk Jensen** - aka Jan Foster - younger son of Charles and Brenda
- **Morty and Ferdie** - aka Martin and Freddy cousins to Dirk and Albert
- **Chief Richard Sparks** – Germantown Chief of Police
- **Manfred Mickelson** – The Jensen's Lawyer and family relative

**Prologue:**

Everyone has dreams. Dreams often manifested with ambition, desires, hopes, wishes and sometimes fear. A dream can become an overwhelming need. We dream of things we want and must have. Like purchasing a lottery ticket, the ticket is not a chance, but an invitation to dream. If you win, what would you do? The possibilities are endless.

You may dream about a vacation, which serves as an escape from where you are in your life. You may dream of owning a beautiful home or simply have some place to rest your head. If you are an organ patient, you may dream for a critical transplant. If you are a child your dreams may be of a toy or just understanding. Maybe all you're dreaming of, is just to wake up for one more day.

What you dream and what you get may be entirely different things, which leads to disappointment. I know because, like you, I've had ups and downs from ecstasy to depression. I've learned in life, the secret to happiness and mental health, is always having something to look forward to. My advice, dream well, make plans, and follow your dreams!

The execution of a dream is not what's satisfying, it is nurturing a desire for something, that obsession, to look forward to. That is what it was with my cousin, Wolf LeDuc when he scanned web sites for months searching for that perfect car, his dream car. The lesson is, be very careful what you wish for. You may get more than your dreams can deal with.

## Chapter: 1    (A Car To Die For)

Steve Williams, a handsome six foot three man, was dressed in his usual business casual clothing. He was fit for a man of his age. He stood to his full height in order to reach the top of the car cover which spread across a 2018 Mustang Shelby GTR 350 coupe. He gently lifted the cover to reveal a pristine electric blue car with a beautiful white stripe that ran from the engine hood to the trunk. He smiled while carefully folding the cover and laid it on the floor behind the car. He rechecked the number on the windshield. As he did so, his cellphone buzzed. He looked at the caller ID, sighed, and said, "Yeah! What do *you* want?"

"Yes! I understand. You want to increase the price on your car. No I can't let you do that. We sell cars here. You signed a contract to sell your car. Look, I have an important customer arriving today around 9:00. I don't have time for this now."

"Uh-huh. What do you mean I'll regret my decision? Do not threaten me, you understand? I'm hanging up now. Yes, yes, I don't care what you think. Goodbye!" He hit the end call button, shook his head, and began walking toward his next vehicle.

Steve, the sales manager, sold expensive vehicles stored at the Global Classic Vehicles storage facility in Olathe, Kansas. He was annoyed. He shook his head trying to get the irritating call out of his mind. He checked the inventory list on his cellphone and found the location of the Mustang known as the Roush Jackhammer.

In his time, Steve had dealt with a lot of fussy car customers who wanted Global Classic Vehicles to sell their specialty cars. Many of them unsuccessfully tried more conventional methods by listing their vehicles on a variety of websites. In most cases, they simply wanted too much for their cars. Selling through an auction was out of the question for many of them because of the entry fee, but mostly because they wanted to set the reserve higher than the auction would accept. When the car didn't sell, they turned to Global Classic Vehicles to store and sell their vehicles for them, on consignment, for a commission.

This was the second call from this customer demanding that he not sell the car in a week. The man who just got off the phone said he was the owner of the Jackhammer. Paperwork said he lived in Clearwater, Florida. The owner stored the car here 1400 miles from his home and the car had been in Global's inventory for a long time.

Steve was convinced that the owner simply didn't understand the ups and downs of price fluctuation for cars in a weak automotive market. It was like the guy on the phone didn't really want to sell his car. He wanted to raise the price again, then he threatened to sue Global if the vehicle was sold. The man was also behind paying storage fees to Global. Storage fees were okay but a commission on sale would be much better. And Global needed the space. It was time to sell.

Steve thought, *"This owner signed a contract, in good faith, to sell the vehicle to a willing buyer for an agreed upon price, albeit overpriced. There was now someone out there prepared to pony up for a rare Mustang and Steve wanted that commission. The car buyer said he wanted to see the car first, drive it, then make a cash offer to buy."* Steve was more than prepared to please this out of state customer.

Arriving late, Steve noted that none of the other employees had shown up to work yet. Working alone, he found the storage slot for the car in question. He carefully removed the car cover to expose a rare black on black beauty. He folded the car's cover and placed it behind the vehicle. While he was bent over, he heard footsteps approach from behind. He stood up and said, "You startled me. What in the hell are you doing here? And what do you want? I don't have time right now. A customer is coming in today and I need to get this car ready. Go up front and wait at the office until we open."

"What's that on the car?" The person said pointing at the back of the Jackhammer.

Steve's head whipped around. He turned, bent down to closely inspect the side of the car for possible damage. That was the moment when he was shot in the back of his head with a single 9mm bullet. The loud noise echoed in the huge building. The bullet's entry wound pulverized the side of Steve's skull, and he fell to the floor between the two parked Mustang cars.

The murderer simply backed away and said, ". People like you just don't listen." He opened his cellphone. When someone answered all he said was, "Sale cancelled." The murderer hung up, then slipped the handgun into the pouch on the front of his hoodie. Pulling the hoodie tightly around his head, he rapidly walked back the way he had come into the rear of the building, leaving through a rear entrance. Exiting, he kept his head down avoiding as many close circuit cameras as possible.

**Chapter: 2**                    **(A Week Earlier)**

Surrounded by an orange grove, the man currently known as Perry Sanchez angrily disconnected his phone. The salesman at Global Classic Vehicles was being unreasonable. He took a moment to gather himself before making his next call.

He dialed the number, and a woman answered. "What happened Charles? Is she giving you trouble?"

"No Brenda, nothing like that. You know that golden nest egg we've been nurturing for the past three years?"

"Ye-e-e-s, what happened? The price of gold go down?"

"Worse. Those people in Kansas found a buyer for our car."

"Simply withdraw the car from their custody. We'll take it someplace else." She said.

"Can't, Brenda. There is a serious buyer showing up who's already put down a deposit for that car. He'll be there next week to take possession. They won't let me take the car out of their inventory at this stage. They claim that they have a contract that allows them to sell the car. All they see is dollar signs and a sucker whose willing to pay that much."

"I thought you set a ridiculously high price for that car. You said no one would pay that much."

"I wasn't paying that much attention and the market shifted. I priced the car above market, but the car's price is now within range of similar cars."

"Damn, Charles. I told you there had to be a better place to store that car than Kansas."

"You always said, invest into an appreciating asset. That is precisely what we did. The car's worth a lot more now than what we paid."

"How well hidden is our stuff?"

"Dirk hired someone who installed a secret compartment then modified the trunk to cover up the installation. The trunk looks almost like it did before he made the modification. He sent me pictures."

"So, no one knows what we have hidden in that car? The car buyer is simply buying a car at a stupid price. What can we do to stop the sale?"

"Dirk is busy wrapping up a job in Texas. Albert is free. Maybe Morty or Ferdie can go with him to Kansas. If they're lucky, they can prevent the sale. The worse case scenario is they simply steal the car out of the Global Classic Cars inventory, and we store it someplace else."

"Like where?"

"Just a rental storage unit. There are storage units all around Kansas City."

Behind him, Charles heard the woman Gwyn calling his name with a high pitched twitter. "Perry. Oh Perry, where are you? Are you all right?"

"Look, I've got to go. She's looking for me. Get hold of Albert, explain what's going on. Tell him and your nephews to get on a plane for Kansas City right away. And don't waste time."

"Goodbye. Love you." Brenda said.

Charles looked up and Gwyn was standing in the orchard not far from him. He said in the phone. "Love you, too." He turned to face Gwyn.

Gwyn's head tilted to one side, and she asked, "Who *was* that?"

Perry smiled and said, "My son. One of my grandkids fell and they had to take him to the hospital. He was explaining what happened when you came looking for me."

"You were gone so long. I was worried. I thought you might have fallen in the orchard. Is the child alright?"

Charles, aka Perry, tried to shake off his anger and smiled. "Yes. Broken arm. They're putting a cast on him now. Come on, let's finish breakfast. I believe you wanted to go to that flower market today."

"Oh, yes. We'll take the Benz. It's such a lovely Spring day."

"I would like to stop by the hardware store, too. If you don't mind. I need a few things." He said smiling.

"I don't know how you do it. You are so capable around the house, and you raised those children of yours all by yourself after your wife died. I wish my Monte had a father like you. He wouldn't be involved with all of those drugs, like he is."

Charles, aka Perry, looked up and smiled warmly. "Yes, nothing like Pop Warner Football to toughen up a kid to stay on the straight and narrow."

"Oh, Perry, you are my dream man."

## Chapter: 3     (One Week Earlier - Springtime)

To witness Springtime in Germantown, TN, is to experience an explosion of color and floral fragrances. Growing up in the Atchafalaya river basin of Louisiana, spring was just the beginning of a series of very hot and humid months to look forward to.

Colorful crepe myrtle bushes, dogwood trees, magnolia trees, and resplendent flowerbeds were bursting with color all over western Tennessee. Every year they announced a glorious rebirth of life for all of Germantown to enjoy. I miss my home and family in Louisiana, but I have grown to enjoy and appreciate the local beauty and good friends I've made at my new home in Tennessee.

My name is Annette Dupart. I work for my cousin and his business partner at LeDuc and Johnson. We're an automotive dealer consulting firm. After earning my CPA, I was able to move to a nicer apartment in Germantown away from the cramped living conditions near the University of Memphis. My second story one bedroom apartment provides sheltered parking for my Camaro and a short commute to the office.

I frequently travel in my job, providing accounting audits for car dealers. I enjoy the traveling part as it provides me with opportunities to meet different people and to visit places I have never been to before.

I had just returned to our office in Germantown from a trip to Paducah, KY. The dealer there had just changed their computer equipment and was having difficulty with the new accounting program. I left the dealer, and his accountant wife satisfied with my suggestions on how to better manage inventories and cashflow using detailed accounting schedules.

When I arrived at the office, I was greeted warmly by my cousin Wolf, his business partner, Ezra Johnson, and our office manager, Connie Strong. Wolf said, "Congratulations! I received a phone call from George Sonders in Paducah. He tells me that you are an accounting genius! He said you and his wife managed to turn a complex accounting nightmare into an easy to use program. They both agreed, they want you back to continue our services for regular follow-up visits."

I was embarrassed by the praise and said, "Their new computer program was confusing at first, but we managed to simplify the books and create a number of accounting schedules to manage the things they wanted to keep track of. Once Laura got the hang of things, she excelled at the task. I just kind of coached her."

"They were impressed with your methods, and now, we have a repeat customer on an annual contract. Well done!" Wolf said.

I demurred and said, "It was nothing."

Wolf began again, "To celebrate, I've planned a dinner at my favorite restaurant, Southern Social, here in Germantown. Ezra and Lavon will be coming, and Connie is bringing her husband. I've also invited a couple of people you know. Chick and Clarence will be joining us. You'll be the guest of honor to celebrate your second full year as a CPA for LeDuc and Johnson and the fine job you did in Atlanta."

"Oh, wow! A party? Just for me?"

Ezra said, "That's right, Sunshine! You've brought a ray of light to our consulting company. We're all proud to have you with us."

Connie grinned and said, "Our revenues have grown so much, I may need an assistant to help me keep track of our business. Your help with our accounting methods has been a blessing. Th-ank You-u-u, Dear." She said with her true Memphis accent.

"On top of that, with Ezra's skill at warranty auditing and your accounting acumen, I am now expanding our brand by adding new and used car sales coaching consultants to our staff. We are now the go-to people for automobile dealership consulting in the Deep South. At dinner tonight, I have a couple of announcements to make. Unless you have *other* plans. Do you have plans tonight?" Wolf asked giving me a wry grin.

"Oh, I think I can make it. How should I dress?"

Wolf said, "Just be your Annette self. See you there at 6:30 PM." He turned to enter his office.

Connie winked and said, "I think a dress would be appropriate, honey."

**Chapter: 4    (Dinner at Southern Social)**

Our soiree assembled in a private dining room at the Southern Social restaurant. Drinks were served and I ordered an Arnold Palmer while everyone else imbibed with an alcoholic beverage. The room was lovely, conversation was lively, and the table was set for 12. Wolf invited Miss Penelope McGruder, his on again and off again socialite girlfriend.

She greeted me warmly and asked about my new apartment. Wolf's best friend, Chick Farrel, the owner of Reliant Security, was delighted to see me as I was him. But I was absolutely thrilled to see his employee, Clarence Smith, aka The Black Fox. We became fast friends while we were dodging bullets in the Atchafalaya bayous. Clarence was employed by Chick as a body guard for hire and munitions specialist. A couple of years ago, Clarence and I watched in horror while a pet alligator, named Big Hoss, ate its owner after I shot the man. At least we think he did. No one ever found either the alligator or the man again.

I scanned around the dining room and saw two strangers across the room talking to one another. Wolf escorted me to Frank Carlson and Tony Morrison. They both looked to be in their early to mid-fifties and good humored. Wolf said, "These men are both former car dealership general managers. I hired them to work with our firm's clients. Their mission will be to increase car sales volume and trim expenses for our dealers. They're good at what they do and I'm lucky to have them on board."

I welcomed both men to the company. We then sat down to a delightful meal. Connie arranged to have Southern Social prepare an almond flavored sheet cake that said, "Congratulations, Annette" on it.

After cake, Wolf stood up and introduced everyone around the table. He then toasted the firm's success, and told everyone about my work in Baton Rouge, Atlanta, and Paducah, saying, "We're lucky to have her."

He then announced, "Annette, you have driven your coveted Camaro to our clients and put many miles on that muscle car. Starting Monday, you, Ezra, Tony, Frank, and I will be driving brand new leased vehicles, paid for by LeDuc and Johnson. And I'll pay Connie's mileage to the office. The leasing company will set each of you up with a vehicle of your choice from their inventory." Everyone cheered, including me.

"Next, I want to announce that our only void is managing dealership parts inventories. Parts inventory is a burden on dealership overhead and working capital. Ezra will tell you that having the right parts on hand will reduce carry-overs and speed up repairs to keep customers happy. I'm proud to announce that I am hiring a former coworker I worked with at car manufacturer. In my opinion, he's the best guru in the business. His name is Stony Carter. He lives near Kansas City in Leawood, Kansas. I'll be traveling there to hire him next week. And I'll be driving my new leased F150 pickup." The guests all shouted, "Here! Here!"

Wolf grinned. "This move will make LeDuc and Johnson a full service automotive consulting company. We'll be able to work with clients well beyond the Deep South where most of our business now resides. Most of that business, I must add, is thanks to Ezra, my exceptional business partner."

"Now, the next item is not related to business. I want to announce that my long time garage queen, the Mustang GT, known as 'the green monster,' has been sold to a local buyer who promised to keep her clean and running nice. So, while in Kansas City, I'll go see a couple of cars that I have my eye on from the internet. I'm focused on two outstanding cars at a storage facility called Global Classic Vehicles in Olathe, KS. I've been talking to the salesman, and I've put bids on both, hoping to win one of them."

There was murmur and discussion around the table. Wolf looked at me and said, "And Annette? I would be pleased to have you as my traveling mate for this trip. I want you to meet the man I want to hire, Stony. He can tell you a lot about parts inventory management and how it should be accounted for on financial statements." Wolf then looked a little sheepish before he said, "And I could use your skills to drive my truck back home, if I buy a car."

I thought, *"You want my skills to drive your truck?"* However, what I said was, "What about my work schedule?"

"Already handled and rescheduled thanks to Connie." He said grinning. "We should be free to leave next week."

"That's kind of short notice. And, where the heck is Olathe, Kansas? Kansas is all about wheat farms and cows, I think."

"Olathe is a nice suburb of the Kansas City area. You know, home of the Kansas City Chiefs?"

"Chiefs? My Saints loving brothers will never forgive me, but it does sound like a fun road trip. How long does it take to get there?"

"Eight hours, give or take. We'll be visiting Stony and staying in Overland Park."

## Chapter: 5    (The Road Trip)

I now know why Wolf wanted me to come along on his employee hiring and car purchasing journey. I drove most of the trip to Kansas City in his new leased F150 while he snored in the passenger seat. Like he said, we made it in just under eight hours, even with driving through traffic in St. Louis. I was pooped when we arrived in Overland Park. We drove straight to the Embassy Suites and checked in.

Once we settled into our rooms, Wolf called me to say that we would be joining Stony Carter and his wife for dinner at Stony's house, which was not far from the hotel. I sighed. After the drive, all I wanted to do was to soak in the hotel hot tub and call it an evening. But duty called.

Wolf and I arrived at Stony Carter's house in Leawood, KS. He was shorter and a little older than Wolf with a full head of sandy colored hair and a well-trimmed mustache. The two had worked for the same automobile company in Detroit. Stony said he had recently taken early retirement and was ready to apply his parts management skills without corporate interference. He said, "I'll be working to improve car dealership parts inventories. It's a noble calling." He said smiling with humor.

Wolf told me he and Stony became good friends in Detroit. Stony mentored Wolf on how to survive the competitive corporate environment. Wolf said he was eventually transferred to field work in Detroit, but he longed to be assigned to someplace, far away from his Detroit family, where he grew up. Stony had moved around the country, in and out of Detroit, before finally being assigned to the Kansas City Regional office.

On the other hand, Wolf's first assignment, beyond Detroit, was Memphis and he never left.

Recently, Stony had been working part time at a local car dealership in Kansas City, when Wolf called and made him the job offer. He readily accepted.

Stony said he and his wife have children ranging in age from 8 to 18. I didn't really understand how many kids they had or where they all were. But there were lots of young people jumping in and out of a swimming pool in Stony's back yard.

Stony's wife, Sarah, was a cheerful woman. She had reddish brunette hair and a figure going to plump. She smiled pointing, "Those are friends of the boys. I'd rather have them playing here in our backyard than someplace, who knows where?" I nodded in agreement.

Wolf and Stony each held long neck beers while Sarah, was never far away from a glass of pink wine, always smiling and waving at the kids in the pool.

Sarah went inside and was busy in the kitchen preparing a tossed salad. I followed. She is a very friendly, talkative woman and was a font of knowledge about the Kansas City area. Specifically, the Kansas City Chiefs. If I were to believe her, every man, woman, and child within two hundred miles were diehard fans of the football team.

I had no idea Kansas City was called the 'City of Fountains.' Apparently, there are over 200 of them in the surrounding area. She bragged about the local art scene, the theaters, and the music. Honestly, I didn't say so, but when it comes to music, Kansas City has a lot of catching up to do when compared to Memphis in May and the Memphis

Blues. I soon discovered that she was talking about ballet and symphonic music.

Apparently, all of Sarah's children are or have been in some kind of youth sports program. Soccer seems to be the youth sport of choice for children in the area. The Carters have a lovely, good sized home in a neighborhood full of big houses. What struck me the most was, I saw no brick homes. In our part of Tennessee, most of the homes were clad in brick. I was shocked to hear Sarah say that the homes all had basements and porch decks, something alien to homes in the South. She said, "Yep! Always the threat of tornadoes, you know." I didn't and I didn't want to find out either.

Driving into Kansas from Missouri, I was surprised to see the number of trees and hills. I've always thought of Kansas as being a flat, boring landscape only to be flown over. A lot of my predispositions about Kansas and the surrounding area were quickly being proven wrong.

We ate a fun picnic style dinner of barbecue chicken, salad, and potato salad. We ate within sight of the pool and watched children bent on drowning one another. Stony and Sarah have a large friendly golden retriever, a mendicant, who's mission was to relieve me of my dinner.

I overheard Wolf talking to Stony, "That's right, besides making you an offer you can't refuse, I am in town to purchase one of two vehicles at the Global Classic Vehicles in Olathe."

"Really? What are you looking at?"

"Well, the one that caught my eye the most was the 2018 Roush Jackhammer Mustang. The car is black with matt black trim and it's pure sex. But I don't need a car to leave in my garage all the time, so I was also looking at a 2018 Shelby GT 350, electric blue with a white racing stripe. I can use that car as a daily driver. Prices are all over the board for both cars in the open market. I did a lot of research for months but found these two in Olathe with low miles and I intend to make an offer."

Stony grinned and said, "You saw my 67 Shelby GT Cobra in the garage. I've had that since I was a kid. You're right about not wanting to take a classic car out of the garage. I'm afraid of paint chips, glass damage or any number of hazards while driving my car on the road. I trailer it to car shows then carefully put it back into my garage with a car cover."

"I'm running out of garage space, or I would buy more cars." Wolf admitted sipping his beer.

Stony laughed and said, "Wouldn't we all?" Then they clicked bottlenecks to toast the idea.

"I'm going out to Olathe to look at both of them tomorrow. I don't suppose you would like to come along? I know your boss may not like the idea of you taking a day off."

"Ah, she's busy with the kids. Now that I'm officially retired, I have a lot of vacation days. Sure, I'll go with you. Sounds like fun."

"You won't mind if Annette comes along would you?"

"Look, Sarah would come along with us too, because she likes cars, but she has garden club and soccer with one of the kids tomorrow. Sure, the more, the merrier. So, she likes cars, does she?"

"Custom Camaro hotrod, modified by her brothers."

"I thought there was something I liked about that girl."

**Chapter: 6     (Planning our day)**

I slept like a baby in my hotel bed. The long drive and evening at Stony's wore me out. However, I awoke at my normal predawn time and changed into my running gear. Instead of using the hotel workout room, I chose to explore the neighborhoods surrounding the hotel where Wolf and I were staying. My curiosity about a new city and state had me wondering what kind of people live in Kansas.

I stepped outside into brisk, chilly, Spring weather. I was told by the desk clerk that there had been a lot of rain recently. I reasoned that each spring day brings more daylight, but today, clouds filled the skies, and the overcast sky brought wet humid wind. During my run, I saw many nice homes lined along neighborhood streets. I was surprised by the hills which belied my preconceived notions about the Sunflower state.

I crested a hill not far from the hotel, and saw a massive sports complex which, I discovered, was attached to a high school. *"Wow!"* I thought. Running by, I saw a huge football arena, tennis courts, baseball, soccer fields. I took a right on a street named Lamar. This amused me because I have a cousin in Breaux Bridge who had a dog he named Lamar.

I crossed a bridge spanning Interstate 435. Below me the traffic was light but brisk for this hour of the morning. I arrived at a round-a-bout. I had seen these before and wondered if that invention didn't cause more accidents than it was designed to prevent. The round-a-bout was located next to a large high-rise hotel. Curious, I ran past the hotel and discovered this collection of buildings was actually the Overland Park Convention Center. Further up the road, I saw a multicolored building that was a children's hospital. Seeing a busy road ahead, I stopped, made a U-turn, and trotted back the way I had come.

This time, I ran along a street toward an intersection with a stoplight. I had yet to cover more than two miles. I continued across the street up yet another hill into a neighborhood full of what appeared to be lopsided homes. I've seen such homes in Memphis, and I think they're called tri-level's. Anyway, they all looked well-kept. By the time I ran past a new grade school, I saw other runners and people walking dogs who were also out to catch the cool early morning Spring air.

I ran beyond a modern looking grade school and turned on a street that took me past a middle school. I continued to run on streets with houses that, by this time, looked pretty much the same. I checked my watch and had run over three miles. I began to work my way back toward the hotel.

I waved back at other friendly runners, some with dogs and others with jogger baby strollers. I don't know if they were waving at me or my University Of Memphis sweatshirt. I made it back to a main street which would take me back to my hotel.

On my way, I saw a street that said, "Not a through street." "What the heck!" I ran up that hill to find not a dead-end, but the street that turned left and became another street taking me back to the bottom of the hill. I saw a house at the top of this hill with a wall of brilliant yellow daffodils smiling at me which made me happy. Homes on this street were bigger with two stories. They reminded me of homes in Germantown, only they were not brick.

I navigated my way back to the street which went took me to my hotel. Once there, I showered and changed into jeans and a sweater.

Checking my cellphone, I saw a message from Wolf saying he was downstairs having breakfast and to join him.

When I arrived, I saw Wolf and Stony engaged in animated conversation and laughing.

I was greeted warmly by Stony who said, "Annette! I was just reminding your cousin about the time we played car tag in Southfield, Michigan. It's a dangerous game but we were driving company cars, and we didn't care." He laughed.

I sat down and gave Wolf a questioning look. He admitted, "Yep! The way it worked, our field group was driving from a meeting in Southfield. We drove in a line traveling at more than posted speed. The purpose was to get up close to the car in front of you then gently tap their bumper. They would then have to pull out and fall back to the end of the line. It was a game, and all of the employees were having fun with the dangerous sport."

I must have given him a strange look because Wolf laughed and said, "Yep! I did that and so much more. Those were the days. I could have stayed in Detroit for my entire career, but I wanted to see more of the country. Staying in Detroit, I would never have made it to Memphis and Louisiana to meet my father's family. And, I wouldn't have met Ezra Johnson and my cousin Annette.

"So, he's the Johnson of LeDuc and Johnson? I've never met him but I'm glad he helped you get started with consulting. And Annette is a CPA. Your company has the skills to offer exceptional advice to car dealers. But today, when do we go to Global Classic Vehicles to look at those cars?"

"I'm supposed to be there around 9:00 this morning. I'm meeting the sales manager, Steve Williams. He's in charge of selling cars from the storage facilities inventory. He has a team of people maintaining cars for car owners who want to sell their prized possessions. I spoke to him on the phone several times."

"Can't wait to see what you've found. I hear there's a lot of eye candy at Global Classic Vehicles. I've never been there before, but it's supposed to be great! By the way, the Mustang club is having a car cruise this Friday evening. I hope you'll you still be around. If you are, do you want to go?"

"I came here to hire you and see a couple of special Mustangs. Let's see how that works out first before I make any commitment to a car cruise."

"I know you have that pickup outside. Why don't we take my SUV instead? There'll be more room, and I know exactly where Global Vehicles is located in Olathe."

Wolf looked at me, I shrugged my shoulders, and he said, "Sure, if you don't mind."

I added, "Not at all. This should be fun. And I don't have to drive."

## Chapter: 7      (Global Surprise)


When we arrived, I was surprised by the sheer size of the Global Classic Vehicles building. Stony said, "Wait till you see the $2.2 Million Dollar Super Snake Mustang that I'm told is stored here. You're eyes will pop out!"

Wolf said, "Can't wait but a car like that is way out of my league."

When we went inside, Stony was right. People were lined up at the door, and we followed them inside. Cars of every stripe and description were stuffed inside this massive facility. We walked to the office and Wolf explained who he was, and we were here to meet Steve Williams. A middle aged brunette woman said, "Steve is here someplace. I saw a text when I came in. So, you're the guy that's here to look at that good looking Roush Jackhammer?"

"Or the 2018 Shelby GT350 in blue. Is it possible to go to take a look at the Jackhammer now?"

"Sure, I'll draw you a map so you can find the Jackhammer. I'll call Steve's phone and telling him you're here. If he doesn't answer, I'll escort you to the car myself."

Steve Williams didn't answer his phone. So armed with the directions and our Global guide, we began a long walk past rows and rows of cars. Wolf would remember this as being the experience of his lifetime. I was also getting excited to see a special car with such a strange name.

We walked passed many exceptional looking cars, both beautiful and exotic. Apparently, the one we were looking for was way in the back of the huge facility. Before we got to it, I could see the black nose of the car from twenty feet away. As we approached, we admired and commented on the shiny black nose of the sinister looking car, with a matte black racing stripe, trimmed in red striping in front of us.

Wolf and Stony rushed passed our guide to the left side of the car to peer in the windows. While they were drooling on the paint, I walked around to the right side and stopped dead in my tracks.

I said, "Uh, guys!"

"Not now Annette. This is so cool!" Wolf said.

"No, Wolf, you need to see this, now!"

"Oh no! What is it, a scratch?"

"No. Not a scratch."

Wolf, Stony and our guide, arrived beside me. When they did, no one said a word. The brunette woman suddenly began screaming with a shriek that could peel paint.

Before us, between the Jackhammer and an older Mustang, we saw a man lying on his side in an unnatural position with sticky looking blood oozing from a head injury.

"I think we should see if he's still breathing." I suggested breathlessly.

Wolf said, "Stony, call 911. Annette, and you too Miss, stay back, I'll check for a pulse."

Wolf carefully straddled the man on the floor and used the Jackhammer for balance while he bent over to place two fingers on the man's carotid artery. I heard Wolf sigh. He said, "Still warm. No pulse." He stood up and retraced his steps to my side. "We need to back away and wait for the police. Don't touch anything." Wolf muttered.

The woman guide was next to me with her arms folded and was shivering. She had tears streaming down her face. In a shaky voice she said, "Oh, Steve."

Stony held up his phone saying, "The police and an ambulance are on their way. I'll go to the front with this lady and inform the office staff about the man."

Watching Stony leave, I asked Wolf, "Do you think that was the man you were supposed to meet?"

"I don't know for sure. Our guide called him Steve, but I couldn't read his name badge. There's a bench. Let's sit there and wait for the first responders while Stony goes up front."

Saddened by what we discovered, I was ready to sit down and regroup. I'm sure Wolf was, too.

## Chapter: 8     (Recovering From Shock)

Wolf and I studied our cellphones while waiting for EMT's and police to arrive at Global Classic Vehicles. I couldn't help myself as my eyes kept drifting to the corner of the black Jackhammer Mustang where a man lay dead. I noticed Wolf looking up at the ceiling and the walls. I asked, "What do you see?"

"It's what I don't see. There are no video cameras in this section of the building."

"Don't you think that's unusual? I mean with so many expensive cars here on the floor, you would think cameras would be everywhere."

"Yes, I do. It'll be interesting to see what the local police have to say."

Wolf and I believed that we would be questioned for hours by the police to find out what we knew about the man who was killed and what happened to him. As it turned out, they understood we came into the building at 9:00 this morning just to look at cars and found the dead man with an employee. They took our names and contact information and said they would be in touch if they had any further questions. We never got to ask them about what they thought about cameras. I overheard one officer mention the place had a couple of break-in attempts in the past.

We stopped by the office and talked to the Global staff. They told us that the dead man was indeed Steve Williams. Wolf was crestfallen he said, "I was to meet him this morning and make a decision about buying one of two cars in your inventory. Is there anyone else who can help me?"

The brunette woman who took us to the Jackhammer, told us her name was Mandy and said, "As you can see, Global Classic Vehicles is not in business today because of what happened. Can you come back a day or two from now?"

I spoke up, "Actually, we drove all the way here from Memphis just to look at those two cars and need to return home. It would be a shame if we didn't even get a chance to at least look over both cars."

Mandy nearly choked when she said, "Steve was our sales manager, but our general manager also sells cars. Give me your phone number. I'll talk to him, and we may be able to set something up before you return home."

We thanked her and left the building. On the way out, police were busy rounding up everyone who was inside the building when the doors were opened. I knew that Steve's blood had not yet coagulated on the floor by the time we saw it. Which told me, he had been killed just before we set foot inside Global's building. If so, where did his killer go? Was he still inside the Global facility?

We three disgruntled car enthusiasts piled into Stony's SUV and drove back to Overland Park in a funk. We re-grouped in the Embassy Suites common area and sipped on bottled water. Wolf was in a mood, for not getting to even sit in either one of his car choices. I wasn't feeling too good either about discovering a dead man lying next to the Jackhammer.

At the hotel, we were all quietly reading our cellphones and I interrupted the silence by saying, "Okay, what now?"

Stony was trying his best to be an upbeat host. He said, "Look, I know you came to see me and to potentially purchase a great car you found online. Maybe I can make your day a little better. It's starting to rain outside, or I would take you to the Kansas Speedway track today. They planned to hold time trials for a road course race today with some Cobras. Since we can't do that, what say we go to a car museum? I know some people, and we should have no problem just showing up."

"What kind of cars?" I asked.

"All kinds. The first place I'm thinking about has mostly vintage classics. It is located just west of here. The other place is the Kansas City Car Museum, located not far from Olathe."

I looked at Wolf to see what he wanted to do but he seemed distant and self-absorbed, probably sulking about making a 500 mile trip only to have his car buying plans squashed by an unfortunate death. I said, "Wolf?"

"Huh? Oh, sure. The Vintage cars sound like fun." Wolf said.

On the ride west to the museum I asked Wolf if he thought we should simply cut our losses and go back to Germantown. He said, "No. I really enjoy spending the time with Stony. He and I still need to work out a compensation agreement. Who knows, someone at Global may yet call about the cars. Besides, we have a Mustang cruise to attend Friday night, right Stony?"

"You bet, brother. I think there'll be at least 75 Mustangs of all shapes and sizes there. I'm guessing you'll enjoy yourself. Sarah has made plans for the smaller kids to be at a sleepover. My son, Jacob, is going to a Spring Formal. So, my wife will be joining us."

Wolf appeared to be less than enthusiastic about doing anything other than shopping for a car, but we went to the museum anyway.

The museum was located in a cluster of commercial buildings. The cars were spectacular. We took a walk through automobile history. There must have been 50 cars on display, and my understanding was, the owner had that many or more stored in barns on his property. There was not a car in sight newer than the 1940's. They had been meticulously restored and they all looked like they had just come off the showroom floor. What I saw was impressive. I was standing next to Wolf studying a placard describing a 1932 Auburn Boattail when his cellphone rang. I overheard his end of the conversation.

"Who? Oh, yes. Thank you for calling me. What? You can? When? Yet this evening? I'm riding with someone, let me ask."

With cellphone in hand Wolf rushed over to Stony and explained "The general manager from Global called and was asking if we could come over to the Global building yet this evening. He said the place closes about 5:00 PM but he and a mechanic would still be there if we wanted to come and look at the two cars that I'm interested in. You can take me back to my truck or you can come with me. Your choice."

Stony looked absolutely surprised and said, "I'm in brother. Let's do it!"

Wolf said into the phone, "Yes! We'll be there."

# Chapter: 9    (The Quest Continues)

Before it was time to go to Global, the three of us ate an early dinner at a place called Jack Stack Barbecue. I was turned around and asked Stony where we were. He said, "Overland Park, not far from your hotel."

I ordered my barbecue meal harboring low expectations because Memphis is well known for exceptional pork barbecue at places like the Rendezvous, Corky's, and the Germantown Commissary. I have to admit, I was pleasantly surprised. Stony insisted I try something called burnt ends. What I was served was crusty, blackened chunks of beef served with a side of unique BBQ sauce to add to the meat as I saw fit. The coleslaw was tasty and not served on a sandwich, though the server said they could do that if we asked. The fries were great, and the meal raised my opinion of barbecue outside of Memphis. I kind of missed the bread pudding though.

While eating, Stony said, "Not far from the museum we visited, Panasonic recently built the largest EV battery plant in the United States in a community called DeSoto." He went on to explain the economic impact on the area while I thought about a town named DeSoto in Kansas. I was amused because we have the Hernando DeSoto bridge in Memphis. The historical myth in Memphis was that the Spanish Conquistador visited the Chickasaw natives there centuries ago. I doubted that he made it to Kansas.

We arrived at Global's facility shortly before 7:00 PM. Wolf knocked on the front door while Stony simply pushed on the door and walked in. Wolf yelled out, "Hello! Anyone here?"

I mumbled, "I hope we don't find another dead body."

Stony gave me a horrified look, and I smiled. Then we heard a voice. "Coming!" I saw a man in his late 40's with premature white hair ambling toward us from our left. "Hello! I'm Connor Franklin, the general manager and co-owner of Global Cars. Come on in." He strode over to Wolf reached out with his right hand and said, "You must be Wolf LeDuc?"

Wolf enthusiastically shook his hand saying, "Yes I am. This is Stony Carter, a close friend, and this is my cousin, Annette Dupart. You bet! We're here to see the two cars I was talking to Steve about."

"Sad news about Steve. I asked the police and all they would tell me is they are following up on several leads. The only thing they said, was that the crime looked like a break-in at our back door, and it must have been an attempted car theft. They took last night's security camera recording with them. I have no idea who they're looking for." Connor said.

"I thought, *Why would someone try to steal a car just before the place opened up? And why just kill a guy who was working there?*"

"Well, come on. I have a golf cart to make our trip to the cars easier. Tyrone, my head mechanic is at the cars now, shining them up a bit. The crime scene tape is still around the Jackhammer, but we should be able to slip the car out of its parking spot with no problem."

When the golf cart arrived at the Jackhammer's location, Tyrone had already pulled the car into the main aisle. I couldn't take my eyes off the pool of coagulated blood that had small yellow crime scene tents with numbers on them where Steve Williams had been shot.

My attention was drawn to the shiny black monster which looked very impressive. Tyrone stood next to the car with a rag in his hand and a smile on his face. He beamed with pride as though the car were his own.

"Have you had the car out much since it came to Global?" Wolf asked.

"This car has sat at Global for over three years. We start all of the cars every 30 days, and we check for fluid leaks and air pressure in the tires. This is the first time the car has been out of the storage bay since we moved it to this spot two years ago."

Tyrone smiled, spoke up, and said, "It started right up and purrs like a kitten."

Wolf gave a head nod toward the car and Connor smiled and said, "Sure! You bet! I'll ride with you, and Tyrone will follow in the golf cart with your friends to open the garage door to let us out. Good time to go, rain's supposed to come again tomorrow."

Stony and I stood to one side of the large open garage door, with envy in our eyes, wishing it were us behind the wheel. Wolf slipped the car into gear and the engine rumbled like thunder. We stood back out of the way when Wolf and Connor rolled the Roush Jackhammer Mustang out of the garage and watched it slowly creep out of the parking lot and into the street. They took off, rubber burning and we grinned hearing the loud engine changing gears well beyond the Global building.

I felt left behind. Stony slowly shook his head. I turned to look at him and said, "So, tell me about your parts inventory experience."

"Huh? Oh, yeah. For the past several years, my assignment with the company was to travel to car dealers who complained about never having the right part on hand even though they had huge parts inventories."

"I've heard that complaint before." I said.

"My job was to hold seminars at Company/Dealer meetings. My seminars were always full because dealership owners loved my message to keep a lean yet effective inventory. Still, I received a lot of push-back from parts managers who defended large inventories because they sold wholesale body parts to area body shops. They simply didn't want to address the daily need to stock auto repair parts in their shops for vehicles less than 10 years old. They make money selling parts in volume. While owners complain about money tied up in parts inventories, they do love the parts sales numbers."

"So, why did you take early retirement?"

Stony laughed and said, "I'm no spring chicken and I had nearly 30 years with the company. They offered an incentive for me to leave. The factory liked dealers stocking large parts inventories because they were in the business of selling parts. My message was a conflict of interest. It was time for me to hang-up my soapbox and move on."

"Do you think you'll be more effective with a consulting company?" I asked.

"I do. Mostly because the dealers and general manager will be paying for the service, unlike free seminars. And they're more interested in the bottom line. To be honest, the factory only had me doing what I did with dealers because they wanted to address dealer complaints and to placate the dealer council."

"Well, our business is based on helping car dealers improve their profit margins. It sounds like you have a formula for doing just that. Welcome aboard." I said smiling.

"I haven't signed my hiring contract yet, but I appreciate your support. That actually means a lot to me. Do you think Wolf will buy that Roush?"

"He still hasn't looked at that Shelby 350, but judging from the look in his eye, I would say he's in love."

When Wolf and Conner returned from their test drive, Wolf was ecstatic. He said, "Wow! What a ride. I'm not sure I can handle a beast like this as a daily driver. I want to, but I'm not sure it's practical."

"You still have that Shelby 350 to look at. They're about the same price. Do you want to look at that one?" Connor asked.

"Absolutely!" Wolf said.

Tyrone parked the Roush Jackhammer while Connor gave us a golf cart ride to the Shelby.

"That car sure is beautiful! I love the shade of blue." I said.

"The leather seats are trimmed with the same blue color scheme, and the electronics are fantastic! You ready?" Connor asked Wolf.

"As ready as a hound at a fox hunt!" Wolf said.

Connor laughed saying, "Come on, let's fire it up and take a ride."

When they returned, Wolf couldn't stop comparing the two vehicles. "Honestly, this is a very difficult decision." He said.

Connor laughed and said, "Buy em both!"

"I only have room in my garage for one. And affording both would be problematic."

"Tell you what. Come back in the morning and I'll have them both sitting side by side in our mini-showroom. How do you want to pay for your choice?"

"I know you have a bid and buy program but I'm willing to do a bank to bank transfer for either one. You or the seller would have the money in your account before you sign the title."

"Sounds fair. Your check or wire transfer would go into my bank. So, see you in the morning, okay? Before it rains?"

"I'll have a fitful night's sleep, but I'll be here to choose my car." The two men shook hands. Stony, Wolf and I all piled into Stony's SUV and listened to Wolf talk about both cars all the way back to the hotel.

# Chapter: 10     (Decisions Decisions)

Wolf and I found a neighborhood bistro and ate a lite meal after Stony let us off at our hotel. He enjoyed a locally brewed beer while I drank my tonic and lime. Oddly, Wolf never mentioned going to Global at all while we ate, but I knew that he would have a difficult night's sleep, thinking about both cars.

The next morning it was raining buckets or *"il pleut à seaux"* as we say in Cajun country. So, I did my five mile run in the hotel workout room. After my shower, I was ready for coffee and a good hot breakfast. I ordered a mushroom and cheese omelette with a bowl of blueberries on the side. I passed on my desired breakfast of a Danish and coffee for this more substantial meal.

When Wolf showed up for breakfast he was red eyed and foggy. I pointed at the coffee urn, and he smiled gratefully. He ordered bacon and eggs over easy and scooped up cantaloupe onto his plate for a side. Waiting for his eggs, he quietly sipped his coffee standing in line and not saying a word. When he picked up his order, he stopped and refilled his coffee on his way back to our table. I said, "Well, you do look a little better."

He sat down, grinned and took another sip of coffee. "You noticed. I had a tough time thinking about the cars last night, but that's not what kept me up."

"Okay, tell me what was on your mind?"

Wolf took a folded up piece of paper out of his shirt pocket and handed it to me. After unfolding the note I read:

*"Picking the wrong car can be murder. Stay away from the Jackhammer."*

"Yeow! How did you get this?"

"It was slipped under the wiper blade on my truck. I went out last night to get my phone charger and found that note. I searched the parking lot and didn't see anyone hanging around. I showed it to the desk clerk, and he showed it to the manager. They checked video coverage of the parking lot"

"What did they see?" I asked.

"They captured an picture of someone wearing a hoodie, who walked into the frame with the sweatshirt pulled over their head. They slipped the note under my wiper blade. That image could be anyone. No recognizable features could be seen. The manager asked if I wanted to call the police. Because it was late and I couldn't make out any facial features, I declined to report the incident."

"So, are going to report this to the police today?"

"The Overland Park police would have no idea what the note was about. I think you're right. I need to contact the police investigators from yesterday and show them the note. They may see the connection."

"Did you get a business card from them? I didn't."

"No. But Connor or someone at Global probably knows who the officers were. I'll call him this morning and ask him to have that Detective show up this morning."

I checked my watch, and it was just a little after 7:00. "When do you think Connor will be in?"

"I'm guessing he'll be there close to 8:30, maybe 9:00 this morning.

"You know, I'm thinking that you should forget buying a car from Global all together. There's too many warning signs. First, there's a murder and now, a warning off of a specific car. What's so special about that one Mustang?"

"That concerns me too. I've checked and double checked the Mustang market in all of the standard and custom websites. The price on the Roush Mustang is high but consistent with the market. Actually, there's nothing really unique about the way it's equipped, compared to other Roush Jackhammer Mustangs. However, the mileage is very low, and it looks pristine. Don't get me wrong, it's a special car alright and to be honest, I am leaning more toward that car than the blue Shelby."

"But at what risk?"

"That's what we need to find out."

"How?"

"By going back out to Global this morning at the appointed time. We need to go over that car with a fine tooth comb. Somebody has a reason to keep me and probably anyone else away from that car. I'm thinking it could be drugs."

"Or it could be someone hiding evidence. Maybe someone committed a crime with that car and is storing it at Global as a way to prevent people from finding the car." I said.

"You do have a diabolical mind, no doubt about that. Are you thinking there could be blood evidence in there? Something they tried to clean up but could be found under a luminol light?"

"Now, who's thinking murder beside me?"

"Well, someone has already committed murder, and it may not be their first. So, your murder evidence theory may be accurate."

"Is Stony going with us to Global this morning?"

"No. He had something else to do. It will be just you and me. He may show up if he thinks I'm buying one of the cars."

"You know, if you get one of those cars, you could drive it to the Mustang Club car show tomorrow evening. That would be fun."

"That thought was in the back of my mind, too, but I need to acquire a car first without risking life and limb."

"Well, I'll keep my eyes open and my Nano handy."

"I thought you preferred your Beretta 1911."

"I do for range shooting, but the Nano is for close-up and personal protection. Since we're talking about danger, did you bring a weapon with you?"

"I do have my Sig Sauer locked up in the truck, if I need it."

"Don't worry, I have you covered."

"I bet you do."

## Chapter: 11     (Eye On the Prize At Global)

The rain let up some and I had an uneasy feeling when Wolf and I puled into the Global parking lot. The clouds were still threatening when I got out of the pickup. I visually scanned all around the parking lot and the streets that led to the building. I saw nothing untoward. Standing next to the front door of the building, I heard Wolf ask, "You coming in?"

"Yes, of course. Just looking for bogeymen."

Wolf did a doubletake and grinned. The door had a sign on it declaring, "Global Closed Due To Maintenance." We tried the door, and it was open. Once inside, Connor sprung from his office and greeted us.

"Global Classic Cars is officially closed today. I gave the staff a paid day off, due to Steve's death. Tyrone is here with me, and I've asked him to bring the cars to our mini showroom. By the way, I got your message. I called and left a voicemail for Detective Mace Robertson at the Olathe Police Department. He and his partner will be here sometime this morning to look at your death threat and to inspect the car in question."

Wolf nodded and said, "Have you checked your close circuit footage of the building today? I'd like to see if anyone may have snuck inside before you got here this morning?"

"No. I didn't think to do that. Tyrone didn't seem to have any trouble locating the cars and bringing them up to the mini showroom."

"Is anyone else at all in the building?" Wolf asked.

Connor blew out some air and said, "Yes, I have two maintenance men who check dust covers and shine exposed cars. They arrived about the same time that I did. They're somewhere on the floor. Tell you what. If it makes you feel any more comfortable, you can check the video coverage with me. I have 10 cameras inside the building and 4 outside. We can use two computers to look at all of them if you like. We'll view split images on the monitors."

"Sounds fair. I would feel better. Thank you."

Connor, Wolf, Tyrone, and I hovered around two monitors and began looking at video footage beginning at midnight and scanned forward. Tyrone and I studied the outside camera images while Wolf and Connor inspected the interior images.

Looking at the same nighttime images of the building's exterior was boring work. We saw the same image from each camera. The cameras covered all of the access points to the building, so if someone were going to get into the building, a camera would pick up their entry. We scanned the  timeline pretty fast when Tyrone suddenly said. "Stop! Go back."

"Which camera?" I asked, He pointed at number 4, a side door showing the back of the building. I slowly rewound the image backwards until I saw what he saw. Two men, dressed in dark clothing wearing hoodies looked like they were picking the lock to get into the building. We saw just a flash of facial image, white guy. But we saw nothing special to identify the intruders. They appeared to use lock pick tools and a screwdriver.

Tyrone said, "Wow! That was quick, they're in!" He was right. They got in and quickly shut the door.

I said, "The time on the video is, 5:48 AM. Wolf, Connor, you need to see this. They've been in the building for hours and must be hiding in the building with us now."

Connor said, "That's camera 4, at the back of the building. I'm calling 911 now."

Connor had only dialed 9 when two armed men stepped into the office where we were reviewing video footage. I turned my back to the two men and slipped my Beretta 1911 out of my purse. I heard one of them say. "Get away from those screens. And I want everyone to turn around and face me."

We did as he asked. I turned around, concealing my gun at my side behind my rain jacket. Both men wore black balaclava's to cover their faces, and their handguns were pointed at us. One man appeared unsteady with his, waving an older model Smith and Wessen revolver around like a fairy wand.

The man who must have been the leader said, "You don't take no for an answer, do you Mustang man? You were warned. Now, this is your final offer. Buy the blue one. I am taking the black one with me now. Nobody move, or my friend and I will put bullet holes in all of you."

No one moved and no one said anything. I knew I could take the one closest to me with the revolver out, but the other one would surely fire his gun, and someone would get hurt. I had to wait. I knew Detectives would eventually get here, but when? Our 9-1-1 call was not completed so it may take a while. The two armed men unaware that law enforcement was coming, both looked uncertain about how to proceed.

I said, "Hey, it's just a car. Would you really kill someone just for a car?" I said stalling for time.

The lead guy looked at me with shiny brown eyes, like he just saw me for the first time. He said, "You there, shut up! What do you know about cars anyway?"

*"Kind of a sexist remark."* I thought, but I said, "I know that if you don't know the access code to the ignition on this special Mustang, you're not going anywhere."

"What are you talking about, access code? All I need is the key. Which one of you has it?"

I said, "These high-tech cars are theft proof. You need a special Lo-Jack access code and a key fob. Without that, you have nothing."

Connor gave me the funniest look. Wolf's eyes just went wide. I said, "If you don't believe me, Connor, toss him the key fob."

Connor didn't know what my play was, but he dug in his pocket and threw the fob at the guy who was talking. The key fell short and while guy one was fumbling to grab the key, guy two was watching him. I turned and shot guy 2 in the arm holding his gun. The gun flew out of his hand, and he fell to the ground holding his arm. Immediately, I swung the barrel to guy one and said, "This shot will go through your temple, and will scramble your brain. You'll be dead before you hit the ground. Your choice. Now, drop your weapon and put your hands on your head. Wolf, Tyrone, pick up their guns. Connor, do you have any zip ties?"

After Tyrone picked up guy 2's gun and handed it to Wolf. He said, "I have some. I'll be right back."

When he returned, Wolf and Connor zip tied the men's hands behind their backs and ripped off the ski masks.

Connor gasped and said, "Mark? What on earth are you doing?"

Mark sat on the floor and sneered at Connor, not saying a word.

By this time, I put my Nano back into my purse and said, "I'm calling 911 to report a break in and a gunshot."

Mark's buddy asked, "Just who the hell are you lady?"

"Thank you. I appreciate being called a lady. I Sir, am the lady that just took you down. You and Mark will probably do a lot of time for breaking and entering along with the murder of Steve."

Mark tried to get up shouting, "Wait! We didn't kill anyone." Some guy just paid me to get inside and steal the Jackhammer."

Guy two moaned, "Man, I ain't going down for some murder I didn't have nothing to do with."

"How about it Mark?" I asked. "How come you don't have the Lo Jack code for the car? Someone didn't give it to you?" I taunted.

Wolf laughed and said, "You amateurs don't know anything. There is no code. This Lady here," He said pointing at me. "is smarter than both of you put together."

"Who paid you?" Connor demanded.

Mark looked away saying nothing. Wolf said, "He'll break when the Detectives get here and tell him he's facing more time in prison than he wants."

"Oooh! Lansing! I wouldn't want to do time there." Connor said shaking his head and laughing.

## Chapter: 12    (Police Procedures)


The rest of our morning was taken up with questions from local police and the Detectives who were investigating Steve's murder. I knew the moment I fired the Beretta, I would have to surrender the 1911 to the police. When they asked, we each repeated our stories in separate interviews.

Mark refused to talk. Guy two was spilling his guts. They were both arrested and taken to the police station. Detective Mace Robertson addressed Wolf, me, Connor, and Tyrone. He turned to me and said, "I spoke to each of you, and you confirmed the same story." He nodded at me and said, "You had a gun that no one else saw and kept it hidden. Then you shot one man in the arm and pointed it at the other one saying you would put a bullet through his head if he didn't drop his gun."

"All true." I said matter-of-factly.

"What gave you the confidence to handle a gun like that?"

I sighed and said, "Louisiana State pistol champion. I am certified by the FBI as a contract employee." I showed him my credential.

The Detective looked at my credential, then looked at me, then back to the document. He said, "I've taken your fingerprints, we'll check your story out. You're not to leave the area. We'll run your gun through ballistics. You say you're here with your cousin to buy a car?"

"That's right and I have to ask. What is so special about that Roush Mustang that's worth killing people for?" I asked.

The Detective tilted his head and said, "Funny, I was about to ask you and Connor over there, the same question."

Connor, feeling on the spot, said, "The Roush Mustang is a specialty car and it's worth several thousand dollars, but it is not that rare. There are several out there in the market."

"Who owns the car?" The Detective asked squinting at the business owner.

"Got it right here." Connor fumbled on his desk through paperwork then handed the title to the Detective. "Here's the title, and the contract he signed when he sent the car to me on consignment. Do you think these guys may have killed Steve, my sales manager?"

Ignoring the question, Mace asked, "Mr. LeDuc, may I have the death threat note someone slipped under your wiper blade last evening? We'll review the hotels' video coverage to see if we can identify who left the note."

Wolf handed the note over, saying, "I looked at that video, but the image was inconclusive."

Mace nodded and said, "Our lab will run the guns those guys used through ballistics and the fingerprint lab. Hopefully, we'll be able to wrap up this murder case for the prosecutor with what we have."

"Do we need to go to the police department to make a statement?" I asked.

"That would be helpful, Miss Dupart. So, Mr. LeDuc, I understand you were looking at two Mustangs. One almost got you killed. Which one will you choose?"

"With everything that's happened, I gotta take the black Roush Jackhammer Mustang. The car is a story I can't pass up. I'll be telling my friends all about this when I get back to Memphis."

"Before you do anything rash and buy the car, let me get in touch with the car owner first. I need to know if these guys were working on their own, or if the owner had second thoughts about selling the car."

Connor shook his head and said, "That guy kept calling me trying to raise the price. It was like he didn't want to sell the car. He could have cancelled his contract before I found a buyer. All he had to do was come and collect his car. But he didn't. The contract clearly states a price and if we find a buyer, we sell the car. He paid me storage fees, but he missed a few months lately. If he didn't want the car sold, he had options. Why kill my sales manager and why threaten Mr. LeDuc?"

"That is precisely why I want to speak to him. I plan to call a detective counterpart in St. Petersburg. He's a friend and I'll have him look into this guy."

"What's this owners name anyway?" Wolf asked.

"Perry Sanchez on the title. I have his address and phone number here too if you want it." Connor said.

"Good! I'll check him out." The Detective said.

"So, you don't need the car as evidence or anything, do you? Connor asked hopefully.

"I can't think of why we would. Are you going to close your deal on this car yet today, Mr. LeDuc?"

Wolf looked at Connor and said, "I could, but I think the car is safer here than sitting in a hotel parking lot overnight. I'm in town through Friday. I'll leave a good faith deposit with you today, Connor. Then I'll make a bank transfer tomorrow, if that's okay." Wolf said.

"That's okay. But let's do the whole thing at once. Friday's fine with me." He looked at the Detective and said, "Does that timeline work for you Detective?"

"Yes. I should have the information I want by then."

## Chapter: 13     (The Interrogators)

Thursday afternoon, Detective Mace Robertson was able to speak by phone to the Chief of Detectives in St. Petersburg, FL. "Got it! Clearwater is a suburb of St. Pete, and we use the same computer software. I'll check him out and call you back with what I find."

"Thanks, Bob."

All Mace could do at this this point was to wait for ballistics technicians to tell him if any of the guns match the bullet that killed Steve Williams. He spent time with Cory, his partner, putting together a list of questions they wanted to use with both defendants they arrested. The perpetrators would spend the night cooling off in a holding cell to be interviewed in the morning.

Midmorning the next day, Mace had run a background check on both men's fingerprints and DNA. Mark Dvorak and Jerry Bonner both had rap sheets for local misdemeanors. Mark had been arrested three times for DUI, and once for assault a few years ago. He was release from probation since he was unarmed at the time. Jerry had been busted for his second DUI, and two counts of breaking and entry. Jerry made it clear that he definitely didn't want to go back to County. Neither of the men had ever been arrested for the use of a gun or weapon.

Mace's partner, Cory Sanders asked, "What made them up their game to carry guns and commit these violent crimes? They've both been clean for the past few years. So, why do this now? We've got them for the break-in, brandishing weapons, and attempted car theft, but we need to nail them for the murder."

"Good question, Cory. Mark was recently fired from Global, but it must be either money or extortion that forced them to carry guns. We'll save that question and start with the easy ones first during our interviews."

"You're the lead. Am I good cop or bad cop?" Cory asked.

Mace laughed, "I think with these guys, we're both bad cops."

The ballistics report came in around 10:00 and Mace holding the report said, "You ready to go to work partner?"

"You bet!"

"We'll interview them separately and use their testimony against each other."

"Sounds like a plan, partner."

The Detective's decided to interview Jerry first. They entered the interview room and slapped an inch thick file folder on the table. Mace identified himself and his partner. Then, for the recording equipment he added, "Suspect identified as Jerry Bonner and his attorney, Gary Jones."

Jerry, in his late 30's, was a dirty blond with tossed about hair wearing a two day growth of beard. He looked absolutely miserable. Mace began by saying, "Jerry, do you understand how much trouble you're in?"

The attorney said, "If you have proof of some crime my client committed, this is the time to lay it out Detective."

Mace smiled and said, "Fair enough, Counselor. You are charged Jerry, with breaking and entering Global Vintage Cars, then brandishing a gun for attempted car theft, both are felonies. We pulled your prints from the Smith and Wesson six shot revolver."

The attorney spoke up and said, "Possession of a gun is not illegal in the State of Kansas, Detective."

"True enough counselor. His use of the gun is illegal and this gun, however, has a history. You see, ballistics has matched this weapon to the murder of two young men across the state line in Kansas City, Missouri last August at a gas station. No other prints were found on the gun. So, we must believe that it was you who murdered those two men, Jerry."

Jerry's face blanched registering shock and horror. He burst out, "Woah! Wait. I ain't shot no one with that gun. I just got it. Mark knew some man, the man who hired us and gave Mark those guns."

The attorney immediately admonished Jerry and said, "I told you to not say a word." He turned and addressed Mace, "My client told me he just acquired that gun from a man he had never met before."

Mace nodded looking down at a police report. "Well, your prints are on a murder weapon that was used in another shooting. That crime has never been solved. I think the prosecutor will take an interest in clearing a double murder, albeit across the border with Missouri. We do cooperate, you know."

"I need to speak with my client." The frustrated attorney said.

"Interview is put on hold pending an attorney client conference." Mace said for the record.

Mace and his partner stood up. picked up the file folder and walked out of the room. Outside, Mace looked at his partner and said, "That went rather well, don't you think?"

"I do." Cory said laughing.

They went to their desk, put one folder on a desk, and picked up the second one. "Let's go see what Mr. Dvorak has to say."

They entered the second interview room and repeated the ritual of identifying themselves, the perpetrator and the attorney, Nancy Combes.

This time, Cory Sanders took the lead. He put the thick file on the table and smiled at the defendant. He began by saying, "Violence is nothing new to you, is it Mark?"

The attorney said, "If you have something to accuse my client of, let's hear it."

"Well, Counselor Combs, I will do just that, but you wouldn't make a case in court without foundation, now would you?" Before she could reply Cory said, "Mark, you were caught red handed, brandishing a weapon at three people with Jerry Bonner at Global Classic Cars. We have both of you on video tape breaking and entering into that building at 5:48 AM. And again on video pointing a gun at three people." He pulled a photograph out of the file, turned it around and showed it to both the lawyer and Mark."

She immediately said, "That could be anyone, they're faces are covered, wearing a mask."

"You are not in court, Ms. Combs. The mask was subsequently removed after your accomplice, Jerry was shot, and you were told to put your weapon down. Just to be fair, we have video footage of exactly how that happened. I'll share the video with both of you at the appropriate time. Our forensics team has removed DNA from a black ski mask that matches your DNA, Mark. There is no doubt, you are the man in the video."

Mark looked at his attorney then at Cory and said, "Okay! I had a dispute with Global about coming to work late. They fired me. I was given those guns to use as leverage by a man who wanted that car, I just met him at an AA meeting. That's all. I didn't shoot anybody."

"How did you and Jerry come up with a plan to steal a car?"

"I barely know Jerry. He and I met at an AA meeting some months ago. He was sent up for a breaking and entering charge. He told me one night that he knew how to use lock picks. Then this strange blond dude, calling himself Bill Joyner, came to an AA meeting and introduced himself to me."

"Can you describe Mr. Joyner?"

"Oh, just under six foot, he had blondish hair with a short beard. Kind of a skinny guy with bright blue eyes. He always seemed to be smiling. He wore jeans and a t-shirt which both looked new. Not like those of us in AA who were down on our luck and unemployed. He did produce an AA chip that said he was sober for one year."

"It was after the AA meeting when he offered to buy coffee that he asked about what kind of work I did. I told him that at that I was looking for a job and crashing with friends temporarily. He asked, what would I do for $200 in cash. I told him I wasn't that desperate. The guy just smiled. He asked me, 'Who do you know that can pick a lock?'."

"Not me, I said. Then he told me, 'I'll pay you and a lock picker, $5,000 to break into that place where you used to work and steal a car.' Of course, I thought of Jerry right away. I asked when. He told me Wednesday morning. I mean, $5,000 is a lot of money and it would tide me over till I can get back on my feet again. So, I agreed to do the job. I recruited Jerry, promising him $500. He was on it in a flash. That was the first I ever saw of those guns."

"This is where it gets sticky for you, Mark. You see, ballistics proves your gun was the one who shot and killed Steve Williams. Your fingerprints are the only ones on the gun."

"You'd better check again. Jerry's prints may be on that gun, too. We both handled that gun. He took the revolver." His attorney closed her eyes and slowly shook her head.

Detective Mace almost laughed. He quietly spoke saying, "This is where the plot thickens, Mark. You see, Jerry is now being held on a dual murder charge that took place in Kansas City last August which is tied to the gun that was in his possession. During that double murder, a car was seen leaving the scene with two men inside. We think you are the second man in that car."

"Where are you going with this?" Nancy Combs asked breathlessly.

"We have enough evidence to present to the Johnson County Prosecutor for two men who are suspected murderers in a previous crime across the state line. The evidence suggests they also murdered Steve Williams at Global Classic Cars. They panicked and left, then came back to steal the car later.

"Motive? Detectives?"

"Five thousand dollars in cash to steal the car and whatever they could get for the car. We have it on tape when Mark held a gun on three people saying, 'I'm going to take that Mustang out here.' Then, he said he would kill all three of them if they got in the way. It's all on video,

Counselor. There will be no plea deal, and your client will be remanded for the Capital Murder of Steve Williams. We'll ask for the death penalty."

Mark's face lost all color, and he slumped in his chair. "Then, we're done here. Anything else?" Nancy asked closing her notebook.

"Yes. One thing that keeps bothering me."

Nancy's head tilted to one side, and she sarcastically asked, "And what would that be, Detective?"

"Why would a pair of low end, recovering alcoholics, who are known assault and B&E guys, neither one of which has a propensity for violence, suddenly take to murder and brazenly invade a Classic Car business and hold three people at gunpoint demanding they hand over a high profile classic car? Doesn't make sense, does it?" Cory said, rubbing his chin with his right hand. If I were their lawyer, I would want to find out as much as I could about who that person was. The man who they said gave them the guns and promised to pay them to break into the Global building. Just saying! Who is that guy and did they get paid? Have they been paid anything, yet?" Cory said raising his shoulders.

Exhausted, Nancy eyed her client with disdain and asked, "What you really want to know is who hired them to do this job at the Classic Car place? You're thinking that person used the gun that you have in your possession to murder Mr. Williams then set my client and Jerry up for the crime. Isn't that right, Detectives?"

"Did that happen?" Cory asked straight faced.

Nancy rolled her eyes and said, "Let me talk with my client, please. And I'll talk to the other attorney. You may get a package deal."

Mace and Cory stood up, and Cory said, "Interview put on hold while the defendants and their attorneys confer." Both Detectives smiled and walked out of the room.

When they arrived at the Detectives room, they both broke out laughing and gave each other a high five. Cory said, "That was fun."

"You noticed our defendant flinched when we mentioned the gun as a murder weapon." Mace said.

"Yes and he looked pretty sad. I think we'll prove neither one of these guys killed our victim, Mr. Williams. Now, we need to get the blond guy who used that Ruger for a single shot to the head." Cory said.

Mace nodded saying, "They'll probably give up the guy who sold them the gun. We get the gun guy, and we have our murderer. These two guys will go up for attempted car theft and armed assault. It's always fun when things go your way. I have a message to return a call to the St. Petersburg police department. Let's find out more about this Jeminez character.

"Sanchez." Cory said.

Mace smiled and said, "Whatever."

## Chapter: 14    (Who Owns The Car?)

The next day Wolf and I met Stony for breakfast at the Embassy Suites, and we reviewed our plans for a busy day. I looked up into the sky and clouds were menacing for yet another rainy day. I thought, *"Does it ever stop raining in Kansas?"*

Stony grinned and greeted us saying, "You had a busy day yesterday. I understand the police arrested the men who probably killed the salesman you were supposed to meet at Global."

"How did you know?" I asked.

"It was on the morning news. The details were sketchy, but they said two men were arrested while trying to steal a car and a man was killed. No names were released. Were you there when it happened?" Stony asked.

I looked at Wolf, and he said, "We were there about that time. A lot of police cars, let me tell you. Look, I wanted to review your compensation package and employee benefits. Is this a good time?"

"I thought you would never ask." Stony said.

An hour later, Wolf checked his watch and said, "Welcome aboard. We'll need you to come to the office in Germantown for an orientation week. Connie Strong, our office manager, will coach you on how to fill out our contact reports and of course, get you signed up on our benefits package. Then she'll teach you about our expense reports. You'll get to meet everyone on the team."

"We'll set you up at a hotel suite near the office. Now, if you don't mind, Annette and I need to meet a couple of Detectives in Olathe and give them our statement about what happened yesterday."

Wolf and I left the hotel in his pickup and drove to the Olathe police station. We waited for 10 minutes until Detective Cory Sanders met us in the waiting area. He said, "We've been pretty busy the last day or so. I'll take your statemen. Follow me."

When we sat down at his desk and Wolf asked, "Do you have any more information to tell us about the man who owns the Jackhammer? After we leave here, I'm going to Global to purchase that vehicle and I really don't want any further trouble."

"I'll take your statements first, then tell you what we know about the mustang's owner."

Thirty minutes later, Detective Sanders said, "Thanks again for coming in to give your statements. This will help the prosecution with their case against the men involved. And here's your gun back Miss Dupart. Everything checked out."

"Thank you." I said taking the gun and checking the chamber and magazine.

Cory picked up a piece of paper and said, "Now, you asked about the owner of the Mustang, Perry Sanchez. The police department in St. Petersburg, FL told us that the name Perry Sanchez is an alias. He is known by several names and has been dodging arrest in Florida for years. He is a known scam artist who cheats widows and divorced women out of their money and property. The word the St. Petersburg police department gave us for what he does is called Bunco."

"You mean Bunco, like the card game?" I asked.

Cory said, "No."

"Does he actually own the Roush Mustang or not?" Wolf asked excitedly.

"Did he steal the property? We've run the serial numbers, and no one has reported that vehicle stolen. It's titled in the name of Perry Sanchez and Global has a clear title in their possession. So, I would say, the car is good to be purchased. That's not to say someone couldn't come looking for that vehicle in the future with some proof, claiming it was stolen from them."

Wolf looked at me and said, "Is he living at the Clearwater address?"

"The phone number doesn't work and the address in Clearwater has a different tenant."

"So, is this a guy on the run?" I asked.

"He's probably operating under a different name and is currently milking money out of some poor woman's account as we speak."

"How about the bank account that Global has on file to deposit money for a car sale? Can't that be traced?"

"That is an off shore Cayman's bank account. We don't have access."

"Wait a minute, I know someone in the FBI's cyber security department. Maybe they can track him down." I said.

"Good luck with that. We think this bank account is used to transfer and launder money. It's just a pass through account. He probably invests his money into hard assets that are difficult to trace."

"Hard assets, like what?" I asked.

"Like expensive cars, for one. Things like art work, jewelry, first edition books and even real estate by using different names where he can hide money. He's a pro and the St. Petersburg police would be thrilled to catch this predator."

"Do you think he'll come here or to Memphis to claim this car?" Wolf asked.

"Anything's possible. We have his prints on file but no real name or a good photograph to identify him with. We do have an arrest picture taken several years ago, but I imagine he disguises himself. Mr. LeDuc, my advise to you, is to pass on the Roush Mustang and let the Olathe police keep the vehicle in our impound lot to see if he shows up."

"Okay. Thanks for the advice. Do you think anyone at Global is connected to this man? I mean, is someone there contacting him and telling him about interest in the car? If the guy hired these men to come to Olathe and discourage people from buying the Mustang, someone must have tipped him off." Wolf speculated.

"We're working on that angle. Right now, I cannot comment on what we know."

"I really want that car. It's a showstopper. If I do buy the car, how do we stay in touch, if  someone should come after the car or try to harm us?" Wolf asked.

Detective Sanders slowly shook his head and said, "I've given you the best advice I can offer. If you do buy the car and take it to Memphis, you're on your own. My partner and I are always available by phone should you need to contact either one of us." Cory said, handing Wolf a business card.

Digesting what Cory had to tell him, Wolf was quiet while driving the pickup truck to Global. I kept quiet during the ride. I could tell he didn't like the idea of not buying the Roush Mustang. But I could see his desire was exceeding his common sense. I finally said, "What do you think? Are their drugs stored in the car someplace? After all, the car did come from Florida."

"Yeah, I've been thinking about that, too. If drugs or some other contraband is hidden in the vehicle, some government agency will just impound the car. I could simply lose my money."

"Then, don't do it! Buy the blue Shelby." I said.

"No. I've got another idea. I'm calling Stony, then I'll see what Connor at Global has to say.

## Chapter: 15    (Okay, What's Inside?)

Wolf's asked Connor if he could meet us at a local restaurant to talk about the car purchase. He agreed. When he arrived, Wolf said, "Thank you. I'm glad you agreed to meet us this way."

"No problem. I'm pretty busy with the business being closed for two days. I'm preparing for the upcoming weekend sale, but what's up?"

Wolf began, "As you know, I am very interested in buying the Roush Jackhammer. But there's something not quite right about killing your sales manager and with Annette and I being threatened by two men with guns."

"I agree, but the car's good. In fact, if you want to drive it out of the building again, I have no problem with that. You can see for yourself what you think of the vehicle's performance."

Wolf nodded and said, "I have faith in the car's performance, and I don't want to take it to the racetrack. But I do want to hand you a good faith deposit. I want to this, so I can get that car on a lift for a complete inspection. Why someone would risk so much for that car is unbelievable. Did the police tell you that Perry Sanchez does not exist?"

"Yeah, they called me. But the title is clean and good. I called the state of Florida DMV to verify ownership. Sanchez is on the title alright. The police assured me that the vehicle has not been stolen." Connor said.

"Not stolen as reported in the National Insurance Crime Bureau, but what if it was taken from an estate and this guy simply transferred the title, illegally to himself." Wolf asked.

"Then the title is still good, free, and clear. A family member might complain, but the car title will be legally transferred to you. You buy it, you own it. And you title it in your name." Connor reasoned defensively.

"Still, I want to perform a complete inspection on the vehicle."

"What are you looking for, if you don't mind my asking?"

"A secret compartment." Wolf said mater-of-factly.

Connor accepted Wolf's deposit check then thought about it. "Okay, I'll agree to drive the Roush Jackhammer Mustang to a shop near my Global building. I understand it's someone your friend Stony knows?"

Wolf nodded saying, "The owner is a personal friend of Stony's, and he offered to help inspect the Mustang with Stony, you and me, on very short notice."

"Okay, I'll meet you there with the car to watch and make sure no damage is done to the vehicle." Connor said.

To be on the safe side, Wolf called Detective Cory Sanders and said, "We're going to give that Mustang a full thorough inspection on a car lift. Think you or your partner might want to be on hand in case we find something?"

"Can't. We're in the middle of preparing a case against those two guys who attacked you. I'll send over a uniform officer and if anything important turns up, he'll let us know."

"Fair enough." Wolf said.

We drove to the body shop and Stony's Latino friend, George, was waiting for us. Connor showed up with the Jackhammer and an Olathe uniformed police officer arrived and introduced himself.

George and Stony went through the interior of the vehicle with a flashlight and a magnifying glass, looking for fittings that didn't look right and possible trap door releases. The officer watched every step. They didn't find anything obvious with the first inspection. George then pulled the Mustang onto a two post lift and brought it up to head height. He and the officer walked back and forth underneath the vehicle, using flashlights seeking anything that looked odd or out of place. It didn't take long. George stopped, then using his flashlight as a pointer he said, "There! See that steel plate?" He said directing the flashlight beam.

"You know, I didn't see that on my first pass under the car. What do you think that is?" Stony asked.

"It's above the fuel cell and below the trunk. It sits lower than the frame and is welded on."

"Okay, then let's check the trunk." Stony said.

They lowered the car and lifted the trunk lid. Next they pulled out the trunk mat and the spare wheel along with the jack. Stony's friend, Geroge, literally crawled up inside the small trunk space with his flashlight. We heard him beginning to chuckle.

"George, what is it?" Wolf demanded.

"Whoever did this, built up the back of the trunk with some kind of putty or foam and painted it the same color as the trunk's interior. I can guarantee you this is not a factory paint job."

"It looks normal from here." Wolf said.

Connor was beside himself with disappointment. He said, "We checked that trunk out when the car came in and we didn't notice anything, but now that you point it out, it looks as obvious as a bear in the pantry."

Stony's friend, George, turned to Connor and said, "I believe the car is in your care and custody, Sir. What do you want to do? It's obvious, something is under that pile of goo."

"If it's okay with the potential buyer, it's okay with me." Connor said looking at Wolf, "Open it up." He nodded at Wolf.

As for me, I couldn't wait to see what was hidden below that trunk. Wolf said, "One man is dead because of this car, you bet we open it up. Officer, you are a witness to this."

"Yes, Sir. I cannot tell you whether you should do this or not to do this. If there's anything there, I'll report it to the Detectives squad."

George said, "If it will make things easier and if damage is done, I'll repair the damage and return it back to factory specs, for a price of course."

"In for a penny, as they say. Let's see what's in there." Wolf said.

## Chapter: 16     (Body Shop)

It took a good hour for George to scrape and remove the Styrofoam like material. Once he did, we saw a steel box lid that had hinges on one side and a clasp on the other held together by, of all things, a cheap key lock on a hasp.

"This is just too good. You can't make things up like this. We've got to see what's inside." I said excitedly.

"Whatever it is , it's enough to get one man, who I considered a personal friend, killed. Not to mention the three of us nearly getting shot. Hell yes! Open it up." Connor said.

"I have a bolt cutter around here someplace. Hope it's not too big." George walked off to find the bolt cutter while we waited in anticipation.

I watched George try the bolt cutter. It was too big. George had to use a hand held rotary tool. It took a little longer, but the lock was cut free. Then came the big reveal. Would it be drugs, diamonds, bones of one of Perry Sanchez's victims or nothing? I wondered.

George, using a small flashlight in his mouth was crammed inside the Mustang's trunk. He slowly raised the lid of the box. He immediately dropped the flashlight from his mouth and raised his head hitting it on the top of the trunk lid. "Ay!" He exclaimed.

Everyone around the Mustang asked, "What is it? What is it George?" We all said at once. None of us could see anything because of George's behind being in the way. He slowly backed out of the trunk and stood up holding his head. He said, "No amigos, you gotta see this for yourself."

And we did. Each of us poked our heads as far into the trunk as was possible and we were amazed by what we saw. Packed inside the compressed space we saw white Styrofoam cradling an aluminum box which held what appeared to be gold something. When I looked, it glistened in reflected beam of the flashlight. I couldn't tell just by looking but after everyone had a good look it was Wolf who said, "I'll buy the car, right now, as is."

Everyone in the shop laughed. The uniformed officer grinned and said, "I think I'd better call the Detective Squad. They may want to take a look at this for themselves."

"You mean this might be more important than interviewing a couple of gun toting criminals?" I asked

## Chapter: 17     (My Golden Decision)

Two Detectives along with a couple of uniformed officers arrived and stood around the car gawking at the trunk. Detectives ignored the rest of us and proceeded with investigating the trunk of the Roush Mustang, no one touching the golden objects in the trunk. Photos were taken and everything was documented. Finally, using plastic gloves a forensics expert removed one of the gold bars. He inspected and dusted it for prints and slipped it into a plastic bag.

Meanwhile, Wolf moved to one corner of the shop and was on the phone with Baxter Grey, our attorney in Memphis. He explained the chain of events and the discovery of what appeared to be a hoard of gold hidden in the car.

Baxter said, "As usual, Wolf, you come up with the strangest things. Strange but interesting. I'll do some research on this. I understand that you put a deposit on the car before you inspected the vehicle at the body shop. So, technically, you have a claim for ownership of the car and it's contents, unless otherwise specified. If need be, I'll get a court order to cease and desist with the removal or confiscation of the golden contents you mentioned. We need to sort this out and pronto."

Wolf said, "I know it's almost a weekend. Thanks for hearing me out, Baxter." And he disconnected.

Wolf turned to Detective Mace and declared, "My lawyer said no one is to touch the contents of that box any further at this time. He's working on a court order to that effect as we speak. From this point forward, nothing is to be removed from the car."

Mace laughed and said, "Sorry to rain on your parade, Mr. LeDuc, but we are investigating a murder case. This car and it's contents appear to be critical evidence, which leads to motive in the murder of Steve Williams and also your assault. This car will be impounded by our department."

I heard wolf and Mace's conversation. I had been busy, too, and now held my cellphone out in front of me and said, "Uh, Detective Mace?"

"Yes? What is it young lady?" He said with a scowl on his face.

"It's the FBI, Sir. They want to talk with you."

"FBI? How on earth did they get involved?" I didn't say anything and just handed the phone over to Detective Mace.

"Hello. This is Detective Mace of the Olathe, Kansas Police department. Who are you and I'm warning you, that it's a crime to impersonate a member of law enforcement with a prison sentence as a penalty."

"You're who? What? You are? What are you talking about? You're in Washington, you have no jurisdiction here or with my murder case. You do? Who? Coming here? When? Well, I may just impound the vehicle now and keep the evidence safe for myself. Are you threatening me? You are? Well, we'll see about that!" He hung up and handed the phone to me with anger in his eyes.

Mace said, "You just did that, didn't you? How do you know the FBI Director?"

"As I said before, I am a contract employee with the FBI. I called my employer and explained the situation. He agreed with me that a cybercrime has been committed, and the internet was used for the interstate transportation of laundered funds. He has assigned an Agent from Washington to fly here today or tomorrow. That person will take charge of the investigation. Special Agents will show up from the Kansas City bureau shortly. I think he probably told you that in the meantime, I'm in charge of all evidence until they get here. I am not telling you, but the FBI is telling you to stand-down, Sir."

Detective Mace Robertson was beet red in the face when he looked at his partner Cory Sanders. Spittle flew from his mouth as he said, "This is not over. I'm calling my Chief on this."

"At the request of the Director and speaking for the FBI, we would request that the Olathe Police remain and post a guard to protect this shop, the Mustang car and it's contents until Special Agents arrive."

Detective Mace nearly shouted, "We don't have enough manpower for your request, Miss!" He said sarcastically. "Get the Johnson County Sheriff's department to do your guard duty." He turned his back on me and stormed out with Detective Cory Sanders who looked over his shoulder, staring daggers at me. The two uniformed officers had no orders, so they just hung around with their thumbs in their utility belts waiting for further directions.

Next, I called Baxter Grey and told him about the FBI's involvement. He listened quietly and said, "Okay, new plan. I'll call the Kansas State Attorney General's office. I happened to know her quite well. I'll ask for her assistance to provide protection for the car."

I waited in George's office to see how Baxter's call would pan out. The Olathe police detectives were mad because they wanted to close what they thought was a slam-dunk murder investigation. They were right, a pile of hidden gold represented a lot of motive to steal the car or even murder for it. Two uniformed officers remained. I said nothing because I wanted them here until the FBI arrived.

## Chapter: 18    (Make Way For the FBI)


Baxter Grey's call to his friend, the Kansas State Attorney General, resulted in a call to the Johnson County Sheriff asking them to take charge of protecting George's body shop and a Roush Jackhammer Mustang. They would do so until the FBI could secure the vehicle for themselves.

I was amazed at how quickly the Deputies showed up. They parked in front of the body shop waiting for the FBI agents to arrive. Deputies said they would assist in any way the FBI deemed necessary. Their arrival was not a moment too soon because news trucks and curious bystanders began to show up. A parameter was quickly set up.

The Attorney General established a media gag order. No one except the FBI in law enforcement was to speak to the press. Failure to adhere to this order could result in serving time in a state penitentiary. No word about the car or its contents was to be leaked to anyone.

Somehow, the word got out, and the press knew something unusual going on at a George's body shop in Olathe. Two TV news trucks parked at the edge of the body shop parking lot. A gaggle of reporters attempted to interview everyone they saw but were chased off the premises by the Sheriff's Deputies. The news trucks and reporters were told to stay beyond a fifty meter perimeter of the property. Sheriff's deputies did an excellent job. The press never had a clue what was going on at the body shop except that a car at the body shop was tied to a murder at Global Classic Cars. Wolf and I believed the detectives, Mace and Cory, were probably responsible for tipping off the press to check out George's Body Shop.

Mid-afternoon, three FBI agents from the Kansas City FBI field office showed up and presented their credentials to me. They claimed the car and its contents. This was now their case and responsibility. A tall man with gray hair and a gray suit to match, introduced himself as Special Agent Larry Singletary. He said, "This is my partner, Special Agent Louis Acosta and this is Special Agent Florence Sallaz."

He turned to me and said, "Since you are the only woman in the garage, I presume you must be FBI consultant, Annette Dupart?"

I smiled warmly, stepped forward, and gave him a firm handshake. "Annette Dupart at your service, Larry."

Agent Singletary said, "Let's go someplace quiet where we can talk alone."

"Are you thinking of a car, the body shop office or a restaurant?"

"The Sheriff's department has deputies watching the place. So, let's talk in the body shop office if that's okay with the owner."

George nodded effusively. "Sure, make yourselves at home, Agents." He said in his best English.

On the way to the office, I said, "You didn't correct him to say, Special Agent."

"Not necessary. First of all, your reputation has preceded you, Miss Dupart. Welcome to the Kansas City Bureau. I spoke to the Deputy Director, and he told me that you're a special contract employee for the bureau, and you have been temporarily activated for this case."

"That's right, I called someone I know and explained the situation here with the car and the gold. And they agreed with me that what has been discovered was definitely of interest to the bureau and the US government."

"Welcome then! My colleagues and I are pleased to have you on board. I understand that you are a sharpshooter. Good with a gun. Is that right?"

"Not bragging but I am a Louisiana State Shooting Champion in skeet and pistol. I've been known to hit the mark a few times and have done so while working with friends at the FBI."

During our conversation, I told both Special Agents all I knew about Wolf trying to purchase a unique Roush Mustang. I said, "He put a deposit on the car this morning before it was brought here to find out why men were trying to kill people and prevent them from buying the car. That was when the gold was discovered. A lot of gold."

"You mentioned that the name on the car's title is someone called Perry Sanchez. You said the Olathe police discovered that the name is an alias. We did some research, too. The man has a thick file with the FBI. Mr. Sanchez has several names in our file, and he is no longer living at the address on the title. In fact, at this time, we don't know where to find him."

"Before we drove to Olathe, our records showed that Perry, or whatever his name is, has a string of victims in cities all across the country where he's left a number of broken families in his wake. He has victims not only in Florida but in Georgia, South Carolina, Ohio and even Las Vegas, to mention a few. We believe he's responsible for several suspicious deaths surrounding people he bilked out of their life savings.

Family members are grieving for lost loved ones and screaming for law enforcement to find this guy so they can sue to recover stolen property."

Special Agent Lou said, "His crimes have crossed state lines, and it looks like money along with property was transferred through a variety of bank accounts using the internet. That makes this a Federal case of cybersecurity.

This man does not work alone, we believe he operates with a gang to assist with setting up his swindles. This is a dangerous criminal organization operating with impunity which solidifies this as a Federal case. The FBI wants this guy along with all of his hidden assets."

"Do you even know what he looks like? How would I know him if I ran across him on the street?" I asked.

"Families of his victims have provided us with snapshots that were taken while he was charming their family member. He's good at disguises. We are working on building a better profile, using a composite of his disguises. We have a team making an attempt to electronically remove the disguises using AI for a generic construction of his face."

"Okay. So, once again, Wolf put a deposit on the Roush Mustang. Technically, he is a transitional buyer of the car. The transaction has not been completed. Legal ownership of the car and its contents are currently up in the air." I said.

"Well, as you know, ownership is a civil matter but the car itself and the contents as you have described will now be seized as evidence in a fraud and murder investigation for the Federal government. What we have with the car and gold, is proof of an obvious attempt to circumvent US tax code. The FBI will take a complete inventory of the contents and will put it into safekeeping. A trust will be created to resolve remedies put forth by the victims' families when the perpetrator is found. Now, I want to look at what you've discovered." Special Agent Singletary said.

"While we do, let me tell you about an idea that I have. It may help the bureau find and nab this guy. I'll outline a plan that may draw out your criminal. And, if you seize the car, I'm hoping Wolf, my cousin, can get his deposit back. And help me here, what will happen with Global's contract for care and custody?"

"FBI lawyers will issue the seizure order. Monetary matters may have to be settled in court." Larry said.

I said, "You might be able to make matters easier if you to talk with Connor, the general manager of Global Classic Vehicles. He may see fit to return Wolf's deposit with your encouragement. Also, I think it would be a good idea to issue a press release saying that a person of interest was arrested in the death of an employee at Global Classic Vehicles. Say he was killed during the attempted theft of a classic car that was subsequently sold to a buyer from Memphis. And you might add that local Olathe Police Detectives, Mace Robertson and Cory Sanders, were key to solving that murder. I'm just thinking it might make good politics to keep the Olathe police on your side if my plan is to work."

Larry gave me a funny look. He put his tongue in his cheek, nodded, grinned, and said, "I can't wait to hear more about what you have to tell me about how to catch our perp."

## Chapter: 19    ( The Plan)

Wolf and I awakened the next morning prepared to put my plan to into action by driving the Roush Mustang back to Tennessee. I firmly believed someone would attempt to take the car during our road trip and expose the man who the FBI was after, allowing him to be arrested. So, Wolf suggested that we take an alternate route to Memphis and not go through St. Louis."

"How does this route work?" I asked.

"I think we should drive south from Kansas City to Springfield, Missouri, then drive east to West Plains, Missouri, where we will take highway 61 South to Hardy, Arkansas. Then it's a quick jaunt over to Jonesboro, and on to Interstate 55 for the short drive to Memphis."

"Okay. I'll just follow you in your truck. You don't mind if I mess with your radio, do you? I mean Delta Bluz music is fine, but I do enjoy other music, too."

Wolf smiled and said, "Of course not. Mess with the radio all you like. Tonight, we go to the Mustang car show. You ready for that?"

"I don't think we should take the Mustang. The FBI's not quite done with it. And some FBI hot rod from Washington, DC is not in town yet either."

"Agreed. It's just you and me tonight. We'll find Stony and Sarah and have a good time. What do you think?"

"Sounds like fun."

Wolf and I arrived at the car cruise and were greeted by the Mustang club president. Stony said, "And he's the owner of a Roush Jackhammer Mustang. He didn't bring it tonight, but he has pictures."

Wolf proudly pulled out his cellphone and said, "I have pictures of my car and my dog but I'm sorry to say no pictures of my girlfriend."

Stony and the host laughed at the joke that only car people understand. The club president said, "Just like all of us, then. Welcome."

"And thank you for inviting us to your Mustang rally cruise."

Stony said, "Sarah and I will be very happy to introduce you to everyone in the club. They're fun people and very passionate about their Mustangs. A few have a stable full of pony's. Up until a couple of weeks ago, you had a green GT, and you just replaced it with another Pony."

Stony was in on my plan, and he let Sarah in on the plot, too. If any peering ears were around, the bait was now set on the hook.

Earlier while discussing my plan with Stony, I said, "I felt that much gold would never go unnoticed. Word would spread fast from local law enforcement to the press. Once out, people whose family member was cheated, would be clamoring for that gold. The gold assets would be frozen immediately, and recovery of additional assets would simply disappear."

"How much was there anyway?" Sarah asked.

"In terms of dollar value, that's hard to say. Most of it was in gold bars with serial numbers stamped on them. There were a lot of gold coins, too. Coins are always purchased with an inflated value. However, by weight, the total was 100 pounds or more." Wolf said.

"Wow! Let me look that up. How much is 14 carat gold per ounce?" Stony asked.

"$2,000 give or take on the market. But many of the bars are stamped, 24 carat pure gold and that is nearly $3500 per ounce." Wolf said.

Stony fiddled with his cellphone. "Let me look *that* up. Wow! There are over 1600 ounces per 100 pounds. We're talking about five and a half million dollars. No wonder they're coming after that car."

Sarah asked, "Why on earth would someone store that much wealth into a car?"

Wolf nodded, "That way, the gold is hidden in plain sight. This is all ill-gotten wealth with no taxes paid on the money."

"Those thieves must be a liquidating machine to convert so much in stolen assets from their victims. As I see it, the real problem they had was to figure out what to do with the gold. I'm sure their plan was to store cash and use it a little at a time." Stony speculated.

"I agree. They acquired so much wealth, so fast, they had to do something. They invested into gold which is always gaining value. It seems they were taking their time trying to figure out how to get the gold out of the country so they can convert it back into currency." Wolf said.

At the cruise, Wolf was impressed with the car eye-candy but not full of envy. I knew he would, at least for a while, be driving a beautiful, black on black Roush Jackhammer Mustang as though it were his own. All we have to do, is get the car safely to Memphis then spring a trap to capture a predator of the weak and vulnerable.

## Chapter: 20    (Hot Shot Arrives In KC)

Sunday morning, the flight from Dulles International Airport landed at Mid-Continent International airport in Kansas City, Missouri. FBI Special Agent, Hop Dickerson, deplaned with his computer backpack and headed to the luggage carousel to pick up his bag. He was surprised to be greeted by fellow agent Florence Sallaz. She was waiting for him with a sign. They had met each other at a cybersecurity meeting in Washington just a couple of months earlier.

"Florence! What a wonderful surprise. I thought I would have to find my own way to a hotel."

"Welcome to Kansas City, Hop. When I heard you were coming to Kansas City, I volunteered to come and pick you up. Once you get your bag, my car is in the parking garage."

"I am not familiar with this city. I believe that I have a reservation at a Sheraton Hotel, in some suburb called Overland Park?"

"That's right! I know the hotel, we should be there in about forty five minutes."

During the car ride to the hotel, Florence reviewed what she knew from the case notes. "Apparently, a car was being sold in Olathe, KS. A salesman at that storage facility was shot to death next to the car being sold. Two men attempted to steal the same car the next day, and they were prevented by some woman who turned out to be a contract employee for the FBI. Before the car was sold, it was taken to a body shop for a thorough inspection before being delivered to the buyer. As a result, a secret compartment was discovered full of gold. It turns out, the owner of the car on the title is using an alias name and phony address. The Kansas City bureau, thinks this is a case of stolen goods being transported across state lines. Using the internet to launder money makes this a cybercrime."

"You say a contract employee discovered this gold?"

"Apparently she has documented proof of her status with the FBI. We checked it out with Washington, and she's the real deal."

"I've heard of contract employees being used on special occasions. I knew one in Georgia who was a former FBI employee. He was a tactical operations specialist who the bureau uses from time to time. What do you know about this woman?"

"Apparently, she's well regarded by the Director and the Deputy Director. Local law enforcement wasn't too happy when she declared the murder, assault of the buyer and discovery of the gold an FBI case. The local police had been working on the murder investigation, and they have two men in custody for the murder. They were ready to wrap up their case when she made her announcement taking custody of the car and the gold on behalf of the FBI. The problem with the police department's case, they had no motive for the murder until the gold was found. Neither suspect had any idea the employee had been murdered. Our contract employee discovered absolute motive for murder when the gold was discovered."

"Well, she is to be commended for her quick thinking. The reason I'm here is my Cybersecurity department in Washington tracks sales of gold in large sums, purchased through the internet. We want to know who's buying and why. A buying pattern developed that we were following. Even with the use of several fake names we could track the gold transactions through the same servers, and we followed the gold registration numbers. The physical gold was shipped to the same address in Florida. When our agents in St. Petersburg went to the address, they discovered no one living there. That name tied to your case, Perry Sanchez, is just one of the many names we were following. When the Deputy Director assigned this case to me, that name was mentioned. Coincidence, right?"

"Why is someone buying all that gold?" Florence asked.

"Gold transfers are always our first red flag for international terror activity. Those organizations may be shifting capital to purchase things like weapons, maybe even weapons of mass destruction. Or the money could be used as payment to sleeper agents and things like that. If it is terrorism, we definitely want to know who is doing this. And we want to know who they are working for and what they plan to do."

"You definitely have a complicated job linked to national security." Florence said while changing lanes.

"I agree and I appreciate the cooperation and assistance from the Special Agent in Charge of the Kansas City bureau for lending you to me. I'm sure we'll do a good job together." Hop said flashing a winning smile.

"The Agent in Charge is out of town right now and he'll meet with you next week. Today, after you get checked into your hotel, you and I will meet with the contract employee. Then, I'll take you to see the gold for yourself. Apparently, our contract employee has some kind of plan worked out to draw the mysterious car owner out of hiding. That plan has the approval from the Director himself. Right now, you're in charge of the field investigation, and I'm temporarily assigned as your partner."

"I couldn't have asked for a better partner. So, this is where the Kansas City Chief's are from? The city apparently spans what, two states?"

"Yes. Kansas and Missouri. There are actually three Kansas Cities, two in Missouri and one in Kansas. You'll be staying in Johnson County, a wealthy suburb of the greater Kansas City area. There seems to be a lot of local rivalry between the Missouri and the Kansas communities. Don't understand it myself, but I heard it goes way back to the Civil War."

"Incredible, that's over 150 years ago."

"I think it's commercially based. Both states are vying for economic development to see who'll become the top dog in the region."

Hop and Florence continued a lively conversation all the way to the Sheraton Hotel in Overland Park. Florence told Hop that the contract employee was staying at a hotel nearby and a meeting had been arranged.

## Chapter: 21     (Yippee Ki Yay)

The weather outside was cool but not rainy for my morning run. I showered and changed into more conservative clothes for my meeting today that was to take place between me and some big honcho from Washington DC. He was to give his final blessing on my plan to draw out the man everyone wanted to arrest.

I could see that everything surrounding Wolf's decision to buy that Roush Jackhammer Mustang had his head spinning. The more complicated the events became, the more obsessed he became with that car. Last evening at the cruise, we met a lot of wonderful people from a local Mustang car club. Wolf proudly flashed his Mustang Club of America card and pictures of the Jackhammer.

We strolled around looking at great vehicles, some of which were trailered to the cruise and really should have been museum pieces. I could see that Wolf was salivating over each wonderful car he saw. I told him, "You know, a Camaro makes a good alternative to a Mustang." All that got me was a nasty look and a roll of his eyes.

After we left the cruise, Wolf was quiet all the way back to our hotel. I could tell he was becoming morose. We had come all the way to Olathe, Kansas, to pick out a car so Wolf could drive it home. For me, it seemed like my only job was to drive his leased pickup from and back to Germantown.

When I arrived for breakfast the next morning, I could see Wolf was in a sour mood. I tried cheering him up by saying, "The sun is out, and it looks like a promising Spring day. Come on, let's make the most of a good day!"

Wolf gave me a dead pan expression and said, "I think you've been drinking too much of the whoopie coffee."

"Is that a real thing or did you just make that up?"

Wolf finally broke into a smile and said, "Guilty as charged! I'm thinking about throwing in the towel and just drive back to Memphis in my truck. You and I should just leave all of this behind I cannot risk you getting injured or even killed because of some car. Maybe I'll go to the auction in New Orleans next month. I might find something I like there."

"Don't quit so easily. I am officially on the FBI clock, and I have a plan that will release the car into your care and custody. The car will be yours, for a while anyway. And you and I have a meeting with the FBI today, here in our hotel."

"You go ahead and do that without me. Discovery of that gold and losing the Roush car has taken all the air out of my balloon."

"My idea has been presented to the Deputy Director. I just need to convince the new investigator. Don't throw in that towel just yet cousin."

Wolf gave me an incredulous look as he sipped his coffee. He said, "What are we doing to occupy our time until 2:00 this afternoon?"

"Let's just drive around town and do a little site seeing?"

"Site seeing? And go where?"

"I hear there's a lot to look at in an area called the Plaza. There's a museum not far from here called the Nelson-Atkins Museum of Art. Supposed to be a big deal. Also, there's a building that's almost 175 years old called the Shawnee Methodist Mission Manual Labor School. This school served not only the Shawnee natives but other native tribes who lived in the area. And there's also a house real close to here called the Alexander Majors home which was built about the same time."

"What's so important about that? We have much older homes around Memphis."

"True enough, but this part of the country was the wellhead of trails that led to the Old West. Last night, I met people who were a font of knowledge about the area. They said, The Sante Fe trail, the Oregon trail, and the California trails west all began at the Majors house. The Majors supplied all of the frontier forts in the Kansas territory before it became a state. They were the go to people providing wagons and stock for whoever traveled west in wagon trains. Majors created the Overland Stage Coach company and the Pony Express. This man and this house was the foundation of every myth and legend we've read or seen in the movies about the Old West."

"Okay, okay, that sounds good, I'm sold. Yippee Ki Yay! Let's go!"

## Chapter: 22    (Meeting The Honcho)

Wolf and I visited the Alexander Majors home on State Line Road separating Missouri and Kansas. The home tour was short but very informative, and I was amazed to find out that Majors hired Kit Carson for the pony express and even Buffalo Bill when he was nine-years-old to carry messages between wagon trains. In Majors later years, Buffalo Bill gave him a place to stay on his ranch in Wyoming. This guy was a true entrepreneur of his time.

Wolf and I had fun just driving around the Kansas City Plaza with its Spanish village architecture feel. We drove to the Nelson-Atkins Art Gallery and went inside. There was so much to see there we hardly had time to see a fraction of what was displayed before we had to leave.

On the way back to the hotel, we drove through neighborhoods of Overland Park and Leawood. It seemed like there were garage sale signs everywhere. The best thing about our time spent was, Wolf wasn't obsessing over that Roush Mustang.

He and I ate a late lunch at an out of the way restaurant recommended by Sarah Carter. Tatsu's French restaurant operates on a reservation only basis. But when we arrived, we were welcomed and seated. I ate the sauteed chicken breast with mushrooms in Calvados cream sauce while Wolf ordered beef served with a shallot red wine reduction. This was exceptional French cuisine one might find in New Orleans. I said, "Please remind me to thank Sarah for the recommendation of a wonderful food experience. Real French food! I can't believe it!"

"I must admit it appeals to my French roots, too." Wolf said with a wry grin. "I know you don't drink but the wine choice was exceptional."

"I did fine without it." I said, then checked my watch, "Oops! Time for our meeting. By the way, our meal will be covered by the FBI." I said winking and paying with my credit card.

"Your part time job is sounding better and better." Wolf said, finishing off his glass of wine."

When we got back to the hotel, I no sooner got to my room to freshen up when my cellphone rang. It was Florence Sallaz. "Hello Florence, the Kansas City bureau said you would be calling. I take it you're here with your Washington investigator?"

"Yes. He's here and anxious to get started."

"Tell him to cool his jets. I'll call my cousin Wolf, and we'll be right down."

I didn't know what to expect by meeting this guy, but I definitely didn't expect what I found. I saw him from across the room. His back was turned to me, but that unmistakable shock of blond hair was obvious. I had met him just last year and he was now here in Kansas City. He is the man who made my heart beat just a little faster. It was Hop Dickerson.

When I approached, Florence stood up, and Hop turned around. His mouth dropped open, and his eyes got wide, and he couldn't get words out. He said, "A-A-Oh-my-goodness!"

Florence gave him a strange look, then she looked at Wolf and me and asked, "You two know each other or something?"

I laughed and said, "You could say that. Wolf and I were in Atlanta, Ga when I met Hop. We went to a kind of costume party together." I turned to Hop and said, "Wow! I can't believe it's really you. How are you? How is living in Washington?"

"Uh, I thought I was meeting an FBI contract employee. What are *you* doing here?"

Wolf stepped in, extended his hand, and said, "Special Agent Dickerson, remember, we met. Glad to see you again and glad to have you helping us out."

"Us?"

I said, "Yes, I am an official FBI contract employee. I work on an as needed basis for the bureau. By the way, where's your bright red Flash outfit?" I said taunting him.

His face turned red, and he said, "Flash? Oh, that! Long gone, I'm afraid."

"So, you're here to root out why someone wants to kill people over a Mustang?" I said baiting him.

"Well, kind of. I'm tracking someone who has been buying gold through the internet and concealing their identity. It seems that you have found at least some of the gold. I'll be tracking the serial numbers on the gold bars while I'm here."

"How about the coins?"

"Was there any paperwork found with the gold?" Hop asked.

"You'll need to ask your co-workers about that. I just got a peek inside the trunk at the glittering pile of gold. The vehicle has been guarded by the Johnson County Sheriff until the Kansas City FBI team showed up and seized the vehicle along with its contents."

Sallaz, spoke up and said, "I'm with the Kansas City bureau but I'm currently assigned to Special Agent Dickerson. And yes, our team did seize the vehicle and the gold, thanks to you." She smiled pleasantly.

I turned to her and said. "Yes. Hop, or rather Special Agent Dickerson and I met in Georgia. I was auditing a car dealership in Atlanta who was trading expensive exotic cars for Bitcoins. Hop was the FBI liaison with the Atlanta police department at the time. We both followed a lead to the source of the Bitcoins. It was a club of computer gamers who actually had stolen thousands of Bitcoins from a wallet. Turns out the wallet belonged to the Corsican Mob. They were pretty mad and came after their Bitcoins. They captured me in an effort to get their money back. Hop and a team of local law enforcement rescued me along with some of the gaming fanatics. He and I have kept in touch by exchanging some emails. Haven't we Hop?" I probed.

Hop grinned slightly and looking at Wolf he said, "Why are you involved in all of this?"

Wolf spoke up, "I'm the one who's to blame. You see, I sold my GT Mustang in Germantown and began looking online for a replacement. I found two that were being stored at Global Classical Vehicles in Olathe, KS. I called and I made an appointment to see them. I asked Annette to join me since she's a car enthusiast like me. We had no idea that a car I had my eye on, a Roush Mustang, would be the source of murder and attempted theft."

"Well, let's find someplace where we can sit down and discuss the current situation." Hop said briskly looking around.

Wolf offered, "Let's use the living room in my suite upstairs. It's private. We can grab some refreshments and take them to the room."

The four of us gathered in Wolf's suite and we began discussing my plan to lure the owner of the gold into the open. Hop said, "Okay, Florence has given me a good grasp of what's happened up to this point. My task is to discover who is behind the gold transfers and where the gold is going and for what use."

"I have an idea, you may not like, but it's sure bound to draw out the person you're looking for." I said smiling sheepishly.

Hop glanced at Florance, and she shrugged her shoulders and smiled. Hop said, "Okay, let's hear it."

I told him my plan in detail and surprisingly, Hop said, "Sounds workable to me. And I already spoke to the Deputy Director. Your plan is a done deal." Hop said flatly.

# Chapter: 23    (Albert Reports In)

Things had gone as planned up to the point where Albert Jensen was unable to lay his hands on the car in Olathe, KS. The Global car salesman, the man who refused to return the car to his father, had been shot and killed. His plan was not to kill Mr. Williams if he refused to give the car up, he would just threaten him and take the car. That's why he hired a couple of men to help recover the car. He just wanted to have the men break in and steal the car and deliver it to him.

Albert used a trick he learned while working a scam in South Carolina. He pretended to be from the Kansas Bureau of Unemployment. He called Global Vehicles to find out if any employees had been fired recently. The woman admitted that one man had been let go a month ago for coming in drunk. Albert knew what to do next.

Albert posed as a recovering alcoholic and attended a local AA meeting. Sure enough, the fired employee, Mark Dvorak, was there. Over coffee at a restaurant, he offered to hire him for $500. Mark refused. Then Albert asked him if he knew a B&E man. That was when he offered $5,000 to break into Global to steal the black Roush Jackhammer.

Mark warmed to the idea of getting back at his former employer and he knew exactly where the Jackhammer was stored. He said, "Okay, for $5,000, getting that car should be a slam-dunk."

Albert used gloved hands to hand over the two guns to Mark. He said, "These are just for intimidation. Your plan is to get in and out with the car. The guns are in case you need to scare anyone who might get in your way."

Albert was disappointed when he found out the men he hired bungled the theft and got caught. They didn't know anything about him, a description maybe but that was all. He still needed to recover the Mustang. After a few calls, he found out that the buyer of the Mustang was from Memphis, TN. He drove by Global and saw police cars. After inquiring, he found out the car was being inspected for purchase. Now, he would have to rely on his cousins to help him recover the Mustang away from this man from Memphis.

After eating breakfast at the Big Biscuit restaurant, Albert sat in his rental car watching rain pelt down on the windshield. Using his burner phone, he dialed another burner phone. It rang six times before it was answered. "Who is this?"

"It's me, Charles."

"Did you get the car and our gold back?"

"Wasn't that easy. The man who gave you so much trouble at Global won't do that any longer. He's dead. I hired these men to break in and steal the car. They got caught in the act. I was going to help them as backup but by the time I tried, the police were showing up. I had to leave or risk discovery."

"Dammit! I said, get the car, even if you have to steal it!"

"I know what you said. But, like you *always say*, save your ass first then come back later and finish the job."

Albert heard Charles exhale hard. "Okay. What's next?"

"The car was sold to some dude from Tennessee. I've been watching the building as they test drove the car a couple of times. They took it someplace to have it inspected, and I think they're having the car detailed for delivery now. I watched the buyer, and some woman look over the car. They appeared to be very impressed."

"So, your plan is what? Just take the car away from him? How? You said the buyer was from Tennessee. How do you know that?"

"Williams told me as much when I spoke to him on the phone, but I asked people at Global what was going on with all of the police."

"Where in Tennessee? And how will you get the car?"

"I'll follow them. I thought about ambushing them on the road between Kansas City and Memphis, which is where they're going. But that is risky. Setting up a trap on an Interstate system is undoable. There are too many cars and lots of witnesses. There is another route to Memphis that's a little shorter and if they take the southern route through Missouri into north-eastern Arkansas I might be able to stop the car on a lonely stretch of road, long enough to recover it."

"What? Run it off the road?"

"No. They drove a pickup to Olathe and if that truck is following the car, I figure I can follow both vehicles. When the opportunity arises, I'll force them to stop. We'll do that by disabling the pickup, and when our Mustang guy discovers the pickup is not following, he'll slow down and stop to turn around. That's when we'll surprise him and take the car."

"And if that fails?"

"Memphis is their home. We should have plenty of chances to recover the Mustang and its contents there, by force, if necessary. Besides,

I don't really want to wreck the Mustang, and I don't think you do either. In fact, I would like to have that car for my own when all of this is all behind us."

"I bet you would. Your mother, Brenda, helped me pick that car out for herself when she devised the plan to store the gold someplace other than a bank safety deposit box. If you recall, she does not trust banks. She wants liquid assets that she can lay her hands on quickly. And that means both the gold and the car."

Albert chuckled and said, "Sure. But she might let me drive it though. Ferdie's now with me. He knows someone and has already recruited a couple of hired hands in Memphis. They'll help us take the Mustang. They'll meet us there. I'll let you know how it goes."

"Definitely keep in touch, Albert. Things are getting sticky here in Sarasota. I might have to make a quick exit. Gwyn's nephew keeps showing up and he's demanding to see her medications, and her will. I've not given anything to him yet. I've had her sign a power of attorney making me her next of kin. That man is a persistent nuisance, a real pain. I may have to do something about him. If you do not get the car and the gold back in a day or so, I may join you with Morty to pull off this job. I'll tell Gwyn that my daughter in Dallas has a serious cancer operation, and I need to join her for a few days. I'll deal with the nephew when I get back."

"Ferdie and I are following the car and the truck now."

"Good luck!" Though Charles knew that luck rarely had anything to do with achieving results in his world.

## Chapter: 24  (Pick Up The Jackhammer)


I knew Wolf was anxious to get back to Germantown. We've both been away from the business far too long. It was morning and we were finally preparing to leave Overland Park and drive back home. Before we departed, Wolf and I drove his truck to the Global facility in Olathe. Waiting for us was Connor, George, Hop, Florence, Detective Mace, Detective Cory, and an FBI technical specialist.

Hop was in charge of the meeting. "I think everything is now in place for your sting. I want to thank Connor and George for their cooperation with this operation. At my request, the FBI has agreed to reimburse you for your storage fees that were not paid by our con man. In all likelihood, you would never have received them from the Mustang's owner of record, Perry Sanchez. Our lab, with the assistance of George's body shop, restored the Mustang's trunk back to the way you found it. Connor has signed the title over to Wolf for the Roush Mustang with the FBI's financing company as a lien holder. He will take temporary ownership of the car."

"Detective Mace I wish to thank you and Detective Sanders for suppressing the story of the gold. Our story of an attempted robbery of the car was released with no mention of gold. Your department is to be fully commended. We believe the men in your custody had nothing to do with Williams death. They were set up as patsies for the murder by the people we're after. The true murderer we believe will be following a tracking device they place on the Mustang. We spoke to your chief. You, and your partner will receive full credit for closing your case. The assault and any other crimes you can link them to should proceed."

Florence said, "The FBI has taken possession of the gold, and it is being held in safekeeping at the Federal Reserve Bank in Kansas City. Only a handful of people involved are aware of the gold and we want to keep it that way. Our technical specialist has placed our tracker in that black Mustang, should the perps ever lay hands on that car, we'll be able to locate it."

"What happens next?" Connor asked, thrilled to be part of a Federal investigation.

"FBI Special Contract Employee, Annette Dupart, has a plan to take the car to Germantown, TN in an effort to draw out the person or persons we're looking for. That person has many aliases and is now on the FBI's 'Most Wanted' list. It's amazing. He has kept that car with the gold stored inside, hidden here for over three years." Hop said.

"Why just leave the car at Global all this time with all that gold?" Detective Mace asked.

Hop said, "We at the FBI firmly believe they intended to reclaim the car at their leisure either by guile or by force or by simply paying the over price value for the car. They thought no one in their right mind would pay that much for a Mustang." He said looking at Wolf. "They probably intended to ship the car by container to someplace out of the country where they could recover both the car and the gold."

Wolf winced.

Hop continued, "When serious interest in the car became a real threat, with Wolf offering to pay the full price, our Perp couldn't let that happen. He or she, panicked and sent someone to kill the salesman and take the car. When that didn't work, they hired local people to use as fall guys for the murder of Mr. Williams. As you know, when those guys attempted to steal the car at gunpoint, Annette managed to foil their plans and that puts us where we are today. Those guys never realized they were being set up for murder."

"Connor, I need to know that no one on your staff is aware of the gold's discovery. True?" Florence asked.

"No. I haven't even told my wife about the gold. No. And thank you for paying the storage fees. I'm not getting my commission on the sale, however."

Hop laughed and said, "Don't press your luck. We covered Wolf's deposit, consider that a tip. Like Florence said, our technical expert has outfitted a tracking devise on the Mustang and on Wolf's pickup truck. An interesting fact, we discovered another tracking device on the Mustang and decided to leave it there. The car is now bait, and we want them to know where it's at and on the move. We'll follow both vehicles from here to Germantown using our tracking software. I doubt if anyone would attempt to hijack the car on the road, but we will be monitoring both vehicles from Washington all the way to Wolf's home in Germantown."

Hop added, "I've been in touch with the Special Agent in Charge at the Memphis Bureau. They'll be providing a surveillance team to keep track of Wolf, Annette, and the Mustang once they arrive. Florence and I will be flying to join them in Memphis. I'm confident, this person will not let five million in gold simply slip through their fingers. They will do whatever it takes to recover the car and the gold. Any questions?"

"For a little background, we're pretty sure  this person is still actively milking funds out of widowed and divorced women. We believe he's continuing his occupation someplace in Florida,. He's left a lot of ruined and brokenhearted families in his wake as well as a few unexplained deaths. Because of this, he's wanted in several states for murder. We've got pictures of him but he's a master of disguise and could turn up anywhere, so be very careful when talking to people you do not know." Detective Mace said.

"Good advice. Annette do you or Wolf have any questions? This guy is dangerous, and he would think nothing of murdering either one of you." Hop asked.

"I doubt this person would just run us off the highway." Wolf said. "He would still have to extract and haul  a heavy load of gold alongside the road. That would be too risky with people driving by all the time. If he does anything, it'll be when we get back to Tennessee."

"Good. I think we're all in agreement. Once again, thanks to the Olathe Police Department. I promise we'll keep you in the loop. And good luck to you and Annette on your road trip." Hop said smiling.

*"Good luck, indeed. So that was all he had to say to me? I thought he and I were attracted to one another. Now, I don't know."* I thought sourly.

## Chapter: 25    (The Road To Memphis)

Wolf and I said our goodbyes to everyone at Global Classic Vehicles. Kansas was nice but Wolf and I were more than ready to move on. We decided to take the southern route through Springfield back to Memphis. Interstate 70 was a quagmire of road repair that we didn't want to deal with. So, we took the route through the Ozarks. Wolf led driving the Roush Mustang, and I followed in his F150 truck. We communicated on speaker phones using our vehicles phone sync systems.

Traveling through southern Missouri was a pleasant journey. Traffic was light and the hilly scenery enjoyable. We easily made it to West Plains, MO, where we ate a fast food meal. We then turned south and drove into Arkansas where we found the twisty roads that wound their way beyond Hardy. Both Wolf and I were keeping a sharp eye out for anyone who might be following us. We discussed our risk at lunch and decided no one had followed us since we left Olathe. We felt the prior owner installed a tracking device and was keeping tabs on our location. Why follow when they could see us live on a computer screen?

Still, while traveling through the hills of northern Arkansas I was especially concerned because if we were to be attacked anywhere, this would be the logical place to do so. The roads were narrow with lots of curves. What I didn't expect was that I would be the target while driving Wolf's pickup.

I didn't hear the shots, but I heard metal on metal noise then I felt the tire blow out. I was on a tight curve about ten miles from Black Rock, AR and I struggled to keep the truck on the road. My truck swerved left and right in my lane while a blue pickup truck behind me kept honking mercilessly. I drifted left and corrected at the last second for a semi-truck passing me while climbing the uphill lane on my left. There was no shoulder to turn on to, just a ditch and a hill full of kudzu. I needed both hands to muscle the steering wheel. Finally, there was a stretch of road that leveled out and the impatient vehicle behind me finally blew passed me in a hurry.

I pulled over and immediately called Wolf. "Wolf, my rear tire is flat, and a light blue pickup is coming your way in a hurry. Be prepared." I then called Hop and told him what happened. He told me the Arkansas Highway patrol was looking for both of us and they would intercept Wolf at Black Rock. I told him that Wolf would probably be speeding when he entered Black Rock. I said, "Send help for a flat." and I hung up."

Wolf recklessly passed a couple of vehicles while speeding downhill. He was slightly above the speed limit when he entered Black Rock. When he saw the Highway Patrol cars waiting at a gas station, he slowed down, pulled into the station, and parked next to the cruiser. After a moment or two, a blue pickup with blackout windows blew by. The highway patrol called ahead and alerted patrolmen from Jonesboro to stop the vehicle.

I waited nearly forty five minutes for a Roadside Assistance truck to show up and change the tire on Wolf's pickup. I paid the extraordinary amount with a credit card and got back on the road. Wolf called and said he was waiting for me now in Jonesboro with the Highway Patrol at a Valero Truck Stop.

When I arrived, I needed a breather and a cold lemonade. Wolf said the Highway Patrol lost track of the blue pickup. I said, "I'm thinking there must have been two of them inside that truck. The tire was a run-flat, but the rear tire blew out due to a large hole in the tread. When the tire was changed, a lead bullet was rattling around inside against the rim. Sorry to say, you also have four bullet holes in the tailgate of your new vehicle. The gunman apparently tried zeroing in on that tire. I'm glad they focused on the tire instead of me."

"Me too. So, the plan was to separate us by taking you out first, then catch up to me. They would probably wait for the perfect moment to shoot me when I got out of the car. How did you ever keep that truck on the road?"

"Emergency driving techniques taught to me by my brothers. We don't have too many hills in the Atchafalaya, so I had to improvise."

"Well, we now know that we are both a target for the former owner of the Mustang and his gunmen."

"Now that we have a moment, how did you like driving the Mustang?" I asked.

"It's not what I thought it would be. The vehicle has a lot of power and torque, great for a quarter mile race track, but suspension and handling is a little too stiff for my taste. Going through those curves coming downhill was not easy. Could be the tires or maybe it was the suspension, I don't know."

We spent some time talking to the two Highway Patrolmen and thanked them for being on hand when we needed them. They wanted to know who we were and why the FBI was involved. All I could tell them was we were working on a sting with the FBI to draw out a murderer and apparently, we did. They were impressed and decided it would be wise to escort us with their lights flashing all the way to Interstate 55.

## Chapter: 26    (Germantown Sanctuary)

It was dark when Wolf and I crossed the Hernando DeSoto bridge. We were both relieved, as we drove into Memphis. Driving the familiar freeways in Memphis was a piece of cake compared to the traffic we saw in Overland Park on Highway 435. We arrived at his house exhausted from the longer than expected drive. My brand new Chevy Traverse company car was parked where I had left it in his driveway. He asked me if I wanted to come inside for a cold Ginger Ale while he ordered a pizza. Pizza sounded good and I agreed. We were both greeted by his dog Roger at the door. The golden retriever was all love and tail wags.

Wolf handed me a plastic glass with ice, and I took the glass outside to his poolside table and let the dog lick my hand while I decompressed from the strenuous road trip. Wolf stepped out with a beer in his hand and said, "Pizza's ordered. I called Becka, Rogers dogsitter, to let her know I'm home."

While relaxing, I sat there captivated by the pool light's reflection in the pool. "We didn't quite get here in one piece but safe is okay with me." I said sipping my Ginger Ale on ice.

"Well, at least the Mustang's owner knows we have the car. He's hired people to come after the car and us if we get in the way. What we don't know is if the man himself will show up." Wolf said.

I sat my soda on the table and said, "I agree, he's our objective but the real question is, when and where will he make his next move?"

"You know, with that much gold, that guy must have unlimited resources at his command." Wolf speculated.

"He did till we came along and took away his golden piggy bank." I said laughing.

Wolf chuckled and said, "Wait till he finds out the gold is gone!"

I was delighted to see Wolf happy and said, "Like you, I imagine he still has a good reserve of cash hidden someplace. That picture of him that Florence showed to us was old and he was wearing a black beard then. I really couldn't tell how old he was. How are we going to recognize him?"

"I'm not sure. But did you notice the cable TV truck parked down the street?" Wolf asked

"I did and I wonder if Roger let them in to place cameras and listening devices around your house?"

"Good point. If the FBI wanted into my house, I'm sure they got in. Your friend Hop should have told me if he bugged the house."

"I think so, too. Oops! That's him calling me now. I'll ask him."

"Calling to make a date?" I asked into the phone.

"Date? What? Oh! No. But you got into a bit of trouble while driving to Memphis. I'm glad you're now home safe."

"Listen, I've got Wolf on speaker phone."

"Hello Hop, we made it!" Wolf said holding his beer up.

"That's a relief. But if they went after you on your way home, you're not out of the woods yet. They'll try again."

"You use the word they. Do you have any further information about exactly who we should be looking for?"

"No, I do not. You reported two people were in that blue pickup. I believe our perp has hired more people to go after the Mustang and you."

"Well, I want to thank you for alerting the Arkansas Highway Patrol to keep an eye out for us." I said.

"That wasn't me, that was Florence. But you made it out alright."

"Yeah, after getting shot at. Wolf's pickup truck has several holes in it." I said.

"These guys must be well paid to play for keeps." Hop said.

I was sitting there thinking, *Is that all Hop has to say? The last time we were together, I got the feeling that he, I don't know. I thought he was interested in me."* I said, "Yeah, I'll keep my eyes open and my Nano handy."

"I thought you had a Beretta?"

"I do. Beretta 1911 and a Beretta Nano along with a Glock. The Nano was given back to me by the Olathe Police Department to conceal and carry."

"Wow! You're armed like a tank. Just don't shoot one of our field agents." Hop said without humor.

"Yes…I'll keep that in mind. Wolf, do you have anything for the Agent in Charge?"

Wolf gave me a knowing look, and he asked, "Is my house under surveillance?"

"Yes. There should be a cable truck parked near you. We will change the shadow vehicles periodically."

"Have you bugged the house?" Wolf asked."

"No. and we would not do so without your permission."

"I'm going to ask Chick, you remember him, to scan the house for electronic devices."

"Former Special Agent Farrell. Sure, I remember him. Good idea, just to make sure no one is listening in. Listen, Florence and I are flying in to meet up with the Memphis Bureau Chief. Keep the Mustang out of sight for a while, in your garage, but take it out and show it off tomorrow. We want everyone to see you in that car."

"Will we need bullet proof vests?" Wolf asked looking at me and grinning.

"Probably not a bad idea. I'll speak to the Special Agent in Charge in Memphis. We'll see what we can do for you."

Wolf gave me an incredulous look. I shook my head.

"Look I've got to go, but I'll touch base with you when I arrive in Memphis." He abruptly disconnected.

I was thinking, *"Yeah, you do that."* I said to Wolf, "I bet Chick has body armor if you ask him for it." I said grinning.

Laughing, Wolf said, "I'm calling him now."

"Your Mustang is in the garage, your Escape is parked outside next to your leased truck with as many holes as Swiss cheese and I am taking my Chevy Traverse home so I can soak in a hot tub."

## Chapter: 27     (Back To The Office)

After a good night's sleep in my own bed, I woke up both hungry and ready for a morning run. I snacked on pizza with Wolf last night and had to satisfy myself when I got home by delving into a heart healthy container of ice cream. Now, I will work off the added calories, one running footstep at a time.

The weather in Germantown was warm and sunny. It felt good to be back home again. I was surrounded by the familiar fragrance of magnolia flowers permeating the air while I listening to Carly Rae Jepsen sing "Call Me Maybe" and Taylor Swift's "We Are Never Getting Back Together" both of which rang true for me thinking about my hopeful romance with the handsome blond Hop Dickerson. Then, I listened to Katy Perry's "Firework." That was when I decided I was going to get Hop's attention, if it was the last thing I did.

My morning run was wonderful and refreshing. During my run, I saw the friendly faces of people I knew, greeting me. My mind turned to Wolf and the Mustang. I didn't really think I was a target. I was just in the way. What they really wanted was the Mustang. With *they* being a mysterious man who believed his golden fortune was hidden in the car. And just who is this mysterious crime boss? Obviously, he was charming enough to convince a load of wealthy and not so wealthy women to give him all their money and possessions.

*"He'd better not try anything with me."* I thought cavalierly. I really didn't think he would be interested in me anyway, I'm nearly broke.

Wolf's black Roush Jackhammer Mustang was parked auspiciously in front of our office building like a road sign that read, "Here I am! Try to take me!" This was an obvious invitation the FBI had encouraged. But was it too obvious?

Connie and Ezra greeted me warmly and I asked, "Well, what do you think of the black monster outside?"

Ezra laughed and said, "Nice car. I have a classic car, too, you know."

"No I didn't. How come I've never seen it?"

"I only take it out of my storage garage on special occasions. It's a 1966 Lincoln Continental, cranberry color, with a white landau top. I keep it in perfect running condition."

Ezra could see the confused expression on my face. He said, "The one with the suicide doors?"

"Oh! I've heard of them, I've just never seen one."

"I bought that classic from a car dealer I called on after I started with the car company years ago. The dealer was a car collector, and he let me have the car for a good price. I bought it because it was a sedan, and Lavon doesn't like riding in convertibles. We take that car when we visit her relatives in Selma."

Stepping out of his office, Wolf joined us and said, "The hook is set. Let's see if we get any bites."

Connie said, "I don't like it. It's a dangerous game you two are playing. One or both of you could get hurt."

"Chick and the FBI have their eyes on the car right now. I'm thinking we need to get our eyes on LeDuc and Johnson business, don't you?" Wolf said grinning.

Ezra smiled, nodded, and he laid out his travel plans for the next few days. I said, "I need to reschedule some of my audits I missed last week because of our little vacation to Dorothy and Toto land in Kansas."

Connie said, "I've already done that for you, sweetheart. Your calendar of rescheduled visits is on your desk. You have the rest of this week to refocus on your work here in the office." She said smiling.

"Why thank you, Connie. That makes coming back much easier. By the way, I drove my new Traverse here today and I think I'm liking it."

Wolf said, "By the way, our new employees will be arriving here this week to for orientation and to pick up their leased cars. I'll call the leasing company and find out when they'll deliver cars for our new people and where to take my pickup for bullet hole repair."

"So, Stony will be flying in? I thought Sarah and the kids would be coming by car with him. I was looking forward to seeing Sarah again. I plan to review financial statement schedules for the parts department with him. I know he is good at managing inventories, but I want him focused on the financial side, too, when he calls on car dealers." I said.

"And... Isn't your almost boyfriend, Hop, due to arrive today?" Wolf said cautiously.

My face flushed and I angrily said, "Boyfriend? What? Do you think I'm in Junior High School or something? I do not do boyfriend/girlfriend stuff. I will admit that I'm attracted to him, but so far he has not responded to me in any way." I said in a huff.

Wolf put up both hands in surrender and said, "Sorry! I must have mis-read the signs. I retract my comment."

"Signs? What signs?" Then I laughed at my own outburst and said, "Okay. I did, too. Not sure if that sign was 'Detour', 'Stop' or 'Rough Road Ahead'. I would like to know where I stand with him. Do I even have a relationship going with Hop? If I do, where is it going?"

I looked around the room at the stunned silence of my three work mates, and I was embarrassed. Frustrated, I stalked off to my office, shut the door, and settled down to focus on work. I began making phone calls to my clients and forgot about my non-relationship with Hop Dickerson.

## Chapter: 28    (Hop To It)

Before I knew it, the work day was over, and I had missed lunch. I stepped out of my office and saw that both Connie and Ezra had gone home for the day. Wolf was still in his office, so I knocked then stepped into his office.

Wolf looked up and asked, "You going home?"

I laughed and said, "I have nowhere else to go. I have nothing left in my refrigerator. So, I'll probably eat out then go to the grocery. Will you be okay with that monster car of yours?"

"The car's okay. It's that goofball who's trying to get it back that's bothering me."

"Well, his goons shot at me. I'm in this, too, you know."

"I know, Annette, and I'm worried about your safety. Chick brought body armor for me and you to use if we want. I have it in the car, may I retrieve the armor for you?"

"That'll make a fashion statement. Where would I wear it?" I said.

"I know, me too. When you're out driving around, I guess. No telling how or when these guys will make their next move."

"Okay."

Wolf turned off his computer and stood up. I said, "I sent you an email with a summary for this month's client financial statement submissions. You'll be happy to know everyone is on track as planned."

We stepped outside and Wolf turned to lock the office door. Just at that moment, a bright flash of red light nearly blinded me. Then I saw the unmistakable flash again of rifle laser light dancing on Wolf's chest. I turned and looked. It was coming from a building roof across the street. I pushed Wolf aside and he, yelled, "What the heck!" He immediately fell to the ground with me rolling on top of him.

I managed a peek around the Mustang and saw no longer saw a rifle or shooter on that roof. There was no gunshot. They didn't fire the weapon. Seeing Wolf and I rolling around on the ground must have awakened the FBI people on surveillance. They came running out of vehicles like ants on a sugar cube.

A Germantown police cruiser suddenly appeared, and Wolf and I spent an hour and a half answering a lot of questions with law enforcement. The potential shooter escaped without being discovered. Wolf said, "That was a close call. I might be dead now if it hadn't been for Annette's quick thinking."

The police, Chick and his team left us, with Wolf and I to rethink our evening plans. Just as we were getting ready to leave, Hop Dickerson and Florence Sallaz pulled into the parking lot. Hop said, we arrived on the flight from Kansas City and went to the Memphis bureau. That was where we heard about the disturbance here at your office."

"Yes, they were here right after it happened. I was getting ready to go grocery shopping."

Hop said, "Our Agents inspected that roof. They found footprints and a place where a gun's tripod must have sat. We found nothing to indicate who the potential shooter was and there is no closed circuit camera coverage either"

Wolf burst out, "I thought you guys were securing a bubble around us. What the hell happened?"

For the first time, Hop looked nonplussed. "Honestly, we missed that. It won't happen again."

"You damned right it won't. I'm hiring Chick to take over our security. You guys stand out like a pregnant bride at a hillbilly wedding." Wolf said.

"I'm afraid you cannot do that."

"Sorry? Do what? Hire personal protection. Just try to stop me."

"I remind you that you are officially working undercover for the FBI. This is our operation, and you do not officially own that Mustang."

Wolf was on a roll now and he wasn't through. "Well, I hate to remind you, 'Buttercup' it looks like your cover is blown! As far as I'm concerned the operation is blown. It's time for you to pack up your toys and go home."

Hop's mouth fell open, he was unable to utter a word. I joined in and said, "Hop, do you have an alternate plan? If you do, we'll listen. If not, Wolf is right. I may be just a contract employee for the people you work for, but even I can see that you or your people did not plan this end of the operation very well."

Florence was incensed by our position, but she kept her cool. She said, "I can understand why you're angry, but I don't think yelling at one another is going to get us anywhere. I agree, if the people wanting this car didn't know the FBI was involved, they may now. But I do not think that will detour them from their goal. They think the gold is still there."

I cooled off and said, "You are right! Calmer heads will prevail. They were probably just checking us out and didn't realize their laser sight was on. If they wanted to kill Wolf or me, they would have pulled the trigger. As far as them knowing about the FBI, you both showed up after the Germantown police already left. I think when we dodged the laser, they just packed up and left. They probably didn't see the mob of law enforcement coming to our aid."

Florence smiled, then said, "Come on you two. Dinner's on us. We're done for the evening. Bring the black Mustang and let's go eat." Hop was just outnumbered watching Florence take charge.

Wolf, mumbled, "Still, I feel safer with Annette than I do with you two."

I gave him a winning smile and said, "Safety in numbers, Wolf. Safety in numbers."

## Chapter: 29    (Planning For The Worst)


The next day, I was groggy when I got out of bed but ready to run. Only this time, I wore my holstered Nano around my waist. I had no idea if my apartment was being watched or not. Stony had calculated close to five and a half million US dollars' worth of gold was recovered by the FBI. No doubt, all of it was from women who had been duped out of their life savings and all of it undeclared income. I knew that was the primary reason the FBI was interested as well as the IRS-CI department who investigates nonpayment of US income taxes.

Last night, we ate our evening meal at Dinner at Daisy's Homecooked Meals restaurant with Hop and Florence. It was a testy experience. Hop was cold and distant, while Florence kept trying to be a mediator. Wolf didn't say much either during the meal, which was unusual for him.

An uneasy truce was declared and we all decided that regardless of the police activity after what appeared to be an attempted shooting, there was no indication that we had discovered the gold. Those coming after us probably believe the gold is still in the car. Wolf and I would continue our role as bait for Perry or whatever his name is, to make his move, so he can be captured. They now know someone is watching over us. That is probably a good thing because they may think twice about making a frontal assault to get the car, we decided.

When I asked Florence, she confirmed that I was in full FBI contract mode and would be reimbursed for my time and expenses working this operation. I was surprised when she said a stipend check would also be provided to Wolf for his role.

This morning I ran my routine five mile route and returned to my apartment for a healthy breakfast of cereal and strawberries with only one cup of coffee. While running, I ruminated over my relationship issues with Hop. I really couldn't figure out what Hop's attitude was all about since he flew to Kansas City. When he and I last saw each other in Atlanta, he was effusive with his attention for me. His signals were clear that he wanted to work on a long distance relationship with me.

He was in Atlanta, and I was in Memphis. We planned a winter vacation to Destin, Florida together but before we could make any serious plans, he was promoted to the Cybercrimes division in Washington, DC and he moved.

I kept sending emails and texts and his replies were spotty. I was wondering if he was in another relationship with some woman in Washington. I couldn't understand why he was keeping his distance from me. It was odd, since he showed up in Kansas City he has been rude, and bossy. I can't figure out why.

Today, my plans were clear. I would pick up Stony Carter, Frank Carlson, and Tony Morrison at the airport. They were all flying in at different times but within an hour of each other.

The new hires visit to LeDuc and Johnson was twofold. We had just implemented a new Health Insurance plan for them to sign up on, and they would pick up their new leased cars. Stony would be coached by Connie Strong using the LeDuc and Johnson company software on how to submit expense reports and fill out dealer contact reports.

When Wolf arrived at the office with the Mustang, he told me that he contacted our friend, Chick Farrell at Reliant Security. He said, "Chick came to my home last night and scanned my house for electronic listening devices and found none. He coached me on evasive procedures to avoid conflict and said he would have people discreetly placed to watch over both you, me and the car and he gave me those bullet proof vests. I told him, thank you and told him that he was good at what he does. I explained that this was not a friendship thing, he was officially hired by me."

"Chick said, he's assigned a friend for your protection, Clarence Smith."

"Really? That makes me feel more comfortable."

Wolf then broke out in a wide grin and said, "Fantastic! By the way, I contacted my friends at the Mustangs of Memphis Club and explained about my special Mustang that I wanted to share with them. They reminded me that this coming Friday night was the Collierville Cruise in the Square night. I told them that I and my Mustang were planning to be there."

When Wolf told me about the Collierville Cruise in the Square, I said, "I think that is exactly the kind of thing we need to do to lure this Perry guy, and his rifle toting buddies out into the open. I'll be there, too, of course."

Wolf asked, "How's that leased Chevy working out for you Annette?"

"I'm still getting used to driving an SUV. It operates more like that pickup of yours, and the gas mileage is atrocious. Still, I can use my cellphone with the phone link, and I can get quite a bit of stuff in the back when I put the rear seats down. That's pretty handy."

"That reminds me, I still need to report the bullet hole damage on the truck. When will you be going to the airport?" Wolf asked.

"Frank Carlson is due in at 10:30 AM. Tony and Stony will fly in around noon. I'll camp out in an eating area near baggage claim and remain there until I've collected everyone." I checked my watch and said, "Rush hour traffic has died down by now, so I'll probably leave for the airport soon."

"I'll call Chick and let him know that you're parking your SUV in the short term parking lot."

"Good idea. It's inconceivable that anyone would make a move at a busy airport with all of that security, but I'll keep a sharp eye out."

## Chapter: 30    (Bang Up Time At The Airport)

I parked my SUV in the short term parking lot adjacent to the airport terminal and walked to the baggage claim area downstairs. I found an uncomfortable plastic seat, took out my computer, water bottle and waited with a sign that said, "LeDuc and Johnson."

I didn't wait too long before I was approached by a man wearing a camel colored sport jacket. He appeared to be in his late 50's. He had salt and pepper hair with a neatly trimmed dark beard. He stopped in front of me and my Spidey senses rushed into alarm mode. In a soft voice he said, "Miss Dupart?"

I looked left and right. No help anywhere. I asked, "Who's asking?"

The man gave me a disarming smile, and he said, "Larry Gorman. I'm with the Shelby County Prosecutor's office. I was at your business yesterday when police were called."

"I'm sorry, I don't remember seeing you there."

"There were a lot of law enforcement people there at the time. Is LeDuc your boyfriend, brother or relative?"

That did it! Wrong question. "You know, I'm not accustomed to talking to strangers. Do you have some identification on you?"

The man smiled again, and he pulled out a wallet and briefly showed a plastic covered ID to me that said, Shelby County Prosecutor

Investigator, Larry Gorman. The ID had some kind of stamp on it to make it look authentic. I said, "What is it you want Mr. Gorman?"

"I just wanted to ask you a few questions about the attempted shooting yesterday."

"I believe the Germantown Police Department has my statement. You may get that from them." I said looking around him.

Larry opened his jacket just enough to show me that he was carrying. He said, "I think you need to come with me. I have a few more questions I need to ask you."

I thought, *"Not on your life!"* I said, "No. I don't think so. I'm waiting for someone who is flying in, and I don't want to miss them. If you have any questions, you can call my attorney, Baxter Grey, and he'll provide you with answers to any questions you might have."

Larry's face turned hard. He nodded and said, "You are not making good choices, Miss Dupart. You either come with me now, or I'll have airport security arrest and detain you."

I squinted at the man standing in front of me. I shut my laptop and put my water bottle and laptop into my backpack purse. I slowly stood up and said, "I am going nowhere with you, Larry. If you touch me, I will scream bloody murder, and it is you who will get arrested. Do I make myself clear? You want airport security? Good! I'll call them right now."

Larry no longer smiled. His eyes narrowed and he pulled out his cellphone and while staring at me said into the phone, "Do it now."

He gave me an evil grin, and while he did, I took his picture with my own cellphone. He reached for it, and I pulled it away saying, "Step away, Larry or is it Perry the car thief?"

He sneered, pivoted, and stalked away. Just a moment later I heard a loud dull thud, then car horns blaring outside. People were screaming and sirens blaring. Something serious had just happened. I resisted the urge to go investigate. I stayed put and waited for Frank Carlson."

When he arrived he was beaming at me with a full grin. "Annette! Thanks for meeting me."

"You are the first to arrive. Stony, another employee and Tony are due in around noon. So, we have a bit of time together." I felt my cellphone buzz, and I said, "Just a minute, I need to get this."

"Annette, it's me, Clarence. You need to know, someone has fire bombed your car in the airport parking garage."

"They what?" I said in shock.

"Your Chevy truck is toast."

"My new truck is toast?"

"Yep! And airport security wants to talk with you."

"Do I come there, or will they come here?"

"I don't think it matters."

"I'll come there. Damn, I had my new shoes in that vehicle."

I told Frank to wait patiently with the sign and to catch both Tony and Stony. I said, "Something's happened to my car in the parking lot."

I quickly called Hop's number and told him what Clarence told me. He said, "We're on our way."

When I arrived where my SUV had been parked, I saw a knot of airport security, Memphis police and fire department personnel standing next to a smoking black hulk of metal and glass. I was stopped by an officer, and I explained that the vehicle in question was mine by lease agreement.

Memphis uniformed officers and airport security officers quickly approached me. A tall man in a sport jacket and jeans asked, "Are you the owner of this car?"

"You can't tell now, but that is a Chevy Traverse, and I just got it last week on a lease agreement."

"May I see your photo ID?" The tall plain clothes officer asked. He read my drivers license and handed it to a uniform officer who said, "I'll run it."

The tall man regarded me with suspicion. He asked, "Do you know of anyone who would do this to your car?"

I sighed and handed my FBI credential to him. The man studied the document, and his brow creased. He shook his head and asked, "What is this I'm looking at?"

"I am a contract employee for the FBI. I work on an as needed basis, and I am currently working on a sting operation for the Feds."

"I don't understand. Are you telling me that you are an FBI agent and this is a government registered vehicle that was just fire bombed?"

"I am telling you no such thing. I am on the clock as a contract employee, right now. Special Agents should be here momentarily, and they will answer any further questions you might have about me. That SUV is leased to me through my employer, LeDuc and Johnson, in Germantown. If you don't mind I will take a picture of the wreck and send it to my employer. They will in turn text a copy of the registration to my phone so you may have it.

The uniformed officer returned with my drivers license and said, "She's been involved in several instances with the use of a firearm, but there have been no arrests or convictions."

"Are you now armed, Miss?" The officer asked threateningly.

I looked at the burned out shell of the Traverse, shook my head, and said, "Somewhere in that glass and metal casket you'll discover my Beretta 1911 handgun and some brand new red shoes, I just bought. Before you ask, yes, I have a conceal carry license."

A uniformed officer escorted me to sit in the back seat of a police cruiser where the windows were up, and doors were locked with no handles. They took my cellphone, computer backpack, and purse.

Twenty long minutes later, Hop and Florence managed to get through the police barricade. They asked where I was. Florence then requested that I immediately be released from the cruiser and given back all of my possessions.

The tall officer reluctantly complied. Recovering my items, I turned on my phone, and it immediately buzzed. I answered, "Wolf?"

"I can't get anywhere near you. What the hell happened?"

"Well, someone fire bombed my leased car."

"Good god! Are you alright?"

"I'm fine but the vehicle is a black pile of junk. Forget me. Call Clarence and tell him to cover you. This may be a plan to grab the car."

"Was anyone watching your car?"

"Clarence got here right after it happened. He saw two men fleeing on a motorcycle fast from the fire. Clarence called 9-1-1 and reported the fire."

"Where's our employees?"

"Frank's inside with a sign waiting for Stony and Tony at baggage claim. Goodness! It's noon already. They probably wonder where I'm at."

"I'll have Connie call them and tell them to take an Uber to the office. How will you get home?"

I looked at Hop and Florence who were talking to airport security and the Memphis police. I said, "Courtesy of the FBI."

## Chapter: 31    (What The Heck Happened?)

When Hop and Florence asked about the man in the airport terminal building, I shared the photo I took of him at baggage claim. "He said he was an investigator from the Shelby County Prosecutor's office. He was five foot seven or eight, casually dressed with a tan sport coat. I believe his facial hair was fake. It didn't look natural to me."

They, in turn, shared the picture with the Memphis police and Homeland Security. Hop checked with the Shelby County Prosecutor's office, and they concurred that no one knew any man named Larry Gorman.

"Fake ID, fake beard" Hop said. "You did right in refusing to go with him. You say he appeared to be in his 50's. Hard to say how old the guy really is. He changes like a chameleon. He could be older, he could be younger. Still, you took the most recent image we have, and we'll put a BOLO out with this photo. We'll attach an image showing him without the beard, using AI."

"Why not blast the internet with this picture and a warning, 'Do not approach. This man is dangerous!'." I said.

Florence smiled and said, "Good idea, but we cannot do that. He could resemble someone else, and our litigious public might sue us. What I can't figure out is why he chose to come to you in person and expose himself. He must have followed you to the airport. He did his research. He knew your name and your car. Did he think you would just follow him out because he asked?"

"Hard to say. He didn't know if Wolf was my brother or my cousin. He did flash his shoulder holster showing he had a gun making an obvious threat. Airport security was everywhere. He even threatened me with arrest. I didn't buy his ploy. He reconsidered his options, and someone was waiting, ready to destroy my car to prove what he's capable of. I'm just glad I wasn't driving my Camaro."

Florence gave me a strange look and asked, "Camaro?"

"Yeah, that's my special car. I paid cash for it after I graduated from Louisiana Lafayette. I earned the money working as a bartender. My brothers took the car, beefed up the engine, suspension, repainted it, installed custom seating, and put on racing stripes. That car is my special baby."

"So, you're an automobile enthusiast, too?" Florence asked.

"You mean car nut! Yes, that and firearms collector. Which reminds me, my Beretta 1911 is lying in that pile of plastic and metal."

"The Memphis police will recover it, run it, through ballistics and it will be held as evidence. Eventually, you may get it back." Florence said.

"Hmmm. Do you think I might be able to file a homeowner insurance claim for the loss?" I asked weakly.

"Doubt it. I'll talk to the local FBI office. They may have a spare old 1911 in their armory. Most of their agents use Glock because of the weight. They might let you use one." Hop said unconvincingly.

"Yeah, that would be great, until I can replace it. A 1911 is more accurate for distance and rapid fire, at least for me."

"You must be pretty good." Florence said.

"Louisiana State Champion for marksmanship. At least that's what it says on my FBI contract."

Florence grinned and said, "I didn't read your contract. Speaking of which, why do you think he targeted you?"

"He probably figured I was a soft target. He could quickly grab me and use me to extort the car away from Wolf. All he did by blowing up the SUV was to show what he was capable of. He's dangerous and getting desperate. Five million is a lot of money to lose in one shot. He probably has more money stashed but this guy is mad as a hornet, and he wants his gold back. I definitely think he believes the gold is still hidden in that Mustang and that we know nothing about it."

Hop walked over and said, "I agree, the car is the target. We need to keep it under constant surveillance. If they make another move to steal it, we'll have them."

"I know this is your case and all Hop, but I disagree?" I said.

Hop gave me a withering look and ask, "Disagree?"

"Yes. I think he's willing to sacrifice that expensive car for the gold. I don't think he's thinking about that Mustang any longer. Did you ever check the serial numbers on that car to find out who the original owners were?"

Hop bit his lip and said, "Yes. The original owner bought the car not too long before he died. Beside His widow in Daytona was the last registered owner of the vehicle after her husband died before Sanchez."

"Did she ever say how our guy got the car away from her?" I asked.

"No. She and a relative died in a boating accident on the inter-coastal. The boat just blew up. Insurance investigators settled with the estate and cut a check to the next of kin, a person named Harry Long." Hop said while looking at his cellphone.

"There you go. A boat blew up, and my car blew up. These guys like to blow stuff up! Harry Long was listed as the next of kin and the car was registered under Perry Sanchez. He must have worked his way into her confidence, killed her then stole all of her assets, including the car, which he decided to keep for himself with a fake name." I said.

Hop looked at Florence and said, "Good guess, but all conjecture. No proof. Once her body and that of her relative was recovered, family members went to her home and everything had been removed, lock, stock, and barrel. The car was gone along with everything else, including her burial insurance policy. There were rumors of a man living with her, but descriptions were sketchy, and Harry Long disappeared too." Hop said.

"Another victim! Harry Long on the prowl. Hope you two don't have plans, because I need a ride back to my apartment." I said.

## Chapter: 32    (Regroup Another Day At The Office)


The first thing I did when I got home was call Clarence Smith and thank him for at least trying to look after my leased vehicle. After that call, I called the office and Wolf explained that all three employees made it safely to the office. Of course, they oooed and awed over his Mustang Jackhammer. Connie helped by giving the three new hires a ride to their hotel in Germantown.

I've lived on my own for some time. I plan and prepare meals only to clean up afterwards which is not one of my favorite tasks. For one thing, I stand in front of my refrigerator trying to decide what to eat, then I consider what it would take for me to prepare that food. Warming and eating frozen food simply does not appeal to my appetite. I went grocery shopping with Florence last evening and picked out things that appealed to me then. Today, not so much. My evening meal tonight will consist of a green salad topped with craisins and walnuts and a light vinaigrette dressing. The salad was good but that didn't quite fill the hole in my appetite. Only the bowl of ice cream I ate later made me feel like I had a balanced meal for dinner.

I thought about opening my computer and working on a dealer file, but I wasn't in the mood. Instead, I turned on my TV and streamed an episode of Candice Renoir on Acorn. The show was broadcast in French but subtitled in English. She was funny, and I enjoyed the best of both worlds.

The next morning I woke up ready to run five miles, then I heard the thunder and saw lightning outside. I've been planning to buy a treadmill for my apartment, but other priorities keep getting in the way. Now, I need to replace my Beretta 1911. I checked my bank account and thought I could make that purchase if I didn't go grocery shopping for the rest of the month. I guess that's what credit cards are for. Exercise will wait for tomorrow.

After a refreshing shower, I drove my Camaro to the office. The black Mustang was nowhere in sight. I saw Wolf's red leased pickup parked next to Ezra's leased black Buick Enclave with a white interior. I parked next to them. What I didn't see was leased cars for our new hires.

I dodged as many raindrops as I could and went inside our office. I shook off the umbrella and smiled at Connie. I said, "I guessing the lease company will bring the other cars today?"

Connie sighed and said, "You'd better talk to Wolf about that."

Wolf was on the phone when I knocked on his doorframe. He waved me in. I heard him say, "Alright Frank, I understand. I'll be there on Monday." He let out an exhausted burst of air.

"Things not going well at Surprise Auto in Dyersburg?" I asked.

"That's an understatement. Apparently someone broke in and stole his business safe."

"Stole the safe? How do you steal a safe? Those things are heavy. They took the whole thing?"

"It was smaller but you're right it was probably very heavy. They broke a doorframe taking the safe out of his building. Thing is, it held his weekly payroll, petty cash, computer back up tapes and the deed to his dealership property. They made a mess out of his building and when he asked his office manager about it, she just got up and quit."

"Quit? Why would she do that?"

"She didn't want to tell the employees that she couldn't meet the payroll."

"Sensitive woman. Do you want me to go and help with the accounting?" I said.

"It's not accounting, it's working capital issues. He was paying his people cash and was barely keeping the business open from week to week. He was trying to get a line of credit from his local bank, and they keep dragging their feet. He wants me to help him find other financing options."

"What does that even mean? Does he need to sell out or find an investor?"

"I think he believes I can do that, but he's wrong. We are facilitators not investors."

"This sounds like a no-win situation. What can I do to help?"

"Stay here and work with the FBI to catch those guys. This is way out of hand. Thank god you weren't in the car when they set it on fire."

"Yeah, and that guy showed himself to me. That was risky. He's over confident, like he's used to getting his way and he's still out there. I notice you left the Mustang in your garage. Are you sure it's safe there?"

"As safe as anyplace. I'm leaving for Dyersburg in my Escape. Chick and his team have their eyes on my place, and I have cameras and alarms everywhere should anyone break in."

"Your dog Roger probably needs back-up."

Wolf gave me a sorry look, and I asked, "What is it?"

"The leasing company cancelled our contract. The pickup has gunshot holes in the tailgate, and your SUV was fire bombed. They claim we're just too much of a risk to do business with. They're coming for the pickup and Ezra's Enclave today. Lavon will pick him up this afternoon."

"Our new hires came to Memphis expecting to drive home in a company provided car. What will we do for that?"

"I'm going to meet with them yet this evening and go over travel schedules for the next month. That's when I break the news about the leased cars."

"How will they get home?" I asked.

"Connie's making return flight arrangements for them. I spoke to Ezra and now you. How do you feel about a monthly car allowance? That way, our people can get any kind of car they want, and we'll cover their travel mileage expenses with gas receipts."

"Uh, that works for me. In other words, they can buy, lease, or drive their old car or a new one and use the monthly allowance as they wish. Will the allowance cover insurance, depreciation, wear, and tear for the miles they put on? If it does, you know, we write off the expense, and everyone is happy. I say, let's do it!"

Wolf gave me a knowing nod and said, "Done!"

**Chapter 33     (Patriarch In Charge)**

"You know, of course, I had to leave the lovely Gwyn in a state of hysteria. She was heartbroken thinking that my daughter was suffering from cancer in a hospital. This whole mess with the car and our gold has cost me time and money." Charles Jensen said.

Sitting in a plush comfortable chair Albert said, "Honestly, we tried, Charles. The Global salesman was not going to be swayed. Our focus then was to discourage the buyer from closing the deal so we could come back and make a counter offer when he left. We didn't think anyone would be dumb enough to pay that much for a car. Heck, I could buy a Porsche for that kind of money."

Charles, his sons Albert and Dirk, along with two of Charles' nephews, sat in the top floor living room suite at the Bonanza Boom Casino hotel in Tunica, Mississippi. Charles called this emergency meeting to plan the recovery of the car and its contents.

His sons almost always called him by his first name. They sat listening to him explain why he came to Mississippi. The two nephews who chose to go by the names Morty and Ferdie. They were there to assist the brothers with the recovery of the car and the gold. So far, all attempts had failed, and the family had recovered nothing but frustration.

Over the years, as all of the boys got older, they were generously rewarded for their roles with each con. There were times when their jobs went well beyond playing a character in a scam. All four boys had been involved with creatively eliminating a mark or taking out key family members who got in the way.

They were inventive with how they made people disappear. Morty had served in the US Army and was an ordinance specialist. A tool he still enjoyed using. He once said, "I just love things that go bang."

But it was Ferdie who did the tough tasks, and he could make things and people quickly disappear. He was quirky and a little off tilt but a cleaver and gifted mechanical savant.

Charles smiled at the boys in the room. "We're here because, some time back, Brenda got the bright idea of investing into assets she could lay her hands on. As you know, she has never trusted banks or any traceable investment. That's why we've only used banks as a device to ship money out of the country where we would have it when we wanted. As you know we do have a few safe deposit boxes around the country with ours and your share of earnings. You all have the codes for those boxes, should something happen to me or Brenda."

Dirk said, "Brenda always said, 'keep your friends close and you're your liquid assets closer. 'Cash is king she said and don't pay taxes'. Her Daddy taught her that. She said the government took all his business and property away when he fell short of cash back in the day."

Albert spoke up. "Cash is hard to hide. I've tried. Brenda was a firm believer in gold. It just sits there and accumulates wealth. Thing is gold is hard to hide, too."

Charles said, "Gold is good but its heavy and very obvious. We talked about it and needed a way to hide and get it out of the country. So, we decided to hide the gold in a car that I retitled from an estate. The plan was to hide the gold, let it sit, and just increase in value. When the time was right we would ship the car and gold out of the country. That Auto storage facility in Olathe, Kansas seemed like the perfect place. I honestly didn't believe anyone would go to a small town in Kansas just to buy a car."

"Your plan did work, for a while Charles. The car was hidden for three years in plain sight. You priced the car well over market, so no one would pay that much. Storage fees were paid automatically out of Perry Sanchez's bank account." Dirk said.

"Yes, a name I've used from time to time. We just weren't ready to ship that car anywhere yet. We needed more time." Charles said.

Charles quietly said, "Listen, our family, has had a good thing going for several years. We have been very successful setting up stings all over the country. When I first started out, it was just Brenda and me. The first few times were sloppy, and we almost got caught. We did okay but over time, with the aid of her brother, Morty and Ferdie's dad, we began to set up fool proof cons to take what we want. The secret, get in slow and get out fast."

"While you four and your sister were small children, all of you played a character in our cons. For you it was a game of pretend. For us, the adults, it was a game we loved. We still love planning and executing the con. Setting up the mark and walking away with our rewards was the best part. As my brother-in-law would say, "Tax free fun."

Charles looked at Morty and Ferdie and said, It was a shame when your Daddy got caught in that car chase and died. It broke Brenda's heart. That's why we must be extra careful how we proceed with the recovery of that car and the gold. The gold is important, but not as important as family. We are all blood and must always look after one another."

There were nods of agreement around the room.

"Let's get down to business. Brenda made it clear, we need to get that car back and that's what we'll do. When Morty scouted LeDuc's business with that rifle scope, all hell broke loose. It looked like private security popped out of the woodwork right away. I'm thinking the excess security is related to his business. He does something with cars, not sure what, so we'll pick a softer target."

Albert said, "Ferdie followed that rube, LeDuc. He lives alone at a nice house in Germantown. That woman, either is sister or his girlfriend lives not far away. I was curious about her. She keeps getting in the way when we go after the car. Strange young woman. Charles you wanted to take her at the airport and use her to force LeDuc to give us the car. She was about to throw a fit, so you gave Morty the go-ahead to blow up her car."

Morty grinned and said, "Boom!" He used his hands to emphasize the explosion.

"So, what do you think the next plan should be?" Dirk asked.

"Yeah, what do you have in mind, Charles?" Albert asked.

Charles grinned and said, "I think a frontal assault will take them by surprise. We go in fast, take out LeDuc and steal the car. I have the spare key fob for the car. While we're there, I'll search for the car title, then we're gone. Ferdie, get busy. I need a diesel pickup. And we need a second vehicle for us and the hired help to ride in. Albert, I need two more street hires. Will you have any trouble?"

"Nope! I'll go to Elvis's old neighborhood. We'll find what we want there."

Charles laughed and said, "If you can get Elvis, I won't tell anyone."

Dirk said, "Use one of your disguises. Maybe you can go as Elvis for the raid at LeDuc's house. That would be hilarious."

"You know, Dirk, you may have an idea there."

Albert said, "First, I'll see if the Mustang is at LeDuc's business. If it's unlocked, we're good! If not, gone in 60 seconds, right? We blew up that woman's car. Wonder what she's driving now? You know me, I love a good car theft. This could be a piece of cake."

"Take one of those street hires with you when you go, for back up. Don't take any risks. If that don't work, we do the frontal assault" Charles said.

"I'll be armed, don't worry." Albert said grinning.

**Chapter: 34    (Don't Worry?)**


Our meetings with new hires at the office this morning was off to a good start. Wolf made a day trip yesterday to Dyersburg and told the dealer it was time to sell his business. Today, he was ready to spend time with his new hires. He broke the news that leased cars was not now part of their compensation plan, but he offered a compensation program that satisfied all of them.

It was around noon when the leasing company came to reclaim their vehicles. They took key fobs from us and drove the vehicles off our lot in a hurry, looking over their shoulders. Stony made the remark, "Looks like they think you're working for the mob."

Wolf said, "In all fairness, we only had three vehicles for a week and two of them are now out of commission. In their mind, we were just too much of a risk." He turned to Tony and Frank and asked, "Sorry about this fellas. Are you okay with getting your own vehicles with a LeDuc and Johnson allowance? I'm afraid it will not be enough to buy that Mercedes Benz you mentioned but whatever you choose, this should help."

Frank laughed and said, "Wolf, we're car guys. Cars are our image when we pull up on a dealers lot. I'm sure we can find something we like with the monthly car allowance you mentioned. It's all good."

"Be sure to raise your liability insurance to $500,000. That way we're all covered. Your allowance will cover that. Your car allowance will be prorated for the remainder of this month and direct deposited into your bank accounts. Then the allowance will come in your first paycheck of each month. Any questions?" I asked.

"Sounds fair. What about those guys who came after you? Do you think they'll come after us, too?" Tony asked.

"Doesn't seem likely. They're focused on recovering the black Mustang they didn't want sold. Just don't get in their way." Wolf warned.

"Where is that Jackhammer now?" Stony asked.

"Home in my garage being watched by Reliant Security. I'm driving my Escape. Let's meet in the conference room to wrap up our business with your upcoming assignments, then fly home and prepare to meet your first dealer."

"Too bad!" Tony said. "I was looking forward to visiting Beal Street while I was here."

Ezra said grinning, "Next trip boys. Wolf has allowed me enough time to cover warranty fraud indicators for you to be aware of when you visit your dealers. You know from being in the business, the dealer may or may not be aware of sketchy things going on in the shop. You'll be the eyes for fraud. Report what you find."

I looked out across the parking lot wondering if I could see any potential danger, like men with guns. Right now, I was seeing danger behind every trash can. Everything appeared to be calm, which had me worried. In the parking lot all I saw was Connie's car, my Camaro and Wolf's Escape. Connie had already ordered transportation for the three men using Uber to take them to the airport this afternoon.

I settled down in my office to work on a financial statement wrap-up analysis for a dealer in Kentucky. I was just about to finish my report when my cellphone buzzed. It was Clarence. I said in a jovial tone, "Hey Clarence, what's up?"

"Annette, You'd better get out to your car. Two men just walked up to it. I'm observing from a second story window across the street. They seem to be poking around your car. Not sure what they're up to. I think one of them may have a slim-jim. I'm on my way."

I immediately hung up, grabbed my purse, extracted my Nano, and walked past the conference room. Wolf saw me storm past with my gun, he called after me. "Annette! Stop! Where're you going?"

I walked past Connie who had a shocked look on her face. I pulled open the front door and saw two men trying to jimmy the lock on my Camaro using the tool called a slim-jim. The one closest to me, a handsome bearded young man, looked up. He dropped the tool in his hand, then reached behind his back and pulled out a gun. The man on the other side of the car panicked and began to run away. I shouted, "Drop your weapon, NOW!"

The foolish young man turned, smirked, and aimed his gun, I fired a shot that hit him in the right eye. His gun flew out of his hand, and he fell backwards onto the ground rolling around in pain. I turned and saw the other man running for all he was worth across the parking lot, and he ran right into my friend, Clarence Smith. Clarence had him on the ground and zip tied in seconds. He pulled the man up and drug him over to the Camaro. When he got to my car, he saw the man on the ground and said, "Think we'd better call an ambulance!"

I heard a buzzing noise, looked up, and saw a drone flying overhead. I thought about shooting it out of the sky but thought better. In the meantime, Connie dialed 9-1-1. In a matter of minutes, the

Germantown police pulled into the parking lot with sirens blaring and armed officers jumping out of their cars. An ambulance soon followed.

By this time, Clarence had holstered his gun, and I bent over and put my Nano on the ground. With both hands above my head, I greeted the armed officers. I said, "I think he may need medical attention."

Standing behind me and gawking through the glass on out building front, Wolf, the three new hires, Ezra and Connie stared open mouthed at the carnage in disbelief.

## Chapter: 35    (What's Up With Hop?)

Tony laughed and said, "I gotta say, Annette, you make working for an auto dealer consulting company *very* exciting!"

I spent an hour and a half with the Germantown police department explaining what happened that caused me to shoot a man in his right eye. They found the Slim Jim and Clarence backed up my story as an eyewitness. Even though I fired in self-defense, they snatched up my Nano for evidence. I was now down two guns.

The two men were both in their mid-twenties. Drivers licenses indicated the wounded man was from Miami, FL. He was taken to a local hospital emergency ward. The other person was a local black man who had priors. Both faced grand theft larceny charges in the State of Tennessee.

When Hop and Florence showed up he said, "We got everything on video using a drone. We'll back you up with your Prosecutor."

"So, you were that drone, and you surveilled me, but you weren't there to prevent a break-in of my car?"

"Not really. We're watching Wolf's house because that's where the Mustang is. We had a drone agent watching you from above." Hop said casually pointing at the sky.

"Did it occur to you the man I met at the airport would come after me because I refused to go with him? I mean, he fire bombed my car, Hop! And now, he sent two guys to come after my Camaro."

Hop nodded and said, "Noted."

"That's it? Noted? Is that how you treat your coworkers and contract employees? I'll see how the Deputy Director feels about that."

Florence quickly stepped in and said, "Look, I can see there's a lot of tension between you two. I understand there's some history between you but let's not lose site of what we're trying to accomplish here."

Florence turned to me and said, "The man at the airport may or may not be the man we're looking for. Our guy's a chameleon. I think he is coming after you for personal reasons. And now, we're putting you under our protection. You're going into a safe-house for your own protection."

"Me? Look, I would need a change of clothes, and I would just be a distraction from watching Wolf and the Mustang. Right now, I'm more important to you as live bait."

Ignoring my protest Hop said, "The second man was armed, and he is now in a Germantown holding cell. Members of the Memphis bureau will be interrogating him." Hop said.

Wolf and the new LeDuc employees all watched the interaction between me and the two FBI agents. I made up my mind and said, "No. I'm not going anywhere with you. Not until you, Hop, and I have a one on one conversation. Is that understood?"

I watched Hop swallow hard. He looked at Florence for back up and she just stared at him waiting for his answer. Finally, he weakly said, "Okay. Where do you want to talk?"

**Chapter: 36     (Face The Music)**


Hop and I needed to air our differences where no one could hear or see what we had to say to each other. I said, "My apartment. Florence, if you come, you may wait outside. We'll take my Camaro."

Hop agreed to my conditions, and he quietly rode with me to my apartment which wasn't far from the office, without Florence. On the way to the apartment, I hoped that I had picked up my discarded clothes from my morning run. And there were still dishes in the sink. Still, I decided none of that mattered. Hop and I needed to figure out what was going on between us. Both his attitude and mine were getting in the way of our assignment to find and arrest a vile man who was suspected of fraud, tax evasion, and probable murder of several innocent people.

When we entered my apartment, Hop said, "Nice place."

I ignored the sarcasm in his voice and asked if he wanted a water, or lemonade. He said, "Lemonade sounds good."

I fixed us both one from a bottle I had in the fridge. I looked at my small dining room table, then the couch and recliner in my living room. I suggested, "Have a seat on the couch. What we have to say to one another shouldn't take all that long."

I handed him the lemonade. He took a sip and put the glass on my coffee table. He asked, "Okay, where do we start?"

I had several sharp retorts for this question but kept them to myself. Instead I said, "Let's start from where we left off the last time we saw each other."

"Fair enough. We had just wrapped up a crime of Bitcoin theft and delt with several international terrorists from Corsica. As I recall, you were kidnapped from a gamming convention dressed as Wonder Woman."

"Yes, and you were dressed in a red suit as The Flash with yellow footwear and a thunder bolt on your chest. It wasn't just about Bitcoins, it was about murder. How could I forget?"

"There was that funny Indian guy from St. Louis dressed as a fancy elephant. You and he were friends, weren't you?"

"VJ Sing. He was dressed as Ganesha, the Hindu elephant god. Thanks to Wolf and his friend Chick Farrell, they showed up with the cavalry to save me, VJ and a couple of gamers."

"Hey, I was there, too!"

"Yes, you were, and you were about to shoot that man from Corsica who was going to shoot me. Then you were hit from behind. You tried to save my life."

Hop exhaled and said, "He was about to kill you, what else could I do?"

"Yeah, Chick shot that guy from Corsica."

"But Pierre's guy hit me hard in the head and gave me a concussion. I remember, you came to visit me in the hospital."

I smiled and said, "You called me a beautiful angel."

"Yeah, I guess I did. We promised to keep in touch."

"What happened?" I asked.

"Not sure. New job, new life in Washington. I thought of you often."

"I sent emails and tried calling you, but you never picked up or answered. I kind of thought we were attracted to one another."

Hop looked ashamed and said, "Well, I definitely was attracted to you. You were just out of my league. You're smart, beautiful, and extremely brave. I almost called you more than once, but I chickened out."

"Chickened out? What does that mean? Out of site out of mind is what I'm thinking. Did you begin dating someone else in Washington and simply forgot about me?"

"No, I haven't dated anyone since I've began managing the Cybercrimes department. My brother recently got assigned to an Embassy post in China, so I've been spending a lot of time with my Mother in Wisconsin. Look, I had hopes of us getting together, at least dating. But you were in Memphis, and I was in Washington, the logistics simply didn't work. Then, a week ago, I was alerted about a contract employee being involved with a man we've been tracking for some time. I went to my boss and asked to be assigned to the case in the field. He agreed and he told me that our employee had recovered millions in gold. It was the best lead we had to zero in on this mystery man. I had no idea it was you, till I got here.

"Yep! I made that call to the Deputy Director and made sure the gold was secured for the government and the victims' families."

"You see. I just couldn't wrap my mind around you being one of us, a Federal Agent. I've had to suppress my feelings and not appear to be involved with a coworker. That's against department rules, you know."

"Uh, a couple of errors there, Hop. First, I am not a field Agent, I'm a contract employee. I am a specialist for sharpshooting. So, I am not a coworker. Second, you should have at least called me."

"I know. I just didn't know how to approach you. Can we begin again?" Hop asked weakly.

I couldn't help but smile at his sophomoric attempt to be romantic. I said, "I think we can work something out. Why don't we discuss a few ground rules, so we don't make the same mistake again."

"Rules? Like what?"

"Like communication which is the key to every relationship. Phone calls answered, emails responded to, just being honest with one another. Pour your heart out and tell me how you feel."

Hop looked like he was going to cry. I put the back of my hand to the side of his face. I smiled, leaned forward, and kissed him gently on his lips. He eagerly accepted. I felt that we had finally broken some ice.

## Chapter: 37    (Interrupted Sleep)

Two days later, Wolf was suddenly awakened. His dog, Roger, was voicing a low throaty growl. Wolf rolled over and whispered, "What is it boy?" You hear something?"

Wolf heard the low rumbling sound of a diesel truck's motor in front of his house. He quickly threw off the covers and padded to the front window. He separated the blinds and saw a diesel truck slowly move past his house. The truck was followed by an SUV. They turned onto the side street where his garage was located on his corner lot.

He grabbed his cellphone and quickly opened the app for the camera above his garage. He watched as the truck and SUV backed into his drive then seven or eight men poured out. "Oh! Not good!" He ran to his dresser pulled out his Sig Sauer handgun then punched speed dial for Chick.

"What's up Bro?"

"I'm under siege. A diesel pickup truck and SUV just drove past my house and backed into my driveway. I have no idea where the FBI is. Several men got out. All of them are wearing black ski masks and they appear to be armed."

"Get to your safe room as fast as you can. We're on our way."

In his pajamas, Wolf and Roger ran down the stairs as fast as their legs could carry them. When he ran to the kitchen he saw movement men carefully walking past his kitchen window on his pool decking in the back yard.

Wolf pulled open the pantry door and released a secret latch. The pantry shelf swung open exposing a stairwell that went into a cozy basement. He said, "Come boy," and Roger followed him. He turned, shut the pantry door then the shelf from his side and heard it click into place. He descended the stairway. The subterranean room was illuminated with ambient computer led lights. He sat in his computer chair, booted his computer, then opened the app which held all of the security camera images.

Roger made himself comfortable on a rug and growled again. Wolf stroked the dog and said, "Shush!" He turned, put a code on a small safe and extracted his Glock handgun. Now armed with two handguns, he put on earphones so he could hear anything the intruders had to say upstairs.

Wolf was startled when he heard a loud crash. He thought, *"I bet the neighbors heard that noise. Surely they'll call the police"* He watched, open mouthed, as the garage camera recorded men pull his garage door off its rails using a wench attached to the pickup.

Wolf heard men walking and talking inside the house upstairs. He turned up the gain on his computer app and through his headphone, the voices began to make sense.

"I don't care. He's got to be here someplace. He's hiding. Tear the place apart if you have to. I want the title on that car, and I want him dead."

"Yes, Sir." A man replied.

"And hurry. We don't have a lot of time."

Wolf heard footsteps running up the stairs above him. Roger growled again but Wolf hugged Roger and whispered, "Quiet, Roger. They won't find us."

Startled, Wolf heard the pantry door being jerked open above him. He held his breath praying that Roger wouldn't give them away. The door suddenly slammed shut and Wolf let out a sigh of relief.

Wolf watched the screen and listened to men chattering. "I've checked every room downstairs." One man said.

"And I've checked all of the rooms upstairs. I looked in closets and under beds and in the bathrooms. His bed looks like it has been slept in." The man who looked like Elvis, appeared to be in charge. He said, "Check again. Someone go outside and look in the pool house. Damn it! I know he's here! I'll go upstairs and check myself."

Elvis ran up the stairs. Wolf could hear him opening and slamming doors closed. Furniture was being turned over and broken. In his earphones he heard, "He was here! His bed is still warm. People like him just don't disappear! You! Check the attic. He's got to be here somewhere. That crazy woman who works for him shot and almost killed my son, Albert. She shot him in the eye. And I intend to take an eye for an eye."

More furniture was broken, pictures torn off walls and dishes smashed. In the distance, Wolf heard the whine of a siren. The intruders heard it too.

"Hear that?" One of the men asked.

"It's the cops. Let's get out of here." Another man said in a panic.

The man upstairs ran down to the main level and said, "Where are you two going?"

"Cops. You're on your own, dude."

"The hell you say? We're taking that car. Here's the key fob. Get out there and back the car out of the garage. Move!"

"Screw you. I'm not going to prison for some car." A man said.

Roger began to growl louder. I tried to shush him, but Roger was having none of it. Wolf heard the man dressed as Elvis in his headphones, "Quiet! What's that noise?"

"I don't hear nothing, man."

"It's a damned dog! Find that damned dog and you find the man!"

"The sirens are getting closer. I'm getting out of here." Then Wolf heard the deafening loud noise of a gunshot. Wolf saw Elvis shoot the man in the back and he fell onto the kitchen floor. Wolf whispered, "Oh no. He shot him!"

The Elvis man shouted, "LeDuc, you S-O-B, I know you're here and I'm coming back to get you."

"What about that car in the garage?"

"Forget it. Get in the SUV. We're out of time, let's go. We'll hide on a side street till things settle down...I'm coming back..." The man shouted as the voice began to get weaker, but Wolf still heard, "When I find that LeDuc, I'm putting a bullet in his brain."

On Wolf's computer screen, he saw the SUV burn rubber leaving.

The house was quiet, but Roger continued to growl while Wolf stayed put. He saw armed uniform police officers enter his house with guns drawn and that was when he called Chick.

"Wolf, I'm outside. The Germantown police department wanted to clear the house before they would let me come in."

"Tell them not to shoot me. I'm still downstairs with Roger in the safe room. I watched those guys shoot a man. Whoever he is, he's in my kitchen. I got it all saved on computer video. That poor man will need an ambulance."

"Do not come out until I get inside, and I'll let you out of your safe room. If you have any firearms, lock-em up."

An hour later, Wolf was still in his pajamas and drinking coffee. Chick was with him, and he did most of the talking. The police were confused as to why someone would so brazenly do such a destructive home invasion.

"It was the car. They wanted the title to that car," wolf said.

"Car? Armed men burst into your house looking for a car and its title?" The Detective asked incredulously.

Chick cleared his throat and said, "This is a little more complicated than that. Wolf is working with the Memphis Bureau of the FBI on a case involving the black car in the garage."

"The Ford Escort?"

"No. The Roush Jackhammer Mustang."

"Why would they break in to steal that car and demand the title?"

Chick could tell the Detective wanted to tie the B&E to a drug bust, the go-to crime when they don't know what happened. Without saying anything about gold, he said, "The FBI seized some contraband that was hidden in the car. These guys were desperate to recover that contraband and as a result, they thought nothing of murdering one of their own in the process."

The Detective asked. "Contraband? What kind of contraband?"

"I'm afraid you'll have to ask the FBI about that. I'm just Wolf's security company hired to protect him," he said smiling.

"Something still doesn't sound right. Are you sure Mr. LeDuc doesn't have some firearms on the premises?"

"I didn't say that. But he did not fire the weapon that shot that man in his kitchen. He has video proof that another man pulled the trigger."

Florence Sallaz walked into the house, and flashed her ID. She said, "Thank you officers for arriving so quickly. You probably saved Mr. LeDuc's life. This is now officially an FBI investigation."

What she said didn't sink in right away but when it did, the lead Detective was angry as a cat in a dog fight. After calling his Chief, he backed down and asked, "What about the man just taken to the hospital?"

"You mean the vic who was shot? I called. He died in route. I think it would be good for everyone in Germantown if your report reflected that some out of town men showed up to the wrong address. They got scared and left. Don't mention the murdered man to the press, it might be problematic to explain." Florence said.

The Detective packed up his things and said, "No kidding."

## Chapter: 38    (The Morning After)


Wolf called and woke me up at 3:50 AM and told me about his home invasion. I got dressed and came right over to his house. I made more coffee for everyone and offered donuts which I picked up along the way for whomever was there. The Germantown Police Chief, Richard Sparks just showed up with chief Detective, Duke Davis. Chick, Clarence, Florence, and myself were munching on donuts around Wolf's spacious living room discussing the early morning invasion.

Richard Sparks conceded the turnover of Wolf's break-in to the FBI. Florence called a forensics team to inspect and inventory the damage to Wolf's house after she arrived. She explained to the Germantown police the plan laid out by the FBI to capture a very dangerous most wanted criminal, she declined to mention the gold.

Florence introduce me as a colleague and FBI contract employee. I had met Chief Sparks before on a couple of occasions. He turned to me with an amused grin and said, "So, I understand you are now working for the FBI?" It was a question to be confirmed or denied, not a statement.

"Yes, I do work for the FBI, as a contract employee. I am not a Special Agent." I said.

"Then you're like Chick Farrell, here, I take it?"

"I wish that were true. He operates in an entirely different orbit than me. I'm asked to help out when the situation calls for my skills." I said.

"I presume those skills are like the one you exhibited when you shot that man at your cousin's business?" Richard asked.

I didn't flinch at the question. I said, "That's right. How is that man, anyway?"

"The medical report I received said he will never see out of that eye again and he may never speak coherently either. That 9 millimeter bullet from your Nano Beretta rattled around in his skull like a BB in a tin can before it settled down. I'll make sure you get your gun back when we're done with ballistics and filed our report with the State."

Wolf shook his head and said, "I can confirm that guy is the son of the man who broke into my house this morning. I heard him scream vengeance on Annette and me for shooting his son."

"What was that young man's last name when he checked into the hospital?" Florence asked.

Detective Davis said, "The last name on his license said Marsh with a first name Cal. His driver's license says he's a resident of Daytona Beach, probably a high rise condo."

"So, do you think Marsh is the last name of our guy who broke into Wolf's home this morning?" The Chief asked Florence.

Wolf shook his head and said, "The shooter called his son Albert by name, not Cal. I doubt if anyone's last name is really Marsh.

"I'll run both names and his prints through our search engine to see if we can find any priors." The Chief said.

"The FBI forensics team is dusting for prints in the house. We'll need your fingerprint data for that man in the hospital, and we'll run it through our national data base, too." Florence said.

"I figure our local high powered FBI girl would have instant access to those FBI files." Chief Sparks said with humor in his voice.

I heard Chick snort while sipping his coffee. I said, "No. And I don't have access either. I'm just like everyone else. I have to fill out paperwork, and request the information, then wait."

Chief Sparks wasn't going to let it go. He said to me, "You mean a high profile FBI person like you is made to wait? That's just embarrassing." He said with sarcasm and a twinkle in his eye.

I took instant offence and was about to say something when Chick sprung to my defense. He said, "I can tell you one thing, Richard, she may not have instant access to the FBI files but if you ever get into a fire fight, she's the person you want on your '6'.

Clarence put his coffee down, grinned and said, "And Big Hoss in a Louisiana swamp can verify that." He said with a wide grin.

Detective Davis looked confused and asked, "Who's Big Hoss? Some drug dealer or something?"

Clarence grinned and said, "If you ever go to New Iberia, Louisiana, stay away from the bayous. Big Hoss is the meanest, toughest monster you'll ever want to meet."

Chief Sparks asked incredulously, "You shot and killed him?"

Clarence said with wide open eyes, "No. She gave him a human sacrifice."

Chief Sparks looked confused and was about to say something. I could see everything was getting out of hand and asked, "Who is the dead man in Wolf's home this morning?"

"African American male, early 30's, no ID on him. We're running his fingerprints. I'm guessing he's probably local hired help." The Chief said.

Chick said, "Wolf, I've contacted a man I know who will come by this morning to give you a quote for fixing your garage door and any other damage done to the house. Also, I have a clean-up crew who'll come by this afternoon and pick up the mess those guys left behind."

"What about that diesel truck in Wolf's drive?" Florence asked.

"Both stolen yesterday. I'm having it hauled to the impound lot." Chief Sparks said, biting into another donut.

"Damn!" Wolf said looking at his watch. "I had a meeting with Ezra this morning."

"Don't worry. I'll call Connie and Ezra to let them know what happened. I'm sure they'll understand." I said. "Just make sure Roger recovers from the home invasion. Where is he anyway?"

Wolf looked around and said, "I don't know. I forgot all about him. He must be in his bed upstairs. I better go check."

"I'll go with you." I said.

Wolf and I went upstairs into his nearly destroyed bedroom. There at the foot of Wolf's upended bed was Roger's dog bed. Roger was curled up into a ball shivering. We both carefully approached Roger and used soothing words as we petted him. The poor dog was traumatized. Wolf said, "He can still smell the intruders who ransacked my house in this room. I need to take care of him. After my guests leave downstairs, I'll take Roger for a walk. I still need to go to the office this morning. Maybe I'll take Roger with me. It would be nice if you could stay here for the workmen who'll be showing up."

I sighed, "Of course I'll stay. I think Clarence needs to follow you in his vehicle, though. It's pretty obvious that both you and I are marked people by this maniac. A guy who's after his gold is now out for blood revenge."

"Hope you don't have a date tonight. Revenge or not, you and I will go to the Mustangs of Memphis car cruise in Collierville this evening."

I gave him a twisted grin and said, "Date? Who would I date? You don't think that guy will try something in a crowded place like the Collierville square, do you?"

"Probably not, but he may try something as we come and go from there. To be on the safe side, I'll ask Becka, my dogsitter, to take Roger to her house this evening."

We left Roger in his bed and went back downstairs to plan tonight's visit to Collierville with our friends who were munching donuts in Wolf's living room.

## Chapter: 39     (Making Preparations)

Throughout the remainder of the day, Wolf's house was beset by workmen bent on putting his house back in order. Some things, like expensive oil paintings and items in his vinyl record collection were destroyed beyond recovery. Papers were scattered everywhere. A favorite rocking chair from our aunt in Louisiana was completely smashed.

I waited in the kitchen and greeted the garage door repairman. Clarence kept an eye on both Wolf and Roger from a discrete distance in his Reliant Security SUV. Germantown Chief, Richard Sparks and his Detective, Duke Davis, left. Florence and Chick stayed with me at the house and discussed how they would cover the car cruise tonight. Hop was simply missing in action. I had no idea where he was.

"Our perp is becoming pretty unstable with killing the hired help. The destruction of Wolf's home was just unorganized meanness. Wolf said he had a key fob. I wonder why he didn't take the car. What do you think his next move will be?" Florence asked Chick.

Chick said, "I think he ran out of time. This guy will stop at nothing until he gets his hands on that car and the gold that he believes is still there. He wants to kill or hurt Annette for shooting his son. I think we need to let him have the car, then capture him later."

Hop finally showed up at Wolf's house. He walked in smiling and said, "Sounds simple, but how do we do that without arousing suspicion?"

"Suspicion? You mean they might figure out we discovered the gold?" I asked incredulously.

"Annette, you and Wolf will be driving that car to a car show tonight, right?" Chick asked changing the subject.

"It's actually a cruise. Yes, we drive the car to the Collierville square, pull out a couple of chairs, sit and talk about the car to anyone who passes by. The Roush Mustang should draw a lot of attention."

Wolf and Roger returned to the house and heard us talking in the living room. He came in and asked, "Did I miss anything?"

Florence said, "No. We were discussing how the cruise would work tonight. We'll all be there watching you, Annette, and the car."

"Is there anyway you can park that car away from the other cars, making it easier to be grabbed by our guy?" Chick asked.

"Look, I've been thinking about this. I don't want to put any local citizens at risk by using the car as bait. I think we need to get the car far away someplace else where no one could get hurt." Hop said.

"Do you have any ideas?" I asked.

"If the car is bait, I'm thinking Big Box Home Repair and lumber yard. They have a huge lot. Annette, and Wolf will leave the car in the parking lot away from other cars. Then go inside and shop for things to repair his home." Hop offered.

"We drove by there earlier, it might work." Florence said.

"I think it might, too. You guys set up in the parking lot and wait for us to show up. Seeing the Mustang sitting alone in a parking lot might be too much of a temptation for him to pass up." Wolf said.

"Okay, I'll contact the store management and let you know if that location works." Hop said, getting up, pulling out his cellphone, and making the call.

Workmen were still busy at Wolf's home when I drove my Camaro to the office. Wolf called and asked Becka to watch Roger this afternoon and evening. Then Hop sent a text saying he was unable to convince the store manager to let the FBI use his lot. The excuse was liability.

Wolf stayed home managing the cleaning crew and reorganizing the mess left behind by home invaders. The crew piled the junk into a trash container at the edge of his driveway while the Germantown police department impounded the diesel truck. A carpenter arrived and was busy replacing door frames and locks on the doors that were broken.

After work, I went to my apartment and changed into a comfortable skort and colorful top for the cruise this evening. Then I drove to Wolf's house and was surprised by how quickly the renovation was taking place. If I needed to hire people, it would take over a week for them to even call me back.

There was a truck in the drive, and I went inside to find Roger in a much better mood. The workman were touching up paint on the new doorframes when I asked Wolf if he still wanted to go to the Mustang cruise this afternoon. He said, "More than ever. You know, Roush only made 200 Jackhammer Mustangs, and I have one in my garage. They are all unique. I can't wait to see what the club members think of the car."

"Should I order food from Door Dash?"

"No. We have time. I was thinking catfish sounds good. You know that restaurant in Rossville, just east of Collierville?"

"I remember the food but not the name of the restaurant."

"The Wolf River Café. In my opinion, it's the best catfish you can get outside of Mississippi. Hush puppies, green fried tomatoes, and banana cream pie. It doesn't get any better than that!"

After the carpenter left, Wolf backed the Roush Mustang out of the garage onto the drive. He parked his Ford Escape at the curb, and I parked my Camaro behind the Escape. Every move we made was being watched by Reliant Security employees. I wasn't at all concerned about vandalism. Wolf's neighbor across the side street facing his garage graciously allowed Chick to have a man watch both the house and the cars from her property. She even provided him with snacks and homemade sweet tea.

I was in the passenger seat when Wolf started the Mustang. It purred like an angry tiger. I could tell he wanted to cut loose and speed all the way to Rossville, but he grudgingly kept the car under control.

Ww drove Wolf River Boulevard to the Collierville Arlington Road, then took Poplar to Rossville and our restaurant. I rode with the window down.

Wolf was right, the Wolf River Café served fantastic catfish and sides. More than one customer asked, "Is that your car out there?" And Wolf proudly explained that it was. Although, technically, the FBI owned the car but that was our secret.

# Chapter: 40    (Collierville Car Cruise)

After our dinner in Rossville, we drove the Mustang a short distance to the Collierville Car Cruise at the square.

Even though we were early, Cars were already parked around the square in a diagonal parking pattern. Wolf was directed to a spot near a corner, where he carefully backed his Roush Mustang next to a 1964 ½ vintage red Mustang sprint car.

We got out of the Mustang, set up our chairs in some shade and I was simply happy to relax quietly, sipping water and watching all of the activity with cars arriving and parking. I kept my eyes peeled looking for our protectors, for I knew they were already in place.

Wolf carefully polished the beautiful black car with flat black accents on the hood and side. He put the engine hood up and placed a fire extinguisher next to the right front fender of the car. Satisfied, he sat down and said, "You know, my Roush may not get as much attention as that 64 Mustang sitting next to me."

It didn't take long for Mustang owners and people who just love cars to begin pouring by. They stared, gawked, and photographed Wolf's car. Everyone wanted to talk about cars. I've displayed my Camaro a couple of times and it's fun to talk to the people who always seem to know more about your car than you do.

The president of the Mustang Club couldn't stop talking about the black Roush Jackhammer. He had never seen one before and he escorted a steady stream of people by to ogle at the car.

Wolf was right. While his car was a show stopper, everyone wanted to see the near original condition 64 ½ beauty sitting next to us. Lots of people took photos of themselves next to both vehicles.

Colorful streamers were hanging all around the square. A local rock band was playing soft rock on a music gazebo in the square. Children were running and young parents were pushing strollers. All in all, it was a pleasant late spring afternoon outing for families to enjoy.

I saw police officers casually walking around and talking to car enthusiasts. Food trucks were parked in a section of the square vending everything from deep fried snickers bars, hot dogs to tacos and gyros. I admired the fun festival feel of the atmosphere.

Wolf and I were busy talking to people about his car, when I noticed a man walking by who looked vaguely familiar. He wore a loose Hawaiian print shirt with a car pattern, and tan shorts. He had no socks and wore boat shoes. He sported a white men's Panama hat that shadowed his features. This man had a light blond beard and a bushy mustache. What caught my attention was the way he looked at Wolf's car then kept looking over his shoulder. He didn't seem nervous, just cautious. He looked strangely familiar, kind of like an older version of the man I shot.

I stood up and moved to approach him, but he simply walked away, melting into the crowd. I quickly called Florence and described the man. She said, "We'll check him out."

I walked back to the car and noticed a six-year-old approach Wolf's car with an ice cream cone in his hand. I desperately looked around for the parent. Having seen none, I ran over and intercepted the child and said, "Whoa there big boy! Where you going with that cone?"

"A man paid me a dollar to drop the cone inside that black car."

"He did, did he? Well, I'll give you two dollars to point that man out for me. Can you do that?"

"Sure! The boy turned around, taking the cone with him and he ran away ahead of me and from the cars and crowd of spectators. I watched as the child dodged into and around people. I spied him running toward the corner of a building and followed. My Spidey senses then told me, *"this does not look good."* I whipped out my cell phone and speed dialed Hop. "Hop, do you have eyes on me?"

"No. Where are you?"

"Near the store that sells fudge. I'm following a kid who almost put an ice cream cone in Wolf's car. He said a man paid him a dollar to do it. I told the boy that I would pay him two to point out the man to me. Now, the kid has gone down a side street."

"Do not follow the kid. Stay put at the fudge store. I'm coming."

I edged toward the side street to see where the kid had gone. Suddenly, I felt something hard pressed into my back. I instinctively began to turn, and the voice said, "Do not move. I will pull the trigger, and your kidney will be instantly destroyed. Now, walk slowly into that alley next to the fudge store."

"Why should I go with you? You've already threatened my life. Just shoot me now in public and get it over with."

"Don't stop! Keep walking and stop talking. Those are brave words from a young woman. You're so right, I should just kill you now for shooting my son. But none of this is about you. It's about my car in case you haven't figured that out by now. Keep moving."

We rounded the corner of the Fudge Shoppe building. A couple of people were walking toward us. This was an opportune distraction, I thought about making a move but feared that one of those people might become collateral damage. The man sensing what I was thinking said, "Don't slow down, ya hear? Wounding you is no problem for me. I'll shoot you and drag you to that car over there."

"What? And mess up your car seats? That's a terrible idea." I said.

"What? Are you some kind of comedian or something?" The man said.

"Maybe." I said.

"Where did you get that gun from when you shot my son?"

At least he was a talker and that was to my advantage. I said, "It was given to me. Shooting him was a lucky shot. After your son was taken to the hospital, the police took my gun." I didn't want him to know I was armed.

"Good for them. Guns are not playthings and shouldn't be in the hands of inexperienced people."

"So, I take it, you are experienced?"

"Don't make me prove it."

He pushed me toward a silver Dodge Charger. He used his fob to unlock the car door. He said, "Put your hands behind your back. Now!"

I did as he asked, and he slipped a zip tie around my wrists. I tightened my wrists putting pressure against the zip ties. The ties were loose, but my hands remained secured. Using his free hand, he opened the door and shoved me inside and said, "Get your feet inside. Do it or I'll stomp on your ankle and break it. Understand?"

I quickly pulled my legs inside the car and righted myself on the seat. He quickly ran around and got in on the driver's side and started the engine. He didn't bother with seat belts for either of us. I thought, *"Uh oh! He's not a safe driver."*

He backed out of his parking spot then floored the accelerator, thrusting the car forward, leaving gravel flying behind us.

## Chapter: 41     (The Wolf Chase)

I didn't know it, but Hop had just rounded the corner of the Fudge Shoppe and saw the man in the Hawaiian shirt and I walking forty feet in front. He could tell that I was being abducted at gunpoint. He had a decision to make. He could shout out to the man and order him to stop and to let me go or continue to follow us while calling for backup. Hop chose to call for backup. He speed dialed Florence and quickly explained the situation.

Hop said into his cellphone. "He's zip tying her hands now and is standing next to a silver Dodge Charger, late model. I'll try to get the tag number."

Florence said, "Hang up, Hop. I'm on the way."

Florence was standing next to Wolf when he heard her tell Hop to hang up. Wolf now on high alert asked, "What?"

"It's Annette. Our guy's got her, and it looks like he's getting away."

"Why take Annette?"

"Bargaining chip for the car and the gold would be my guess." Florence said, while dialing her phone.

Wolf made a split decision. He said, "Get in."

"In what?"

"In the Mustang. If he's taking off, we should be able to catch him. Where are they now?"

"Behind that building over there, called the Fudge Shoppe."

Wolf quickly put the engine hood down, picked up the fire extinguisher, opened his door, and strapped the seat belt. Florence quickly got in the car with him. Wolf started the rumbling engine of the Mustang Jackhammer. The crowd yelled and applauded. He laid on the horn and slowly moved through the crowd, and they moved aside, like the parting of the red sea.

The Mustang slowly weaved through the pedestrian crowd. He drove past the Fudge Shoppe and found the alley. Wolf turned into the alley and saw Hop ahead standing in the parking lot with his hands on his hips.

Wolf saw Hop, rolled down his window, and asked, "Where are they?"

"They just left, in that direction." Hop said pointing.

Wolf put the car in gear and stepped on the gas leaving Hop behind. Florence ruefully smiled and said, "It's okay. He'll call in a BOLO with local authorities. Do you think you can catch this guy?"

Wolf grinned and said, "You bet! He knows I'll follow. I'll run after him until he catches me."

Florence looked confused then she said, "So, you think this was his plan all along? I'll call for air cover."

Wolf carefully threaded his way back to Poplar, which is also Highway 72. He took a right and kept the car under the limit as he approached the Interstate 269 interchange. He entered the on-ramp for South then recklessly floored the Roush modified supercharged 5.0 engine to life and sped forward.

Feeling the acceleration and the rush of adrenalin, Florence shouted over the noise, "Where are we going?"

"Toward Hernando. If I know this guy, he's staying in one of the Casino hotels in Tunica. We should be able to catch up with him before he gets there. We'll see what kind of driver he is. Sit back and enjoy the ride." Wolf looked over at Florence with a cocky grin.

It didn't take long for Wolf to spot the silver Charger a mile ahead. He backed down off the accelerator to blend in with traffic.

Florence was on her cellphone and said, "That's right, we're traveling west on Highway 269 toward Mississippi and Tunica. Road block? Not wise. He has a hostage and will shoot her to get away. That's right. Yes, aerial surveillance. Tell the pilot to look for a silver Dodge and a black Mustang about one mile behind. That's right, Wolf thinks the perp has a hotel room in one of the casinos. Right. Thanks, keep me informed."

Florence hung up and looked admiringly at Wolf. She was surprised by his assertiveness, and she thought he was handsome with his black curly hair and looking totally relaxed. He had a half-smile on his face. She could tell he was enjoying the chase. *"Too many car chase movies. But not bad."* she thought.

Wolf's thoughts were, *"I've got you, you S-O-B! You'll pay for the death of that man in Olathe and the man you killed at my house. You better not touch a hair on my cousin's head. You know I'm following you, hoping I'll catch up. I'm not playing your game. You're playing my game now."*

## Chapter: 42  (The Delta Blues Highway)

Eric Clapton recorded 'Going down to the Crossroads' in 1968 with his band Cream. Since then, the junction of Highways 61 and 49 in Mississippi is marked with a sign memorializing the birth of the Mississippi Delta Blues. Wolf and I once made a pilgrimage to Clarksdale where that sign sits in homage to his passion for the musical genre.

My cousin is obsessive about the harmonica and guitar riffs which blend with the emotional blues lyrics of singers that go back to the 1930's. Clapton was one of many devoted fans of the Blues and the Faustian myth of selling one's soul to the Devil for musical genius. I knew where we were headed. My captor had done his homework rummaging through Wolf's vinyl record collection while ransacking his house.

I was pretty sure he was taking me to a plantation not far from Rosedale, MS, close to Clarksdale, where it is said, Robert Johnson, the father of "Delta Bluz" is buried. I looked over at the crazy man in the Hawaiian shirt, driving the car in the seat next to me. He must have studied the mythology surrounding the Blues and linked it to Wolf's passion for it. He was going to make a dramatic gesture by killing both Wolf and me near Robert's grave, then take the car and his gold.

The man driving was quiet. He hadn't said a word since we left Collierville. Now, close up, I could see the short beard was real and the bushy mustache was fake, and I smelled a fragrance I could not identify. In a way, I could see how this older man might attract some women. He was soft spoken, his smile, almost smarmy. Like an actor, he probably used a lexicon of poetic words to swoon the women he stalked.

I noticed he kept checking his rearview mirror. I figured Wolf was following but not too close. I finally asked, "You're going to kill me anyway, why not tell me your name, your real name. I know you're not Perry Sanchez. Who are you?"

He turned his head and there was that smarmy smile again. He looked back at the road. I didn't think he was going to say anything. But he said, "I've got to say, you're a feisty little gal. I bet you don't take any guff off of anybody."

Guff? He actually used that word. I shrugged and said, "That includes you too, murderer."

He snorted and said, "In my experience, most women would be crying and begging. If you hadn't shot my son, I would be thinking about recruiting you. You would be good working the cons with me."

I laughed out loud and said, "Recruit? Who are you, Jim Jones? Recruit for what, exactly. You say most women! I bet you're speaking about all of the several women you've captured and killed? Am I wrong?"

He didn't respond. He looked over in my direction. I thought with fear in his eyes. I had struck a nerve. He didn't like being challenged and found out for his evil deeds. I probed, "Come on, what do you have to lose? You're in control, what's your name? Rumpelstiltskin?"

He shouted, "Shut up!"

I had him now and continued to probe. "I bet you prey on the devoutly religious. Woman who have just buried a husband. Most likely someone wealthy. I think you're a deviant predator and proud of it. I believe you actually hate women. I bet you can't even get it up in the bedroom."

That did it. He used his free right hand to hit me in the face with a decisive slap. My head bounced off the passenger window. I could feel blood flowing from my nose. *"That'll leave a mark."* I thought. Since my hands were still uncomfortably secured behind my back, I shook my head back and forth, spraying my blood on the door and dash. If he killed me, at least my DNA and blood would put him in the electric chair.

He shouted, "What are you doing?"

"You broke my nose. Blood is dripping and I don't want to ruin my top."

The man looked confused, "Your top? You won't be needing that much longer."

"Still, a girl's got to look good, you know." I said.

"I think you're crazy as a cat with turpentine on its tail. Stay quiet or you'll get another smack."

*Smack?* He couldn't use words like hit, smash or even crush. The man was an odd psychopath, which was what he was, an unfeeling killer of women. He definitely had a lot of pent up feelings against the fair sex. "So, I guess you are so delusional, that you have buried your name and past so deep you cannot even remember your childhood name. What did you do? Kill Mommy?"

I was ready for a second blow. He barely grazed me with his hand because my head was just out of his reach. I thought he was going to wreck the car as it swerved. He was weaving from lane to lane nearly out of control. That was when he used his balled up fist to swing back to punch me in the gut.

I thought I was going to throw up. In fact, I would have preferred that to the pain I felt. After the wave of pain and nausea passed, I rolled my head in his direction and gave my abuser a maniacal grin. I was mad and thought, *"You're not going to break me, you asshole."*

He just stopped talking and looked very angry while still checking the rearview mirror. I had definitely gotten under his skin. Not seat belted in, I moved in my seat again and thought about shifting my weight to free my legs and kick him while he drove. At this point, I considered wrecking the car was a viable option.

The zip ties were loose on my hands but cutting into my wrists. I had some room to move, and I thought that if I were on my back, I might be able to pull my arms over my butt and up in front of me. What he didn't know was that my Nano had been returned to me and was strapped to my thigh. If my hands were in front of me, tied or not, I could reach my gun.

## Chapter: 43  (Where *Are* We Headed?)

Wolf could hear the beating rotors of a helicopter tracking him above the highway. He turned to Florence and asked, "Can you tell them to back off? I know where he's headed. I think the helicopter will just spook the guy."

"You said Tunica. They'll stay above us in case he chooses someplace else." Florence said tightly.

"Yes, I'm sure we'll go through Tunica on the way. This guy is looking for a revenge showdown. He wants to punish me for taking the Mustang and he wants to see my face when he claims the gold and kills Annette."

"Yeah, when he sees there's no gold he'll kill everyone in sight."

"He plans to do that anyway." Wolf said shrugging his shoulders.

"You're not even armed. How are you going to face him?"

"My Sig Sauer is in the trunk of the Jackhammer. Everyone will be armed but it may not come to that."

"What makes you say that?"

"Even with your best efforts to surround and subdue him, he will try to slip through your net. He has help, lots of help, probably from family members and he's that good. He's going toward Clarksdale, but he's found someplace else. He'll make his move to dodge your surveillance. I'm sure of that."

"How will he do that?" Florence asked.

"That, Florence, is for both of us to find out."

I remained quiet and watched the familiar countryside slip by the car. The four lane Highway of 269 became Highway 68 when we crossed Interstate 55. The road petered out and became Mississippi Highway 61, a road I had been on a few times before with Wolf.

We drove by signs luring passersby into the world of casino gambling. I do not drink but I have tried my hand at playing Craps, a game my brothers coached me on, and with a little skill, I managed to walk away with more money than I came with. To me, gambling is foolish diversion, not an obsession, with a remote chance to win the big one.

Wolf told me that Tunica has been on a downward slide for several years. Many casino owners gave up and left. Still, a few are busy gleaning dollars from gamblers who come from far and wide to leave their cash behind. The glittering signs along Highway 61 are physical evidence that big gambling still exists in the Magnolia State.

My mind drifted, wondering how the man sitting next to me was going to elude law enforcement who were probably everywhere around us. And I wondered how he was going to slip the car away from Wolf then disappear without anyone following.

We passed the famous sign at the intersection of Highway 61 and 49 as we drove through Clarksdale. The colorful pole with three huge blue guitars supposedly marked the spot where Blues Legend Robert Johnson got on his knees to ask the devil for musical genius. My captor never glanced at the iconic sign.

Instead, we drove on through Clarksdale, south on Highway 61 into the murky history of the Mississippi delta. We passed fields of farmland, roadside shacks, and huge estates within sight of each other.

During the drive, I my mind wandered to the poor plantation slaves who were given their freedom only to return to the plantations because they had no way to feed their families or get by except by sharecropping. They had no job skills, no education, and no helping hands.

If my history was correct, racism during the reconstruction era was rampant and it lasted well into the 20th century. Black families in the delta were dispossessed of all of their worldly goods and forced into menial labor, just to feed their families. Some escaped to cities like Memphis and Jackson only to find work at the bottom of the job barrel. Nothing improved for poor black families through 170 years of strife. The lucky ones got out of the delta and moved to the industrial north.

The man next to me was a user, a con man, who only thought of himself and what he could take from others. He shot that young black man in Wolf's house and thought nothing of it. And now, it looked like he planned to take my life and Wolf's, too.

Highway 61 soon became Highway 278. Our car left Highway 278 and went through the small town of Shelby. From there we drove on a twisted two lane road with a road sign that read 22. Trees now crowded both sides of our road while we moved south toward the Mississippi River. Many of the trees had branches with boughs hanging over the highway sheltering us from the eyes in the sky I had heard earlier.

Through the trees, I could see broken down barns and old farm houses begging for paint. I looked up at the sky out of the passenger window and could no longer see the helicopter tracking our route. That saddened me. My saviors were losing us.

My captor slowed down again and entered another highway with a sign that read 'Mississippi '1'. Encouraged, the man sped up a bit. This paved road was used primarily for farm traffic. Our car passed a tractor pulling a manure spreader driven by a black farmer. He had three kids hanging on for dear life. They waved, I smiled, but I couldn't wave back.

My mind drifted again. Daylight was dimming. I was thinking that it was still springtime, and I wondered if it would rain again tonight. Our car drove through three hamlets, and he didn't slow down. I glanced at the man driving, he kept checking his rear view mirror to make sure Wolf was still following. We passed a sign that said, Davis Plantation. He slowed down. He was about to make his move.

Wolf saw brake lights on the silver car in front of him. He thought, *"It's time."* Wolf watched as the silver Dodge slowed down and turned left up a dirt road ahead of him. Wolf no sooner pulled onto the road when a silver Subaru, pulled out to drive south on Highway 1. Behind that car a black Toyota drove passed and followed the silver one. Wolf turned to Florence and said, "Damn! A diversionary tactic to confuse law enforcement. Keep your eyes open. Anything can happen in a hurry on this dirt road I'm turning on."

Wolf stopped at the dirt road and watching the taillights of the two diversion cars disappear down Highway 1. Florence asked, "What just happened? You aren't going to follow that car up this dirt road without back up are you?"

Wolf turned in his seat and said, "Get out."

"You don't have to get mad. I just asked a question." Florence retorted.

"I'm not mad. I want you to get out and direct law enforcement to follow us up this road. Get on your phone and tell them not to be fooled by the two cars going south."

"This is not fair. You're dumping me alongside a road while you wander into a complete trap? I'm the FBI agent here. You will do as I say."

Wolf smiled and said gently, "Get out. I cannot be responsible for you. I need you to keep in touch with those who are following us. Do you understand? Phone coverage is spotty here. Hurry! They're getting away, ahead of me."

Florence saw the logic of Wolf's decision, but she was reluctant to comply. She checked her cellphone and had no connection. She sighed, opened the car door, and stuck the phone outside and saw bars weakly appear.

She angrily looked at Wolf then stepped outside to get better phone reception. She was miffed at Wolf, a civilian, making decisions for her. She was the FBI and should be in control. She moved toward a mailbox and got a good connection. She quickly called Hop. "Hop. We're at a dirt road near a plantation called Davis outside of Rosedale. Where are you?"

"We lost you when the road became Highway 278."

"We turned off 278 at a town called Shelby. Turn around and take a road called 22 to Mississippi 1 then go south. Wolf asked me to get out of the car so he can face these guys alone. I'm not having that!"

"Well, don't let that happen, then" Hop said. "The Highway Patrol and I are just turning around now, and we are coming your way. Do not engage alone."

Florence disconnected with Hop and turned around. Wolf smiled, waved, then pulled her door shut. He put the car in gear and took off up the dirt road in a cloud of dust toward what dangers Florence could only guess. She angrily stomped her foot in frustration.

## Chapter: 44     (Curious Business)

The dirt road my abductor took had huge ruts and holes making for a very uncomfortable and bumpy ride. We blew passed an abandoned derelict farm house with a front porch barely hanging on its last nail.

We went around a curve and suddenly, in front of us, was a large blue metal building with an opening big enough to drive a MAC truck through. I saw a group of armed men standing just inside on a concrete floor. I thought, *"What the heck is this in the middle of nowhere?"*

I looked to one side, squinted, and saw other buildings that looked like greenhouses stretching beyond my sight on the far side of the blue building. Suddenly, I knew. We were at a clandestine pot farm hidden in the rural Mississippi Delta sticks.

I decided that my captor must know somebody in the illegal weed growing business. Made sense. Crooks and thieves often make strange bedfellows. Only Perry, or whatever his name is, was more than that. He was a psychopathic killer and abuser of women.

The men I saw standing in the large opening were a scruffy collection from all races and armed to the teeth. The AR15 Bushmaster seemed to be their weapon of choice. I did a quick headcount and calculated 10 but there could be more inside the building. I was suddenly stabbed with fear. I was not in fear for my own life, I was afraid for Wolf who was driving into a death trap with the black Mustang.

My driver stopped immediately in front of the building on the far side of the opening. He smiled, opened his door, waved as he got out. Then he opened the back door and reached into the back seat grabbing something. He stepped away from the car with his hands in front of him clutching what he took from the back seat. He walked over to the men. He chatted then handed a package to a man.

The man appeared to be their leader. He was talking and waved his arms around toward the road. Then nodded toward me sitting in the car and said something. My captor nodded and gestured toward our car.

Two of the nastiest looking goons walked over and jerked my passenger door open. They yanked on my right shoulder in an attempt to dislodge me from my car seat. They pulled me out hitting my head on the doorframe. I said "Ouch!" Then they literally dragged me to the big blue building.

I heard my captor say, "Stash her inside someplace. She's not going anywhere. She's the bait I mentioned for the car I want. It should be coming up this road any minute." He grinned and the men took up a position with their Bushmasters at the ready. They stood around shifting weight from one foot to the other in the doorway, smoking weed or cigarettes. I couldn't tell which. They looked like a bunch of skinny escapees from a rehab farm with two big fat ones in the middle. If they started firing those weapons, I wondered who they would hit first, their intended target or each other.

When the two men drug me into the large building they pushed me to the floor saying, "Sit and be quiet."

Once I was on the floor, I surveyed my options. I was sitting next to a row of large tables. My guess was this place is where they packaged the buds of cannabis plants to be illegally distributed as legitimate medical marijuana.

As the two men walked away, one of them looked over his shoulder and said in his Mississippi slang, "Y'all move there, pony tail girl, and I'll shoot you myself." They turned around and walked to the open door. They stood and waited with my captor, laughing at some joke. It was probably a joke about me. I didn't care.

All of the men were nervously animated, busy talking and joking with one another. I could now smell the distinctive aroma of weed being passed around.

Now, it was my turn. I am not double jointed but there was just enough slack with the zip ties holding my wrists together for me to get my rear end up enough to slip my bound arms under my butt and over my feet. It was difficult and I may have pulled a muscle, but my arms were now in front of me and I had access to my Nano.

I was thrilled that I chose to wear my skort shorts and loose top this morning. The skort concealed my thigh holster with my Nano. I could now reach it, but I could handle the gun much better if both of my hands were free. I looked around for something to cut the ties. And saw nothing from my sitting point of view.

I kept my eyes on the road outside of the building door, beyond the men. I saw nothing yet. I wondered what was taking Wolf so long. Every so often one of the men would look back my way to make sure I was behaving. No one noticed my arms were now in front of me. Still, I needed to risk standing up to find a sharp instrument to free my hands.

Putting my arms out in front of me I squatted and stood up. I carefully backed further into the room keeping my eyes on the door with the men. I scanned the tables and boxes around me searching for something, anything, to cut my zip ties.

Then, I saw on the other side of the big table a box cutter knife. Darn, I was on the wrong side of the table to reach the knife. I let out a breath then scrunched down to get onto my hands and knees. I began crawling under the table on the filthy, dusty floor. Putting my clasped hands in front of me, I pushed forward and drug my knees to advance forward.

When I got to the other side of the table, I was shocked to suddenly see two jean covered legs standing beside the table, right in front of me. I was confused. A man was standing, right there, next to the table. He didn't shout out to anyone that I was not where I was supposed to be. So, using both hands, I reached under my skort and struggled to undo my holster strap. Carefully, I withdrew the Nano. I was now prepared to shoot the man in front of me.

## Chapter: 45    (Florence, An Army Of One)


Wolf checked his rearview mirror and saw Florence throwing up her arms in anger as he left her behind. He slowed down dodging sizeable holes and truck ruts in the dusty road. Ahead he saw an abandoned farmhouse. And he made his decision.

Wolf stopped in front of the old house and backed the Mustang next to the dilapidated structure away from the direction he had been driving. He backed into tall grass and weeds. The car was parked far enough off the dirt road to be hidden by the building.

Wolf sat in the car and took a moment to collect his thoughts. He said quietly to himself, "Hopefully, help will arrive soon with the FBI and local law enforcement." At first, he thought this Perry guy was leading him to the grave of Blues legend, Robert Johnson, for some kind of ritualistic killing. But this place was not close to where Johnson was believed to be buried. Wolf decided to follow the dirt road ahead to see where it led.

After he parked, Wolf stepped out of the mustang into knee high overgrowth. He immediately kept a sharp eye out for snakes and knew that coral snakes, rattlesnakes, copperhead, and cottonmouth were found everywhere in the delta countryside. He walked behind the Mustang and opened the trunk to retrieve his Sig Sauer. He checked the chamber, pulled the slide then grabbed an extra magazine, leaving the trunk lid open in case he needed something else in a hurry.

With his gun in both hands, Wolf stepped onto the rutted dirt track and cautiously walked up the road. He was spooked, thinking he saw this

Perry Sanchez guy around every tree and bush he encountered. He was prepared to shoot at anything that didn't look right. His only concern was shooting Annette while trying to save her.

Through the tree branches, he saw a patch of bright blue. At first, he didn't know what he was looking at in the distance. He stopped walking and stood behind a tree just staring. He focused on the patch of blue. Then he understood. It was a blue metal building maybe fifty yards away.

Wolf couldn't see much from this vantage point, so he moved closer. He carefully studied the terrain on both side of the road. What he saw was farm fields that had long since gone fallow to weeds and thick woodland.

He moved off the road into a copse of walnut trees and found an old rail fence. He knelt behind the fence and was now close enough to clearly see the blue building. Men stood in the opening of the building. The door was big enough for trucks or farm equipment to be stored inside the structure.

Wolf studied the area around the building and saw greenhouses on the opposite side. He didn't see Annette, so he figured she was inside the building. He needed to get closer to try and lay his eyes on her. He backed off and began trudging through rough ground and overgrowth to get closer to the metal building.

Meanwhile, near the mailbox at the highway, Florence was steamed and frustrated. Hop was nowhere close, and Wolf had left her behind. She needed to do something decisive. Fortunately, when she exited Wolf's Mustang she grabbed her purse because it held her cellphone. She was armed with her gun safely secured on her waist in a holster. She made a decision and marked the mailbox next to the dirt road by tying several tissues together into a string and stuck one end into the mailbox. She hoped it would be recognized by Hop when he arrived.

She looked down at her feet and wished she had worn athletic shoes instead of her FBI street shoes. Resolved, she began walking up the dirt road, athletically hopping over holes and muddy tire ruts along the way.

After a short walk, she saw the black Mustang parked away from the dirt road next to a wooden shack. She mumbled, "So, he left the car here and went up the road on foot. I'm guessing he's trying to catch the guy off guard, the silly fool."

Meanwhile, Wolf decided to approach the blue building from the side opposite the greenhouses. He was watching the building in front of him. He needed to get closer. He was ready to move forward, and his heart stopped when he heard a distinctive sound. His foot stopped in mid-air. What he heard was the unmistakable sound of a rattlesnake tail. His eyes got big, and he quickly looked around. Then he saw the coiled camouflaged reptile, just five feet in front of him. He slowly moved his elevated foot and stepped backward, away from the snake, hoping it would not strike. He breathed easier and thought, *"That was close. Change of plan."*

Watching the ground closer, Wolf stepped over dead tree branches and trash until he reached the back corner of the metal building. There he saw an abandoned orange tractor and a yellow skid-steer loader.

Moving next to the back side of the building, he did his best to remain as quiet as he could. He found a white door and tried the doorknob. It turned effortlessly and he eased the door quietly open.

Carefully moving inside he slowly walked past several cardboard boxes and cultivating equipment that that he figured were used for the pot farm outside. He moved toward the front of the building. In the distance, he saw several men silhouetted by light on the building. They stood impatiently talking in the doorway. He heard one of them say, "Where in the hell is this guy?" You said he was coming, right?"

"Look, you got paid. He was right behind me. Maybe he followed one of the decoy cars by mistake. Don't worry, he'll realize his mistake and will come up this road looking for the girl."

Wolf suddenly felt something pressing against his rear-end. He looked over his shoulder and saw two arms tethered together with zip ties and holding a Nano. He smiled.

## Chapter: 46    (Shots Fired)

Wolf immediately squatted out of sight of the men in the doorway and whispered, "Don't shoot, it's me."

"Oh!" Annette exhaled and she said, "I thought you were one of them. Hurry, cut me loose."

Wolf put the gun down then placed a hand in his pocket and found a knife. He opened it and quickly cut the plastic bonds holding my arms. I sighed in relief. We were now both armed facing an army of armed pot farmers with AR15's and a crazy man from Florida.

It was getting dark outside when we heard one of the men say, "So what's up dude? You said some guy was following you and you want to take him out. So, where is he? We can't wait here all day."

"Look, I paid you well to let me use this place and to back me up in case he was armed. You got your money and the girl too. Just be a little more patient. Smoke another joint, he won't leave her here for me to kill her, believe me."

One of the men turned around and said, "Yeah, the pony tail girl. Hey! Where'd she go?"

Perry turned, looked, and said, "Did you just leave her there?"

"Yes, but her hands were tied. She can't get too far. She's got to be in the building someplace."

Another man said, "Hey! Who's that woman walking up the road?"

Wolf and I were now both armed and hiding under the tables. Perry and the men had the advantage of numbers. Wolf and I had the advantage of stealth and surprise, hiding under a table, behind boxes, with at least 16 rounds of ammo, counting my six and Wolf's 10 to take down a few of them. I didn't know at the time he had an extra magazine.

We heard one of them shout, "Who's that coming up the road?"

Wolf sighed and whispered, "Damn! She followed me."

"She who? Florence?"

"Florence."

Florence suddenly found herself standing on the road in front of a large metal building with a flood lights illuminating the entire area. She saw several rough looking armed men. They stood in the doorway looking confused. Seeing the armed men she immediately raised her gun and shouted, "FBI! Drop your weapons!"

She heard them laugh and gunfire began rattling away. Fortunately, the stoned pot farmers were bad shots. Florence immediately ducked and rolled away from the gunfire to the side of the road behind a log. She took up a prone position and began firing.

Wolf and I heard her shout "FBI." So, we immediately stood up and aimed at the men in the doorway. I said, "I'll take left you take right."

Wolf said, "Done."

Trapped between gunfire in front and behind them, the AR 15 armed men jumped in every direction, like fleas off of a wet dog. Those that sought shelter inside the building were immediately cut down by Wolf and me. A couple of those who went outside ran to get behind Florence and she shot one of them.

The man named Perry, simply ran for his car, got inside, ducked his head, and started the engine. He made a donut U-turn and drove rapidly past Florence leaving the area in a cloud of dust down the inky dark road.

He was driving so fast, bouncing up and down on the uneven road, that he blew past the old farm house and the Mustang parked on the far side. He groaned when he saw the Mustang in his rear view mirror illuminated by his tail lights and he said, "Shit!" But he kept driving. He hit paved road, turned left, and heard sirens blaring on Highway 1 behind him. He didn't look back while flooring the Charger and just kept going toward Greenville and the bridge to Arkansas.

The gun battle at the pot farm didn't last long. Out of ten semi-stoned men, six of them were on the ground bleeding and four simply gave up, with hands in the air. Florence stood up and knocked the dust off her dark pants suit.

Wolf and I stepped out of the blue building into the light and dusty area in front of the building. With our guns in front of us, we saw four men standing with their hands in the air. I said, "Nice shooting, Special Agent."

I actually saw her smile. She said, "Mr. LeDuc. You have disobeyed a direct order from a law enforcement officer. Once we settle all of this, you may consider yourself under arrest."

I grinned at her and said, "Technically, I am FBI, and he assisted me with the take down of these pot farmers who were paid to help our murderer, who just got away. Better call an ambulance, Special Agent."

**Chapter: 47    (After Math)**

It was dark when emergency vehicles and ambulances rolled off of the pot farm, Hop and the Mississippi State Highway Patrol sat in their cars attempting to reconstruct the chain of events that occurred earlier. They kept counting the sheer number of people who were severely wounded by gunfire, although no deaths were reported, yet. The Highway Patrol photographed the crime scene and logged incidence reports. It was suggested everyone reconvene in Greenville at the Highway Patrol field office where there was more light and more comfortable accommodations with fewer flying, biting insects.

Using a flashlight, Wolf and I walked down the dirt road away from the blue building. We arrived at the old derelict farm house that was in ruin. "It would take some doing to put this place back in order." I said.

Wolf walked past the house and around to the black Mustang and grinned. "I'm not even sure the lumber could be salvaged for anything." He said looking at the house while using a hand to push down the trunk lid which he had left open earlier.

"That house was good enough to hide your Mustang long enough to come and rescue me." I said grinning.

"True enough. Let's go see what these Highway Patrolmen need in Greenville. Honestly, I'm kind of worn out and could use a good meal and a bath."

"Now, you're talking." I said.

Wolf, Hop, Florence, and I sat in a conference room at the Greenville, MS Highway Patrol office. The Highway Patrol Captain said, "The Mississippi Attorney General's office called here seeking answers about a report of gunfire and several wounded people in the Delta country. We referred him to the Deputy Director of the FBI. The AG's office called us back and repeated the complaint asking us why the Justice Department was declaring war on Mississippi."

"And what did the Deputy Director tell the Attorney General?" I asked the Captain. I knew he was just a go-between for his boss at the Attorney General's office. The question was not from him.

The Captain nervously fiddled with a pen and said, "From what I gathered, your Deputy Director told him that the jurisdiction of the Justice Department extends across state lines, especially in cases of kidnapping. He further explained that armed men at an illegal pot farm, began firing automatic weapons at a Federal agent who identified herself. She was investigating and searching for the kidnapped victim she believed was on the property."

Hop flashed a covert smile and said, "Our Special Agent and a contract employee of the FBI simply returned fire until the criminals were subdued and surrendered. Several heavily armed gunmen were wounded during the exchange, and they will face Federal charges for firing on a Federal Agent."

Hop was about to say something, and I quickly said, "Right. And how on earth was the Attorney General able to draw such a rapid conclusion about a supposed war with short notice? Who notified him?"

The Captain looked away and said, "Well, I don't know. Our troopers were in pursuit of you and your abductor. And we notified our superiors about the chase. And while we're at it. What gave Mr. LeDuc and Miss Sallaz the authority to go chasing after an alleged abductor? You left lots of wounded men in those woods. And what happened to the guy who kidnapped the victim? Where did he go?"

Hop's eyes narrowed and he said, "Special Agent Florence Sallaz commandeered and deputized Mr LeDuc and his vehicle to follow Miss Dupart's abductor in hot pursuit. In case you didn't know, the Director is correct. Kidnapping across state lines is a Federal offence enforceable by the FBI. She had every right to go after the kidnapper of a Federal contract employee."

The Captain looked stunned and asked, "Who is this contract employee again?"

I smiled and raised my hand.

The Captain asked, "I'm confused. You were the kidnappee *and* you were the contract employee? You were captured and tied up! How did you get free and where did you get your gun? From what I understand, you were actively involved with the shooting those men. I'm not accusing you of anything, you understand. I just have to report this to my boss in Jackson."

It was Florence's turn, and she spoke up saying, "I arrived on foot and was confronted by several heavily armed men who were waiting in that blue metal barn to shoot and kill Mr. LeDuc. They saw me, I announced that I was FBI and told them to lay down their arms. Instead, they began firing their weapons at me."

"Did you have a warrant to enter that property?"

Hop said, "Hot pursuit! We have a right to follow a kidnapped victim onto any property. Wolf found Annette, freed her from her bonds and it turns out she had a concealed handgun that she used during the shooting."

"Those men were caught in a bloody crossfire. It must have been like a shooting gallery. They didn't have a chance," the Captain said in defense.

I couldn't hold back any longer. "Excuse me! I'm the victim here. There were 10 of them bad boys. Most of them armed with AR15 Bushmaster automatic weapons. They had the advantage in manpower and firepower."

"If they had the advantage, how come so many were shot and wounded, and you and your friends were unharmed?"

I gave him a withering look and said, "You mean a bunch of stoned pot farmers with guns they didn't know how to use? I've got to ask, who in your State Government has a vested interest in this pot farm operation? That's who you should be looking for."

Hop and Wolf both said at the same time, "Annette! That's enough." Florence was trying to hide a laugh.

Hop said, "I think we're done here. We'll let your Attorney General deal with the Department of Justice on his own."

"Just one more question. Where's that man who kidnapped Miss Dupart?"

Florence said, "When the shooting began he ran to his car and fled in a hurry. It took you another 15 minutes to arrive because you missed your turn. I'm guessing he and his helpers slipped through your impermeable net in Greenville. They probably crossed the river there and they're roaming the hills of southern Arkansas as we speak."

The Captain had been recording our interview to cover his butt and would share it with his superiors and, eventually, the Attorney General. The question still lingering in my mind was, how did the Attorney General find out so fast and who in the Mississippi government told him? I was betting on a State Senator or some politician who probably had a financial interest in the pot farm and a portion of the profits.

Wolf and I had a long and lonely drive in the dark back to Germantown. Florence and Hop rode quietly in the Mustang's cozy back seat with Hop snoring and Florence reading her cellphone. We made it to Collierville and dropped Hop and Florence off, promising to have breakfast with them in the morning.

We didn't mention to the Highway Patrol that the FBI officially confiscated the thick package of cash that was handed to the pot farmers before the shootout. Hop decided this was critical evidence in his FBI investigation, which could be used for the conviction of the pot farmers to prove they were paid to shoot at law enforcement. The FBI lab would dust for fingerprints to match one of the pot farmers.

On the ride back to Collierville, Hop called the Jackson, MS office to have US Marshalls take custody of all of the healthy and injured pot farmers to face charges in Federal court.

## Chapter: 48    (Eggs And Rehash)

The next day, breakfast was delivered from the Toasted Yoke Café in Cordova so we could eat while we met in the LeDuc and Johnson office conference room.

Digging into his breakfast, Hop said, "These pancakes are good and still warm."

Everyone seemed to enjoy the hearty breakfast with tasty fresh coffee. Ezra and Connie joined Hop, Florence, Chick, Wolf, and me for our breakfast meeting.

Wolf began by holding his fingers up and counting, "In summary, One, we have one dead car sales person in Olathe, Kansas. Two, Annette was confronted by this Perry whatshisname at the Memphis airport. Three, Annette's Chevy Traverse is firebombed in the airport parking lot. Four, Perry's son foolishly tried to steal Annette's Camaro, he drew a gun and Annette shot him. Five, my house was broken into and trashed. Six, during the break in Perry murdered one of his men in my kitchen. Seven, Annette is abducted at the Collierville car cruise. Eight, which resulted in six stoned pot growers getting shot with two in critical condition at a Jackson, MS hospital and four under arrest."

"In other words, this Perry Sanchez is a one person wrecking ball." Connie said.

Still exhibiting the shiner Perry gave me in the car, I shuddered and said, "Kind of hard to imagine him using subtle language to charm unsuspecting women into giving him access to all of their financial affairs. This guy is extremely dangerous, and he has a very bad temper."

"Remember, there are three women we know of who probably died at the hands of this man. There are probably many more we don't know about. He left enough of them alive to provide information to law enforcement in several states. The FBI has drawn up a profile for this man, but we still don't know where he originally came from, what his real name is, or how many people he's bilked or murdered." Florence said.

"The Director has ordered this man to be put on the FBI's most wanted list. The latest photo we have was from a picture Annette supplied. Annette said he had a real beard and fake mustache during her abduction." Hop said.

"We have an all-points bulletin being distributed to law enforcement agencies nationwide with this man's picture. He's on the run but he still believes we have something he wants. So, I suspect we've not seen the last of Mr. Sanchez." Florence said.

Wolf looked at his friends and the FBI around the conference table. "So, I'm looking for ideas on what our next course of action should be. Our guy's got five million reasons for not giving up."

Hop shuffled through some papers then said, "The FBI's mantra has always been 'Follow the money.' Figuring out who this guy is, and where he's stashing cash, is the FBI's top priority. If we know where, we can take preemptive action to freeze his assets. I called Washington this morning and spoke to Deputy Director, Doug Simmons and he said tracing money transfers from Perry's victims is a top priority for our Cybercrimes department. They are working on those transfers as we speak."

Florence was curious. She asked, "What have they found out, so far?

"So far, funds have been washed through two off shore accounts and we think we've finally found the mother account. It seems there are several banks in and out of the US who have received funds in cash up to the $30,000 limit. That is the limit before banks report cash transfers to the Financial Crimes Enforcement Network or (FinCEN). Breaking up deposits into smaller units is called structuring. These transfers appear to be just that. They are washing the money through banks before it's sent on to the Caribbean." Hop concluded.

"Our Mr. Perry seems to be drawing on those accounts and transferring money between banks to stay liquid." Florence added.

"What can be done?" I asked.

"Our next move is to get a court order to put a hold on the accounts we know of. This will essentially freeze the money from being transferred or used. Once it's out of the country and at the final location, we cannot touch it. We think there's enough cash in these accounts to fund his ongoing operations here in the US for some time to come. Freezing them could put him out of business." Hop said with some satisfaction.

"That'll bring him out of the woods." Ezra said while sipping his coffee.

"Let's say he acquired the gold. What could he possibly do with it? Certainly, the government would be notified of any gold transactions, like sales and shipment through required reporting procedures." I asked.

"Yeah, he's not doing that. I'm thinking he was planning to smuggle the gold out of the country, then deposit it in a foreign bank. If he sold it in the US, he would reveal himself and have to pay capital gains on the difference between the purchase price and the sale price. Once again, a paper trail. This guy doesn't pay tax so, he won't do that." Hop said.

"How then would he get the gold out?" Connie asked.

"Not sure. He lived in Florida, perhaps by boat." Hop said.

"How soon will his accounts be frozen?" Wolf asked.

"Not sure about that, but it shouldn't take too long." Hop said.

"Has the FBI been successful with interviewing the shooting victim in Baptist Hospital?" I asked.

"The son? Doctors have restricted access to him while he's in intensive care. We have a court order to find out who is financially responsible for the hospital and doctor bills. The hospital hasn't responded yet." Florence said.

"What about the young man you captured after Perry's son was shot?" Wolf asked.

"Germantown Police confirmed that young man was local, like the man who was murdered in your house. Both had rap sheets for misdemeanors. A casino security employee in Tunica recruited the men and they were hired by a blond man in his late 20's, who we think is the man Annette shot and the son of Perry. We think the son is from Daytona. Fingerprints turned up a rap sheet for domestic violence and car theft in Charlotte but under a different name. We still don't know who he really is." Hop said.

Florence spoke up, "We asked the local man for hire what Perry looked like. The young man just laughed. He said, 'Man, that guy kept changing his look, you know. One day he had red hair and the next jet black. He always looked different, but I could always tell it was him'." She said mimicking the young man.

Florence said, "I asked him how he could be so sure, and he said, 'The mole on his left cheek next to his ear. It was always there.' So, we are now scanning the FBI database for visible features, like tattoos and moles. I think this is a significant break." Florence said.

"You know, with the money he's scammed over the years he could have had that mole removed. I'm thinking he keeps it on purely for vanity. He believes he's smarter than everyone else and he'll never be discovered." Ezra said.

"Well, we know one thing. He left Mississippi in a silver Charger, and he hired two more people or had family drive stolen cars as decoys. The Arkansas State police reported finding a black Toyota and a silver Subaru abandoned in Little Rock. They said the cars were reported stolen in Memphis. The Charger hasn't turned up yet. He's probably changed plates anyway." Hop reported.

"He wants that Mustang bad, so he's probably circling Wolf's house like a raptor seeking carrion as we speak." I said.

"The bottom line is, we don't know who Perry really is. We think he's probably back in Tennessee or even Tunica at one of the casinos. But we don't have a name to search for him at a hotel. The Memphis Police have an officer guarding Perry's son at the hospital Intensive Care unit. So, if Perry turns up there to see him, we'll know." Florence said.

"My house along with the car, is under constant video and personal observation at all times. My tormentor's only way to gain access to the car is when I take it out of the garage and go someplace. Chick and the FBI will have eyes on the car at all times. What is his next move?" Wolf asked. No one had an answer.

Wolf nodded and said, "This guy has a grudge against me and Annette. I'm afraid that he may come after her any time. Because of this, I am suspending her road trips to our dealers until this matter is behind us." He turned and looked at me. "You and your car will be watched, like my house at all times."

Chick said, "Yes, we're watching you at all times, but be very vigilant about where you go and what you do. This guy is slippery as a bag of wet ice, and he thinks he's more clever than the rest of us. I think he's planning some kind of diversion to take our attention off the car so he can snatch it."

"What? Not another diversion? I'm going to say this now, thank you to everyone here, for helping the FBI to take this crazy man down. I'm just a contract employee but I have faith in the bureau and the Deputy Director, Doug Simmons, that this guy will get caught." I said.

Everyone around the breakfast table agreed. Hop grabbed the last Danish.

## Chapter: 49    (Dirk and Albert)

Albert Jensen, was checked into the Baptist Memorial hospital as Cal Marsh. He laid in his hospital bed dealing with severe head pain. He had a patch over his right eye that he kept touching. He shouted out, "Can't you do anything about my pain? My head hurts like it's in a vice." No one was in the room to hear his complaint.

He was on a drip of pain medication. This kept him in and out of consciousness and his brain was a little fuzzy. He found it difficult to form a complete thought. The doctors in Memphis, told him they could not safely remove the bullet that was still lodged in the parietal lobe of his brain. That was why he had difficulty putting numbers together, like his father's cellphone.

He had difficulty measuring distances using his one good eye. And he could barely manage lifting a plastic container with water and a straw to hit his mouth. It was frustrating because he was able to think and reason things but didn't know how to put that thinking into action. Talking in sentences was difficult.

Albert kept wondering if he would die here in this hospital bed, in Memphis, with a fake name, and he was scared.

Now, five days after he was admitted, a young man in blue scrubs and a surgical skull cap showed up with a clip board in his hand at his intensive care hospital door. He stood in front of the officer on guard for a moment and said, "Cal Marsh?"

The officer looked at the young man's ID badge and asked, "Who are you and what do you want with him?"

"I am the speech and motor response specialist. I'm here to measure the patient's ability to speak and form words. I was told by the floor physician that it was okay to go in and ask my questions."

The officer stood up to open the door and the young blond man wearing a surgical mask asked, "Do you need to come in with me? I have several questions."

Knowing this would be of no interest, the officer said, "Uh, no you go ahead." He smiled and thought, *"Good time to take that bathroom break and get a candy bar."*

Once inside, the young man pulled down his surgical mask. He leaned over Cal, who was awake, and said in a low voice, "Hello, brother. You don't look so good."

"Oh, Dirk. I sorry."

"Sorry for what Albert?"

"Messed up, got shot."

"Hang in there. We'll get you out of here when you're better. Are you in a lot of pain?"

"Oh, yes. Head hurt. Slug in brain. No help."

Dirk bit his lip and looked over his shoulder, checking the door. He said, "I understand. Hang in there for a little bit longer, little brother."

"Okay," Albert said weakly.

"Charles is working on a plan to get the gold. He's just sick about you getting shot by that woman. I'm staying not too far away, just down the road. Don't know how often I can get in to talk, but we need to get you out of here and taken to a place where they can fix you up."

Albert began crying and said, "Love you, Dirk. You all I got."

Dirk asked, "Tell me, why did you go after that woman's car?"

"I don't know, it was there, and the Mustang wasn't. I guess, I just wanted to take it. Gone in 60 seconds!" Albert tried to laugh.

Dirk Jensen exhaled, nodded, and still did not understand Albert's reason for attempted car theft. He then reached into his pants and showed Albert a pocket knife and said, "This is in the drawer next to your bed. Don't use it unless you have to. I'll be back."

Dirk turned from the bed and walked out of the hospital room. The police officer was no where to be seen. *"Good to know."* Dirk thought.

**Chapter: 50    (Bonanza Boom)**

The Bonanza Boom casino opened their doors late last year replacing its predecessor who cut their losses and shifted their resources to other gambling properties around the US. In order to boost profits and make a name for itself, the new casino owners recruited known gambling whales from some of their other properties. They used incentives like free room and board, airfare, and a limo to and from the Memphis airport. And the big incentive was they offered a 'no betting limit' on some tables.

One such known whale was Charles Jensen who was a gambler from the Caribbean. When he called to make arrangements to check into the Casino hotel, he said he had business in the States and was willing to visit Tunica for their grand opening to help out his casino buddies. They willingly complied.

The Caribbean casino corporation considered Charles Jensen as a shadowy character who claimed residence in Aruba with Dutch citizenship. He was a popular gambler in a number of Caribbean casinos. He spoke several languages and was often seen in the company of different women, most of whom were on the far side of fifty. He owned a modest home on the island of Aruba, and he always paid his gambling debts. He gave generously to the Aruba law enforcement widows' fund and was frequently invited to island social functions which he never attended. He always begged off explaining he had other interests elsewhere. Which, in reality, he did.

The gambling consortium who owned Bonanza Boom in Tunica was based in Aruba and Brenda, Charles wife, was a member of their board.

On his official Aruba residency paperwork, he listed his employment as Import/Export dealer, and no one questioned the authenticity of this claim.

In reality, Karel Jensen was his real name. He was from South Africa, not Holland. He anglicized the first name to make it easier for people to remember. However, he had many names on passports, credit cards, and drivers licenses. He had supporting documentation for all of them. He could be anyone, anywhere at any time. Under one of these names, he held Venezuelan citizenship. He always figured if he had to run from the law, he would take the short flight to Caracas, using his Hispanic name. All of his and his family's documents were stowed safely away in Aruba bank lock boxes for use when they traveled.

Whenever he brought his women marks to the island, he always said he rented the house from his landlord, Charles Jensen. He never took any of the women to the casinos while in Aruba. He didn't need someone recognizing him during a scam.

Charles, Brenda, and the rest of his extended crime family enjoyed this sanctuary far away from any law enforcement who might be in pursuit of them. The Jensens also owned a couple of beach side properties.

Brenda lived a life of luxury in South Beach Miami and was the key to his success. She chose likely marks and helped to set up the con. She had other family members to rely on. Her sister-in-law Carla, who had been married to her brother before his death, was a superb artist. She was also the mother of Morty and Ferdy.

Carla's brother, Manfred Mickleson, practices law as a Defense Attorney in New York. Using various names, he too, frequently played various characters in the family swindles. He used his legal acumen to help pry funds out of family estates that Charles and Brenda victimized.

When a family member was arrested for some breech of the law, he or a member of his law firm was always there to pluck the family member from the jaws of the Justice system.

Altogether, the Jensen crime family worked in lockstep under Brenda's supervision to amass a vast fortune. They never considered themselves common thieves, even though they frequently relied on the services of such people. They did what they did for the love of setting up the con and making the sting come to a profitable end, then move on to the next victim.

Carl Jensen sat in his hotel suite, waiting for family members to show up, with a pencil and pad working on details to recover over 100 pounds of gold that he and Brenda had stored in an expensive car. The gold was important, but revenge now occupied much of his plans. That woman, Annette, would pay dearly for getting in his way.

## Chapter: 51    (Plotting A New Plan)

Karel Jensen, aka Charles Jensen, Perry Sanchez, and user of several other names, sat in his Tunica casino hotel room brooding about the recent turn of events. Things had not gone as planned. To make matters worse, one of his sons was suffering with a brain injury in a Memphis hospital room. The other one, Dirk, narrowly missed getting picked up by the Mississippi Highway Patrol while leaving the Mississippi pot farm. He was pulled over and used his cover story of being a traveling salesman selling door knobs to hardware stores. The lie worked and he was quickly across the Greenville bridge into Arkansas. He met up with Morty, and they dumped the cars with the keys in them, just the way they were found in Memphis.

Charles put his note pad down and was melancholy, immersed in daydreams, thinking, *"Do not get emotionally involved with a mark. I stupidly loved that black car when I got it from that widow. That was why I chose it to store Brenda's gold in it. Destroying the car would be easy enough to get the gold, but, like my son, I want that car. There must be a better way to capture that vehicle."* He was startled out of his thoughts when someone knocked on the door. His heart began racing and he shouted out, "Who is it?"

"Dirk. Let me in."

Charles caught his breath, sighed, and said, "Coming."

"Thank God! I was afraid they caught up with you." Dirk said.

---

"It was a narrow escape. Some woman showed up and said she was FBI. Gunfire broke out and I thought it was World War III. I was in such a hurry to leave, I drove right past the black Mustang. I didn't stop because the FBI had the place surrounded. I'm glad to see that you and Morty made it out safely."

"Yeah, Morty and I are safe and checked into our room here. I think we're good, at least for now. I didn't have a chance to tell you. I went to see Albert in the hospital."

"You did? How did you get in?" Charles asked.

"I wore scrubs and a surgical mask and impersonated a speech therapist. No one seemed to care."

"How is he?"

"Not good! At least when I saw him. The bullet is lodged in his brain. He can barely talk and he's in a lot of pain. I think he understood what I was saying. He shed a tear when I left, something I've never seen him do. I told him I would punish that woman who shot him. You know, he actually said 'It's just the cost of doing business'. Security at his room door is weak. We should be able to get him out, if and when we want to."

"If and when?" Charles asked.

"At this stage, he's a risk to the whole operation. If we got him out, we would have to take him someplace where people could take care of him. I'm not sure how or where we would provide for him."

Charles sat in the comfortable chair concentrating on what Dirk was telling him. He finally said, "You're right of course. So, are you saying we just leave him and move on?"

"He knows too much, Charles. You know that. He's now a liability. Cut your losses. Isn't that what you have always preached?"

"How should we do it?" Charles asked.

"Security at the hospital is weak. It shouldn't take too much to get into the room and add a chemical of some sort into his IV tube."

Charles thought hard for a moment then said, "If we can recover that gold quickly, you know we can get into the hospital and take him with us to the island. We'll find someone there to take care of him. He's your little brother, Dirk."

Dirk looked at the ceiling exhaled then said, "Okay, so, we get the gold. Are you just thinking about quitting the con and living out your years in retirement then?"

"I would be lying if I didn't say it's crossed my mind. I just don't seem to have the edge I used to have. How could we have let that car slip through our fingers, not once but several times? Something is just not right. We've got this Tennessee rube who overpays for a car and has some female relative who works for him that totes a gun. Who does that?"

"You're right! You are getting old and soft. You never used to be this way. I'm still young and far from thinking about retirement. You have been a good teacher, Charles. I think it's time I took over the family business."

Charles nodded slowly with a thin lipped smile and said, "Yes, son, I think you're nearly ready. You're a little too pushy with the ladies. You need to slow down and play them like a hooked marlin in the ocean. Let them come to you and beg you into their lives. If you press too hard, they'll just shut you out."

"I know. I grew up watching you do your best with the many women you swindled."

Charles grinned and said, "You know it! And I sent all three of you to expensive schools in Florida. When you were old enough, Brenda and I used you boys in the game, too. It always worked perfectly. You were always such innocent looking children." Charles chuckled at the memory.

Dirk grinned and said, "Yeah, we were good cover for your story as a struggling widower trying to make ends meet. Now it's time to turn over the keys to the golden hearse, Charles."

"Okay, help me here. Where do you want to start working the market?"

"I know Miami well and there are a lot of divorced and widowed women living there."

"Remember, the best ones are older, but you're attracted to the young sexy ones. Infidelity will kill you in this game as sure as rain. The young ones do not have the assets you desire. I think you need to give it a few more years of maturity then ease into the market."

"Yeah, well I think I'm ready. Old you say? I can handle the old ones."

"Yes, but can you hump a prune without gagging? What about a fat prune? What about when a wig falls off at the wrong time? I'm not sure you have the stomach for it."

Dirk threw up both hands and said, "That's to be seen. Right now, I'm here to help you get that black Mustang and the gold back. And I have an idea that might work. You still have that spare key fob for the car?"

"Yes, of course."

"Then, I think we may still have a good chance."

Charles smiled at his eager son and said, "You see? We've always worked best when we worked together."

Dirk smiled and said, "Sure."

## Chapter: 52    (Girls Just Like To Shop)

I have not been real comfortable without my Beretta 1911. The Nano works and did a fine job down at that Mississippi pot farm. Then, I was shooting at close range, and it was like shooting fish off a log. Further down range, I might not have been so accurate. If I had shot that blond man trying to steal my Camaro with the 1911, I would have blown a hole completely through his skull and he would not have survived. As it was, the Nano did its job to defend me but not enough to kill the man. So, today I planned to visit my favorite gun store at the firing range to find a replacement.

My last Beretta was a used firearm I got for a good price at a gun shop in Louisiana. Beretta now offers a similar firearm called a 92M9. Not as easy to say as a 1911. I asked to take one onto the range and try it out. The first thing I noticed, it was lighter and targeting with the sights was much better. The salesman wanted me to attach a targeting laser light, or at the very least an adjustable front and rear sight set. He even made me an offer to trade in my trusty Nano for a new Tomcat. The offer was tempting but I was accustomed to the Nano and it's quirky ways.

I was leaning toward the 92M9 which was less expensive than other models. I have a Glock at my home that I've used it on several occasions. But the Glock is mostly plastic, and I prefer the firm feel and heft of a metal firearm.

I bought the 92M9 and busted my credit limit on my credit card. The gun should fit nicely in the holster I used with the 1911. I shot two boxes of ammo before I left, satisfied with my purchase. I felt confident that I could face any challenge with the larger gun at my disposal at any distance.

I had spent most of the day at the gun range purchasing my handgun. Handling of firearms is a comfortable hobby for me and has been since I attended college in Lafayette. While there, I began competing in pistol and trap shooting and I'm good at both. While competing, I was offered a position to shoot on the USA Olympic team in both pistol and trap shooting. I won the Louisiana State Championship in pistol and skeet that year. Unfortunately, I had to drop out of competition because I had no sponsor to pay for additional guns, entry fees, travel, and other expenses. But I continue to sharpen my skills at the range, by poking holes in targets.

My friend, Greg Simmons, the Deputy Director of the FBI, called this morning. He counseled, "Use your skills wisely and without media attention. I went out on a limb when the Director and I appointed you as a contract employee. You are a useful tool in our law enforcement program. The bureau cannot be labeled reckless by hiring people who run around shooting people at will. Fortunately, your incident in Mississippi received no media attention directed at the bureau. That was covered in the media as a bust of an illegal drug distribution operation by Federal Agents. The Mississippi Attorney General was unduly alarmed, in my opinion, but I let him vent."

"The DEA was mentioned for a drug bust?"

"I couldn't do that, but it was implied."

"Those guys just started shooting everywhere with automatic weapons, AR15's. Fact is, they didn't know how to use them. We had to defend ourselves." I said defensively.

"No one in the bureau is blaming Wolf, Special Agent Sallaz, or you for what happened. Yours and Wolf's quick action actually spared the life of Special Agent Sallaz according to her report. The Director and I dealt with that Attorney General who was off the rails about an operation he had very little information about."

"Hop, Florence, and Wolf all agreed with me that someone in local government screamed bloody murder to someone in State Government. We figured someone had a financial interest in that well organized operation tucked away on a remote abandoned farm in the Mississippi delta."

"Now that the hound is loose in Mississippi, State officials are aware and embarrassed about the pot operation. Inquiries will be made into the pot farms ownership. It's now up to State authorities to address the pig in the family kitchen and decide what they want to do about it. We will not get involved. Domestic pot production is not in our wheelhouse."

"I want to say that the Director and I appreciate your role while you're in the field. But, let me emphasize, the investigation into finding a master criminal belongs to Hop. He's an up and comer in the bureau and arresting a high profile perp on the 'Most Wanted' list will set him apart. Your role, and Florence's role is to assist. He will take credit for using the car as bait to catch him, not you. But the people who count know the truth."

"Thank you, Doug. I appreciate your confidence in me. Where are we at by the way? Who is this guy?"

"He's like a ghost. He keeps showing up in places like Atlanta, Hilton Head, Miami, Orlando, and the Villages in Florida. He's a confidence man who works his way into the hearts and checkbooks of women who are recently widowed or divorced. We will continue to use the tracking device to follow that Mustang Wolf has in his possession."

"I was with that guy, up close and personal. I failed to see his charm."

"Who is the guy? The car was titled to a George Franks in Naples, Florida. George died of a massive heart attack, and his widow was tasked with settling his estate. Franks' children live in California and Boston, and another is living in Europe. Not one of the children was on hand to assist their mother during her bereavement."

"According to the family, this guy had no problem selling himself as a concerned manager of estates and probate handling. He managed to transfer the woman's home quickly and efficiently. The bank accounts and the title to both of her cars went to him before she had any clue of what happened. He left her penniless when she died in a boating explosion. She was another victim chalked up by Pierre."

"No. We do not have a name or origin for him. One of the victims reported that she often heard him speaking in some foreign language on the phone. She said it sounded like German, but she didn't know for sure."

"A Jewish widow said he passed himself off as a Jewish jeweler from New York who lived in the area. She said he spoke Dutch, French and German and he had contacts in Antwerp who could value her jewelry. She entrusted her valuables to him, and he vanished. She never saw him or her jewels again. So, he could be Dutch, French or German."

Doug continued, "The main problem we have with nailing this guy is his chameleon persona. Descriptions vary but his method of operation is always the same. Then, we found out that there's the mole on his left cheek. That's the positive identifier. He operates with a woman or two and some younger people who play different roles in his fraudulent stings."

I listened quietly and made notes on an envelope. "The language thing. Do you think he's from another country and not an American citizen?"

"The list of complaints we've received tell us that he speaks several languages, but his English is impeccable like it's his first language but with a slight accent. The people who work with him, according to reports, all speak American English and are believed to be US citizens."

"You know, when he spoke to me in the Memphis airport and in the car, I noticed a certain inflection with his vowels. I didn't think too much of it at the time. People in the South are tuned to accents of one kind or another. We can pick them out. His was definitely different. The emphasis on certain vowels sounds was not natural."

"I'll get our people on that language difference, and we'll make a comparison analysis from interviews with the victims."

"That sounds complicated. Is there anything you want me to do?"

"Just watch your back and be careful. The offer to come and work at the bureau, by the way, is still open. And look after that blond Special agent."

"Oh, I've got my eye on him, alright."

**Chapter: 53     (An Offer To Draw Out A Culprit)**

The next day, Hop visited Wolf at the LeDuc and Johnson office. Wolf asked, "Where's your sidekick?"

"Florence? She's on a video conference with her boss in Kansas City. She's giving him an update and a timeline on how long she may be away from the Kansas City field office. She was assigned to me on an emergency basis. I hope they let me keep her until we catch this guy."

"Speaking of *this guy*, when do you think he'll strike next?"

"Well, one thing's for sure, he's not working alone. He let it slip that his son is in the Baptist Hospital. Will he leave him behind? Unknown. I doubt if he'll take that risk. Everyone at the bureau thinks he knows the FBI is on his trail, but he still believes the gold is in the car. We all are sure he will not leave five million on the table and just walk away. He's coming after that car."

"How come he doesn't think we've already discovered the gold?"

"Because he wouldn't risk everything he's done so far just for a car. He thinks you are just an obsessed car nut who would do anything to keep that car." Hop said.

"Well, I do like the car even though technically, the government, owns it. I do enjoy driving it and showing it off at every opportunity."

"Well, that chance may be coming up again. I'm here because the Meiners Auto Auction has a big event coming up this week at the Renasant Convention Center in downtown, Memphis. The FBI contacted the organizers, and they've agreed to feature your car on a rotating platform. They'll detail the outside of the car and display it on an elevated exhibit with colorful lights under the car. They'll put an outrageous bidding price on the car and except bids. Don't worry, the car won't be sold. It's just there for everyone to drool over." Hop said.

"That might draw the guy out. How will you protect the car?"

"Several local FBI agents volunteered to put on coveralls and work around the display at the auction. Yeah, the bureau has car nuts, too."

"What will I be doing at the auction?"

"You'll be working here in your office while the FBI does their job." Hop said with a satisfying grin.

"And what about Annette?"

"She's on the clock and she'll be working the auction."

"Oh! I see. Even though I'm the owner of record for the car. I don't go?"

"Too much risk. You can take care of yourself but you're still a civilian and we can't be worried about how to cover you, the car, ourselves, and the public all at the same time."

"Look, let's get one thing straight. I'm Annette's cousin but she's more like the little sister I've never had. I know she's got a crush on you, FBI guy. So, watch your step. Do not hurt her, understand?"

Hop was literally and physically taken aback. He stammered, "Y-You mean she likes me?"

"No numbnut, pay attention. She's fallen in love with you."

"Me? I thought she was only interested in the FBI. We went to dinner in Atlanta once and we've exchanged emails after I was transferred to Washington but, love?"

"All I'm saying is, if you do not feel the same, let her know gently."

"She's beautiful, smart and I can't stop thinking about her."

"Gee, you don't think that you might be in love,? Do you?"

"Well, I've never felt that way before. I guess I am."

Wolf rolled his eyes and said, "Tell her how you feel. You seem like a pretty smart guy when it comes to your job. How can you be so dense when it comes to your feelings?"

"When I left Wisconsin to join the bureau, my brother joined the CIA. Our mission was to serve our country the best way we could. Our father was a distinguished Marine sergeant, and he has always been very patriotic. I guess that rubbed off on my brother and me. What I'm saying is, I've never given much time to personal feelings."

"Uh, you've never had a girlfriend before?"

"Sure, in high school. And in college, I dated girls. We went to the movies and such."

"I mean have you ever had an intimate relationship with a girlfriend?"

"Oh, that. No. I guess it never came up."

"I will repeat. Tell Annette how you feel. If it is meant to be, take it slow and you may be surprised by the result."

"You mean like a math equation. Right?"

"Yeah! Just like that." Wolf said shaking his head. "When will we know more about this auction?"

"The auction is in the works now. I expect to know more yet today." Hop said.

"Well, the car is safe in my garage, and I need to get it washed. Our little adventure into the Mississippi delta got it dirty and covered with bugs. When I got home last night, I couldn't even eat. I just showered and fell into bed."

"I spoke to Annette this morning. She had just finished her morning run. She said pretty much the same thing about being worn out from her abduction and escape. She said she had some shopping to do this morning." Hop said.

"I'll keep my ears open waiting to find out about the auction. Give me a call later. And remember what I said about Annette." Wolf said.

## Chapter: 54    (Pretty As A Picture)

A man by the name of Earl Trotter called Wolf from the Meiners Auto Auction and asked, "Mr LeDuc? I understand you have a very special Roush Jackhammer Mustang."

"I do and I'm very proud of it." Wolf admitted.

"Because your car is rather unique, we would like to display your car at our upcoming auto auction being held in the Renasant Center. The reason I'm calling is to make arrangements for the delivery and placement of the vehicle. We have several documents regarding liability and handling that need to be signed by you in order for us to display your prized vehicle. When can we meet up?"

"I'm in town all week. Do you have an office, or do you want to come to mine?"

"I understand that you're in Germantown. I live not far from you in Collierville. Why don't I stop by your office this afternoon?"

"Sounds like a plan. Do you have my address?"

"I do. Do you have the car with you? I want to take some pictures of the car for our advertising department to put into our flier which is going out in the morning."

"Tell you what, I'll go home, run it through a car wash, and bring the car to the office. Meet me here then we'll go to the Southwind golf course to take your pictures. I'll call and see where they'll let us shoot the pictures." Wolf said while arranging some papers on his desk.

"Wow! You can do that? Are you a member there?"

"Not really, but I do know a person or two."

"Great, how about 4:00 at your office?"

"I'll be waiting here with the car."

When I arrived at the office, Wolf told me what he was doing with the auto auction. He said, "It was set up by the FBI."

I asked if I could ride along but only if Wolf bought dinner. He laughed and said, "Sure, but Roger's got first dibs on his dinner. Then we go to the photo shoot and I'm all yours for dinner. You pick the place."

"How about the East End Grill? They have a sandwich there that's become my new favorite."

"Done!"

Wolf drove home and parked his Escape in his driveway leaving room to back out the Mustang. He then walked to the mailbox, picked up his mail, and opened his new garage door using his new code. He was impressed, the door had a good looking wood finish.

Wolf fed Roger, read over his mail, took a satisfactory look around the house and locked up the house saying to the camera, "Keep an eye on the place."

He told me later that he was pleased with the work the carpenters had done with the repairs. Some things were simply lost or destroyed, like paintings and a couple of antique pieces of furniture. He filed a claim with his insurance company for the damage, but his deductible was nearly as high as his claim.

Wolf loved the sound of the Jackhammer's engine rumbling every time he pushed the start button on the dash. He carefully backed onto the drive and waved goodbye at the cameras, which he knew were watching his every move. Then he drove off to get his car washed.

I spent most of my morning purchasing a new Beretta and was in my office polishing my new gun when he arrived with the Mustang. I slipped the gun into my shoulder bag and met Wolf at the door. And said, "I must admit that every time I see that car, I'm in love."

Stepping inside, Wolf eyed me closely and asked, "Speaking of love, how are things between you and Mr. Dickerson?"

I didn't rise to the bait. I said, "Professional, as always."

I didn't say anything more. Wolf gave me an up-chin acknowledgement. He said, "Earl, from Meiners Auto Auction should be here very soon. He's bringing some photographer to do the photo shoot."

Wolf and I waited at the office making phone calls. Two men from Meiners walked into the building and Wolf walked out of his office the same time I did to greet them.

I checked my shoulder bag to see my new Beretta, then threw it over my shoulder and came out to say hello. Earl, was a man in his mid-fifties while the photographer appeared to be close to my age, in his 20's. I walked over and firmly shook hands with both men.

Earl said to Wolf, "Your car's a beauty. It'll look great at the auction this weekend. Will you drive or trailer the car to the Renasant Center?

"I bought this vehicle as a daily driver. We'll drive it there and leave it for the auction."

"Is it okay if we lift the engine compartment hood to expose the engine and rig a light inside?"

"I don't see why not. I don't think there's any reason to get into the trunk, do you?"

"No, not at all. Let me introduce Jan Johnson. He just showed up yesterday with his photographer's credentials and asked if he could take pictures during the auction. I told him, 'I'll do you one better, we'll hire you to take pictures for us, and I have your first assignment'." He said winking at Jan.

I stared at the good looking young blond man who was trim and stood a little over six foot. His grin exuded confidence that bordered on arrogance. But there was something about his face. I said, "I'm sorry for staring. Have we met before?"

That took him aback, but he recovered quickly. He gave me a full grin and said, "No, I don't think so. I would remember someone as pretty as you."

I know he said that to embarrass me and to change the subject. I smiled back and said to Wolf, "I'm ready, if you are."

On the ride to Southwind, Wolf played selections from his collection of Memphis Blues. He said, "Rosco Gordon's, 'No More Doggin' is a Memphis Blues original. Guys like Muddy Waters and Sonny Boy Williamson came later."

I simply nodded listening to the music. I couldn't get the image of that photographer's face out of my mind. Somewhere near the exit for the Southwind Golf Club, the image of the photographer and the man I shot in the parking lot a few days ago merged. The faces were nearly the same, only this one had no facial hair. The revelation stunned me. Wolf and I were getting played by the man we knew as Perry again. My concern now was how this threat might play out.

I couldn't talk over the music or make a phone call to Hop for the same reason. All I could do was wait till we got to the site of the photoshoot then make a quiet phone call to Hop while Earl, Jan and Wolf fussed over the car.

Wolf met his Southwind friend who guided Wolf and the car to a spot at one of the golf holes. Jan used his fingers to picture frame the shot with the Mustang in front of the putting green with the Southwind's pin flag in the background. The car's photograph was enhanced by a late spring golden afternoon hue which lent magic to the scene.

I sent a text to Hop while the photographer was busy shooting pictures from several different angles. Jan suddenly turned to me and said, "I think a car picture could do with a little eye candy, don't you? Annette, would you mind posing on the car?"

"Uh, on the car?"

"Well, at least leaning or reclining on the fender of the car?"

"I can stand next to it but I'm not getting on that car."

The young man looked disappointed. He said, "Okay then, stand next to the car with that big Southern smile!"

"I'll give you my best Louisiana smile. It'll have to do."

I put my fingers through my hair to fluff it out a bit with the wind catching the tendrils over my shoulder and stood next to the car."

Jan shouted out. "The purse. Get rid of the purse."

Reluctantly, I handed the gun heavy shoulder bag to Wolf and went to stand next to the car again. He shot several pictures of me standing and presenting my best smile. He shot a picture with me leaning on the fender and me kind of hugging the car in a suggestive manner. I felt so used.

Jan said, "Great shots. I think we have enough."

Earl asked, "Can we down load those images now? I need to get them off to the printer yet this afternoon."

Jan smiled and said, "Sure, here, you can take the SD card I have another."

I cheerfully said, "Before we do that, why don't we get a picture of our good looking photographer with the car?"

Wolf got my message and said, "Great idea, why don't I take a picture using his camera and another with my cell phone?"

Before Jan could say anything, Wolf was busy taking Jan's camera and ushering him next to the car and began snapping shots. Then he said, "One more with my cellphone. You know, you should be a model. You're very photogenic." Jan offered a weak smile.

Jan sourly went along with the photo shoot. When Wolf was done, Jan retrieved his camera and was about to delete the pictures when Earl said, "I can use that SD card now." Jan sighed and gave the card to Earl.

"Wonderful! Mr. LeDuc! I cannot thank you enough. Be sure to arrive early at the auction on Friday so we have plenty of time to set-up your car on display."

The two men left, and Wolf was talking to his friend at the golf course thanking him when I got a text from Hop. *"Are you sure?"*

I answered, *"Uncanny resemblance to the man I shot."* I had sent the snapshot I took of Jan next to the car to Hop.

When we got into the car and before he turned on the music again, I asked Wolf, "Did that photographer seem at all familiar to you?"

"Strange you should ask. Yes, I felt I had seen him before."

I smiled and said, "You did, but it wasn't him. It was his brother with facial hair."

Wolf gave me a strange look and nodded. I said, "The man I shot in the parking lot. The one who Perry said was his son. Apparently, Perry has more than one son and they look remarkably alike."

Wolf said, "You're right! He looks like the guy you shot in the eye, maybe a little taller, a little older, and clean shaven. What the heck do you think he was playing at?"

"I think he's like his father. Overconfident with a superior feeling that he could never get caught. I think he just wanted to size us up. It reminds me of stories I read about Native American warriors who walked onto a battlefield sometimes unarmed with nothing but a coup stick. They would touch their enemy, alive or dead, with the stick as an act of bravery. Jan was touching me with his camera doing the same thing. He wasn't even interested with keeping the images. What photographer does that?"

Wolf shivered and said, "They're a creepy bunch. But they're counting on the belief that we don't know who they are. It's a slight advantage for us but it may not be enough."

## Chapter: 55    (Well, Hop To It)

Wolf and I spent the rest of the week working from the office while Ezra performed a preemptive warranty audit for a dealer in Nashville who was warned by the factory that they were coming in to conduct an audit for certain types of repairs. The dealer felt it would be better if he put some measures in place to correct codes and resubmit warranty claims before the factory found them and fined him.

Wolf and I were shadowed throughout the day by Chick's employees and by video. This coverage included my routine morning run through my neighborhood in Germantown which made me self-conscious about my every move. I never actually saw anyone follow me, but I knew they were there because I was sent pictures via texts from Reliant Security.

The next day, I thought about Wolf's offer for me to lease a car for travel using my monthly car allowance. A car lease from a car dealer would save wear and tear on my Camaro but many of my out of town trips were getting further and further away from Memphis. I was now renting cars at airports for most of my audits. I could, however, use the extra monthly bump in income to help defray my monthly personal expenses. So, I decided to put off making a decision anytime soon. I have to admit the Chevy Traverse was a handy vehicle to carry things in. Maybe I'll reconsider again soon.

I wouldn't say Hop has been avoiding me, but he hasn't been making any moves toward finding time for us to be together either. That's why I was surprised when he called out of the blue and asked me if I wanted to have dinner and go to a movie. I didn't say no but I wasn't interested in going to a movie either. Instead I said, "Wonderful idea! Where would you like to go?"

"Honestly, this is your city, you know places better than I do. You choose."

"Folks Folly is a local favorite for dinner. I take it you still like beef steak?"

"Well, yeah! What Wisconsin farm boy doesn't?"

"I'll make the reservations. Pick me up at 6:30 and we'll take our time enjoying a good meal. Then, how about we just come to my place and stream a good show or movie on my big screen?"

"Uh, yeah. That sounds good. I know you don't drink alcohol what should I bring?"

"Just bring yourself. If you like wine or beer, I'll get you some at the grocery."

"Oh, you don't have to do that."

"No. I mean it. You may be drinking wine with dinner. I'll probably drink a non-alcohol beverage with you. So, what is it?"

"I do like beer. Can you get Leinenkugel? We call it Linny where I come from."

"Never heard of it but I know a place where they have everything. Remember, I don't drink but I was a bartender for a while."

"You were? You are a very interesting person."

I took that as a compliment and said, "Yes. Florence isn't coming is she?" I asked with some trepidation.

"Florence? No! No, of course not. I just wanted to spend some time with you. That's all."

That made me happy, and we bid each other goodbye. I held my phone and smiled. Maybe there was hope for Hop yet. He had kept himself further than arm's length from me since arriving from Kansas City. I thought he might have a thing for Florence. I liked her but I was glad she wasn't coming to dinner tonight.

Our dinner at the restaurant was exceptional, and I took more than half my steak home in a to-go box. When we arrived at my place, I could tell that Hop was uncomfortable coming into my apartment. I put my go-box into the fridge and told Hop to make himself comfortable in the living room on the couch.

When I walked into the living room with a beer for him he was nervously scrolling through this cellphone. He looked up and said, "You found it! Linny!" And he gave me a wide Wisconsin farm boy smile.

I toasted him with a glass of iced sweet tea. I sat next to him, and we talked about what he might like to watch on my TV. We started with the Sci-Fi stuff then looked for recent movies and he asked, "What do you like?"

"Honestly, mysteries or cop procedural shows. Will you watch a foreign show that has subtitles?"

"Can't say I've ever done that before. Sure, I'll give it a try. Whatcha got?"

"Right now, I'm streaming a French police commander by the name of Candice Renoir. She's kind of funny and the stories are good. You get used to the subtitles and the characters are fun."

"I can guess why you chose a French film to watch."

"The French is a little different than Cajun French, so I rely on the subtitles just like everyone else. But yes, I understand many of the phrases."

After an hour of watching the show, I could tell that Hop was fully engrossed in the storyline. When the episode ended he said, "What happens next? Are we suppose to go to the next episode to see what happened?"

"Yes, I think that was their cruel plan. Do you want to watch another?"

I was disappointed when he looked at his watch. He said, "Oh, what the heck. Sure! More Candice. She's funny and fun."

As we watched I inched closer to him and held his hand. He didn't refuse. In fact, I thought he was going to bend over in my direction for an intimate kiss, but he reached for the beer bottle instead.

I've been attracted to Hop since I first saw him in Atlanta and I thought we may have a thing, but he seems as dense as ironwood when it comes to intimacy. Finally, I could wait no longer. I literally finger climbed up his arm and kissed him on his cheek.

Startled, Hop jumped, turned his head and I kissed his lips. He didn't back off. Instead, he responded. In fact, he responded with more enthusiasm than I thought he was capable of. He used both hands to hold my face and got into the kiss.

I gently pried us loose and said, "That was nice."

"Oh, Annette! I've dreamed of that kiss ever since we were in Atlanta together. You were the most beautiful Wonder Woman I have ever seen."

"Yes, and the yellow boots made you a dashing Flash with the thunderbolt on your chest."

*"Well, don't stop now!"* I thought. He embraced me, and I could tell passion was building between us. Sometimes, you have to chase them till they catch you, as my grandmother used to tell me.

## Chapter: 56    (Who's That Knocking At My Door)

I was dreaming about lying on my back, floating along on a beautiful bayou stream in a pirogue. I was covered in flower peddles. My fingers dangled in the water and tendrils of my hair flowed next to the boat leaving mini wakes in the water. I was a Princess being rescued from an evil knight named Sir Perry. My savior was Prince Hop. Or was it Dickerson, or was it special agent? A bee buzzed and I tried to wave it away with my hand, but the buzzing continued.

My cellphone kept buzzing. I sat up like a corpse in a morgue barely able to crack my eyes open. I kept waving my hand in front of my face until I realized that there was no bee and my cellphone would not stop.

I grabbed my phone desperately trying to focus. "Yeah! Annette! Who is this?"

"It's Clarence and someone is creeping around outside your apartment door."

"Door? Oh! Thanks. Is anyone from Reliant here, at my place?"

"No. We just saw some guy on video trying to peek in your window."

I immediately rolled out of my bed and a thought flashed through my brain. *"Where was Hop?"*

Taking no chances, I reached in my nightstand for my new Beretta. I pulled the slide, chambered a round, and padded to the front room. Hop was asleep curled up on the couch under a blanket.

I slowly walked to the front room window holding my gun in both hands. I moved the shade just enough to peek outside and saw a shadow move. What to do? My front door was metal with a metal frame. They weren't getting in that way. They can't see into my living room. If I open the door to confront them, they might overpower me before I got a shot off.

Clarence was still on the phone. I whispered, "What's he doing now?"

"Just hanging around your door. Looks like he has a prybar in his hand."

"Is there just one of them?"

"That's all I can see. I need to go back and look at parking lot footage to see how he got there."

"What should I do?"

"Stay put and don't shoot anyone unless they break in. The police are on their way."

Hop stirred and moaned, "What is it?"

I shushed him and whispered, "An intruder at the door. Don't get up, the police are on the way."

Hop shook his head and whispered back, "How do you know?"

"Reliant Security." I whispered to my phone, "You still there Clarence?"

"I'm watching everything. There! The police just pulled into the lot. No siren. They're walking up the stairs now to your apartment. Your guy just heard them, and it looks like he dropped the prybar and is trying to run away. They're chasing him. There! They caught him and he's on the ground. They've cuffed him to a railing and they're coming to your place. If you have your gun put it someplace out of sight."

"Good idea." I looked around then stuffed the gun under a chair cushion. The door knocked and I heard, "Police! Open up!"

I opened the door, and they shined a flashlight into my face. They asked, "Are you the homeowner here?"

That was when I realized that I was standing barefoot in a flimsy see-through nighty talking to two armed policemen. I grabbed the front of the nighty and said, "Yes, I rent this apartment."

"Did you call in a disturbance about a prowler at your door?"

"No. You received a call from Reliant Security who has my place under video surveillance. They called you then they called me to let me know I had a potential intruder. Did you catch them?

"We have a man in custody. If you, uh would like to put some clothes on, we want you to see if you know who this man is."

"Yes, just a minute."

The door closed as I turned and walked past Hop who was standing next to the couch wearing nothing but his tighty-whities. I smiled at the thought and rushed to slip into sweat pants, sweatshirt and running shoes.

The two policemen waited patiently outside my door. I said, "Where is he?"

"Handcuffed to the railing downstairs."

I went down the stairs with the policemen, and they flashed their light on the guys face. He tried to shield his eyes from the light, but his handcuffed hands would not let him. I could smell him. He smelled of alcohol. I said, "I don't know him. And I don't think I've seen him before either. He may live here but I can't verify that."

The cop considered what I told him. "How come you have Reliant Security cameras covering your apartment door?"

"Yeah, inside my apartment and on the parking lot, too. My name is Annette Dupart. I am a contract employee for the FBI. We've been working on a sensitive case. Some bad guys know who I am, so I'm being watched all the time."

"I think I've heard about you. You shot some guy in the eye at a parking lot not too far from here. How come you use Reliant rather than FBI gear to watch you?"

I said, "Chick Farrell is a personal friend, and he provided the service. What's going to happen to him?" I asked pointing at the guy cowering on a step, handcuffed to a rail.

"Oh, he's under arrest. Public drunkenness and disorderly. He'll go to jail, sleep it off, then post bond and pay a fine."

"Well, thank you for your vigilance. Do you need me for anything else?"

"Here's my card. We would like for you to come in to the station and fill out a complaint for this disturbance. I've got you on body cam and we know who you are at the station. Sorry you had to be disturbed this evening, Miss Dupart."

I watched while the policemen uncuff the man and take him to their cruiser. They waved and I went back upstairs. Hop had been watching from my living room window. This time, he was fully dressed. I was kind of sad, I missed the tighty-whitey Hop.

I checked the wall clock, and it was 3:45 AM. I walked into Hop's arms and hugged him. He said, "I thought it was best if I didn't get involved with that police call."

"Yeah, especially with your pants down, agent."

He didn't laugh at first then he found it funny, and he couldn't stop laughing. I had to plant a kiss on him to get him to stop. I was hoping he wasn't planning to leave just yet. As it turned out, I managed to convince him it was better to stay and leave after breakfast. It's dangerous out there. Prowlers were loose everywhere in the neighborhood.

## Chapter: 57     (The Jensen's Dutch Treat)

Charles Jensen's mind was a million miles away in a sleepy gossamer cloud of memories. A black Mustang car and gold were nowhere near his consciousness. He was sexually engaged with the beautiful Margaret Montgomery, heiress to the Wilford Bourgoine railroad fortune which was earned in the 19th century. She was busty, lusty and in her fifties. She had recently divorced from a loser whom she found in a spa while traveling in Rio. Charles was only 38 at the time, handsome and appeared to be independently wealthy. He didn't seem to be after her family fortune. At the time, he was using the fanciful name, Raul Windsor and said he was some distant relative of the Royal English family. She believed him.

Their affair was in full blossom, and she had total confidence in his abilities to guide her around grumpy lawyers and trust administrators. He convinced her that in order to travel the world as they planned, they needed full access to both hers and his fortunes to get married and live the life they dreamed of.

In a very short time, he had managed to transfer a large share of her assets into his personal accounts using different names. She trusted him thoroughly. She had not been well recently, mostly because she was ingesting a measured portion of rat poison with her regular morning meal of oatmeal and toast. It was their last embrace when he placed the pillow over her face. She suffocated quickly and he cried at her loss.

Charles was reliving the experience when his burner cellphone rang awaking him. Groggily he answered, "Yes! Who is this?"

"It's me, Brenda, your lovely wife. Remember?"

"Yes, yes, of course I do. Where are you?"

"Still in Florida, dear. I'm with our daughter, Eline, and we're devastated by the news of Albert getting shot and almost killed in Memphis. How could you let that happen? What can we do to get him help?"

"He's under guard. The bullet is still in his brain and they're saying he cannot be moved or have surgery here in Memphis. Dirk went to see him, and he doesn't think there's anything we can do for him."

"I love my oldest son, but he mostly thinks of himself. I'm working on a plan to get him out of there and taken to a hospital where they should be able to help him. Oops! Incoming call. It could be the Doctor I called. Goodbye!" She hung up and Charles stared at his cellphone.

Still sleepy, he was thinking about Margaret. His mind moved to his relationship with Brenda. He had been studying in America on a student visa when he met Brenda while attending Syracuse University in New York. They were instantly like minks, and they married before graduating and moved to Buffalo, NY to find work. His new wife was pregnant, and they struggled to find meaningful employment.

Karel, a student from South Africa, applied for a green card before getting married. He hoped his marriage to Brenda would be enough for him to earn his US citizenship. It was not.

His application for a Green Card was approved quickly, but without a degree, he could only find work with entry level positions. He would need to apply for the naturalization process to become a US citizen.

He didn't have time for all of that. He earned his license to work as an insurance salesman for a broker in Buffalo. He learned the ins and outs of how to close deals and manipulate people for profit. He had some good teachers.

While Karel was working in the Buffalo market, and freezing his tail off in the winter, Brenda soon became pregnant with their second child. It was becoming more and more difficult for them to make ends meet.

Karel was mentored at work by a slick insurance man. One day, the man pitched a plan to Charles that launched his career as a Gigolo con man. The mentor set him up as an attractive date for an older woman. She was an heiress to a Buffalo toothpick fortune. His job was to escort her at public functions. They got along well, and she loved his foreign accent.

When he had to perform romantically for her, he nearly threw up. Still, he managed the deed, and he set his partner up to handle her financial affairs. In a very short time, they managed to strip her bank account, sell her stock portfolio, and put a quit claim on her home. She hired lawyers, and they came after Karel and his partner for fraud and theft.

Karel took his cut of the proceeds and quickly moved out of Buffalo taking Brenda and his two kids with him. He confessed his crime to Brenda and her only question was, "How much did we make?"

The Jensen family took their tidy nest egg and moved to Boston. Brenda pitched right in working with Charles to set up cons with four different women, one right after the other. It finally became apparent that he needed to use different names if they were not to get caught. Brenda came through again and found a person who could obtain fake identification. She schooled Charles on how to overcome his Dutch accent. By the time they were about to be busted again, two things happened.

Brenda was pregnant with their third child, and they packed up and moved to Cleveland, Ohio.

Over the years and several cities later, Brenda and the kids lived very well. She took on different roles to act as a real estate agent, a travel agent, a financial advisor and even a lawyer. She was none of those things, but she was convincing. When things got hot, they picked up and moved the kids to greener pastures, changing their names.

They frequently relied on the brother of her sister-in-law, Manfred Mickleson. He had just finished law school, and he set up practice as a defense lawyer in Buffalo. Brenda's family had operated several shady business adventures, and her father was a devotee of nonpayment of taxes. Manfred was always there to help.

Brenda's key talent was setting up the con. Charles made the con work, and their combined talent was not getting caught. The kids grew up expecting to move from place to place. It was tough because they made friends in school and had to leave them behind every time. Eventually, they understood what was happening and they got into the spirit of the con game. They chose their own names and used that to their advantage.

One of the boys, Albert, almost got arrested for petty theft. Rather than face the music, the family packed up and moved again. When the law got too close they sometimes left possessions behind, but never anything that could be tied to them.

Brenda's sharp mind for finance is the reason they began to invest into gold. She always reasoned that solid assets that don't depreciate were the best security. gold, diamonds, fine art, rare coins, real estate, bearer bonds, and of course, rare cars. They avoided banks and they always managed to be within reach of their ill-gotten gains. Of course, they never paid any Federal or State income tax on their earnings.

By the time the children were adults, the family had become a financial strip mining machine. They were experts at sniffing out wealth and how to take it. They earned enough to pay cash for farm land with mineral rights in the west by using the real names of their children, Dirk, Albert, and Eline with last names of Jensen. When asked by Albert why he didn't invest into cryptocurrency, Charles simply laughed and said, "It doesn't take a con man to recognize a con like that. It's all based on confidence. That's what we do. We sell confidence. We do not become marks ourselves."

Dirk was currently using the name Jan Foster. Albert used the name Cal Marsh. Eline was known as Rita Simpson. All of them had learned their craft well from Brenda and Charles.

They all knew what was at stake. The family, including their uncle, aunt, and cousins, collectively agreed to buy gold, silver, coins, stamps, expensive cars and more then store them while they appreciated. Because they moved so often, it was Brenda's idea to store gold bars and coins they had accumulated in one of the cars, concealed in a secret compartment, then store the car someplace safe.

Charles chose the Roush Mustang from one of his marks and he chose Global Classic Vehicles in Olathe, Kansas as the place to store the car. The Jensen crime family had enough working capital to keep each of them happy for life if they stopped right now. But every one of them enjoyed the game so much, they all said, "Why not keep going?"

The plan with the Roush Mustang worked well for three years. The gold was safely tucked away and kept increasing in value due to a shaky economy. Their cons continued and earnings were invested into the rapidly escalating housing market of Las Vegas. The family knew they were multi-millionaires on paper. Everything ran smoothly until someone, out of the blue, wanted to buy the car with the stored gold. The family became alarmed about losing their liquid asset, worth well over five million and improving daily.

The Jensen children had each gone their own way, working their own confidence games. This disaster quickly united the family. The two boys had been working together on a con in Houston involving a chain of restaurants while Eline aka Rita had been skimming money out of a rock star's business assets.

Charles called Dirk to go after the car before it was sold. When that failed, Dirk called on Albert to help him out. Albert got shot so Martin and Freddy were brought in and they hired street thugs to help. After several failed attempts, nothing worked. So, Dirk, Brenda, Eline and the two cousins, Martin and Freddy all checked into the Bonanza casino hotel with Charles. They put their heads together, to come up with a fool proof plan to recover the car and the gold. And they wanted to discuss what could be done with Albert.

## Chapter: 58    (Two Plans Come Together)

The Bonanza Boom Casino had been very generous to Charles and his family. His suite of five rooms was on the top floor of the hotel which had a panoramic view over the Mississippi River levy and the flowing brown water below. They could see the hilly Arkansas countryside stretching out beyond the western shoreline from their lofty view.

Charles, Dirk, Eline and the two cousins, who were comically referred to by the family as Morty and Ferdie, sat comfortably in the suite's living room while Brenda brought them coffee and breakfast rolls.

Brenda sat down next to Eline and asked, "Is it possible, do you think, that we can go visit Albert?"

It was Dirk who spoke up first. "He's being constantly watched, at least, mostly watched. I was lucky when I slipped in as a speech therapist. He's being held by the Feds till he cracks and turns on us."

"No Dirk!" Eline said in alarm. "Albert would never do that!"

"You didn't see him. I did. He's in a lot of pain and he can barely put two words together. The slug that got him is still lodged someplace in his brain."

"Did he recognize you? Did he say anything at all?" Brenda demanded.

"Yes, I believe he did know who I was. Like I said, he mumbled a few words that I barely understood."

"So, he's not brain dead and there's probably hope. We need to find a way to get him out of there." Brenda said.

Charles and the two cousins remained quiet letting the conversation play out. Dirk said, "And do what? We have no way to take care of a brain injured invalid. Even if we snuck him out of the hospital under the watchful eyes of his police guards where would we take him?"

Eline smiled and said, "If I understand correctly, the only thing he's being charged with is attempted car theft and brandishing a gun, which got him shot. No one knows who he really is. If we can get him out of that hospital, we should be able to transport him to a facility that specializes in this kind of injury, someplace else."

Dirk was skeptical. "How?"

"Morty and Ferdie are both computer jocks. You two get on the web and begin a search for a brain injury facility someplace in the country. Find the best doctor and someplace that can remove a bullet in the brain." Brenda said forcefully.

Morty brightened up and said. "Yeah, I can get on that right now. I'll look for the most qualified brain specialist in and out of the US."

Grinning, Eline said, "And I still have credentials identifying me as a General Practitioner from California by the name of Gloria Fisher. I just need to get some scrubs, N95 face mask and a stethoscope. As Gloria, I'll go in and demand to see his X-Rays." Eline said with authority.

"That's risky. So, you find the X-Ray then what? Can you read it?" Dirk said sarcastically.

"Maybe. But that's not important. I'll explain that his family in California asked me to come and make a recommendation for his care."

"Found it!" Morty shouted out. "The Shepherd Center in Atlanta, Georgia. They rank as one of the top five for brain injuries due to gun shot. Apparently, they have a lot of them there. And the best doctor for bullets in the head is a brain surgeon who works at a trauma center in East St. Louis, Missouri."

Eline said, "See, we need to get his X-rays and take him to Atlanta and admit him under the name Calvin Marsh. I can even arrange for the medical flight that will take him to Georgia. What do you say?"

Charles finally had heard enough. "Saving Albert is something we would all like to see happen, but we cannot lose our focus here. We are here to recover a family fortune. We need that gold! I'm too old to go out and start all over to build another pile of cash. We still need a plan to recover that car and the gold it holds."

Dirk was about to jump into the conversation. He had already cooked up a plan and made the necessary arrangements to steal the car. He even hired local help to spy on the woman who shot Albert and break in if he could. Before he could say anything, Morty said, "Why not do both? We get Albert out of the hospital and police custody, sneak him to a waiting aircraft while we are going after the car? Come on! We've handled more complicated cons than this. Let's do it!"

Brenda was in tears. She looked at Charles and said, "Some things are just more important than money, Charles."

Brenda's comment surprised Charles. She had always been the driving force behind accumulating as much wealth as was possible without getting caught. He said, "Dirk and I formed a plan to create a diversion for taking the Mustang while it's on display at a car auction in Memphis this weekend. That plan would require both Morty, Ferdie and Eline to pull off.

But we could possibly do okay without Eline if she went at the hospital. Dirk will just hire a girl from a talent agency for the task."

Charles stopped talking, looked at tearful Brenda and said, "Alright, we'll do both things. Taking Albert might serve as a good diversion for the law which would take attention away from the car. We will do that first to draw law enforcement away from the car auction."

Dirk said, "My character as Jan the photographer, told me a lot about the owner of the car and the woman who shot Albert. First of all, Wolf seemed totally obsessive about the car. I don't believe he knows anything about hidden gold. Second, the woman, Annette, is very attractive but seems a bit flakey."

Charles snorted and said, "Yes, flakey but resourceful. I think she can be charming, but from my experience, she has a rough side and thought nothing of humiliating me on the drive to that pot farm. Her hands were zip tied behind her back. How on earth she got out of that and produced a gun is beyond me."

"When I took her pictures she carried a heavy purse. When she handed it off to Wolf, it appeared to be heavy. I'm thinking that's where she keeps her gun. Maybe the same gun that shot Albert. We need to separate her from her purse and Wolf from the car to make our plan work." Dirk said.

"Then that FBI woman showed up. I heard they shot and may have killed most of the pot farmers. When I left, it sounded like the place was surrounded by the FBI. Those pot farmers were a tough bunch. They had AR15's, yet they were put down like mangey dogs."

"Was she alone? And how did that FBI woman get there?" Dirk asked.

"Unknown." Charles said. "And that still bothers me. I got out of there as quick as I could when the gunfire broke out. I thought the FBI had the place surrounded."

"Now, let's get down to business. Our plan is to do this during the second day of the auto auction. We simply take the car from the display and put another in its place. We do that and drive the car out of the building and onto a waiting car trailer. This is the old 'Bait and Switch con'." Charles said grinning.

Ferdie said enthusiastically, "That's what I'm talking about! Right under their noses while there's an auction going on. Ka-ching!"

Dirk said, "The talent agency will provide me with a girl in an evening dress to pose next to cars while I shoot pictures. Meanwhile, Morty and Ferdie will set up outside next to a truck and car trailer with what we planned. At the appropriate time when the auction is selling the top car everyone wants, Ferdie will come in dressed in coveralls. I'll hand him the Mustang's key fob. He'll get into the car while Morty sets up the ramps. The car will be backed off the platform and out of the arena area onto the loading dock, then out to the parking lot where we'll hide the vehicle. Trucks like ours will be everywhere. Many vehicles being auctioned are shipped to Memphis. We should blend right in."

Charles grinned, "Dirk, it looks like you've thought of everything. The only wild card is that woman. And I have a plan for her."

Dirk nodded in agreement. "I hired a man to probe her apartment last night to see if we could get in and take her out. Turns out there are security cameras everywhere. It's like Ft. Knox. Our guy, who faked being drunk, got arrested almost immediately. It looks like a security company is protecting her, not the Feds."

"This time, if they get in the way, we just kill Wolf and anyone with him. If that Annette woman gets in our way, I have a plan to trade her for services rendered."

Dirk said, "Good idea. We take her with us. I have plans to torture that pretty little thing beyond recognition." He said grinning and no one in the room even flinched.

Dirk looked at Brenda, Morty and Ferdie and said, "Sounds like we have a plan everyone. Morty, you two will drive the car to New Orleans. From there, we ship the car and gold to us in Aruba."

"I think we should all go to Aruba and lay low for a while. The vacation should do us all good." Charles said grinning.

"Yeah, but, when we get safely away from Memphis, we need to check the secret compartment in the car for the gold. I do not trust that no one has found the gold." Brenda said.

"Of course! And we'll check for tracking devices besides our own. Where could we do that?" Dirk asked.

"I'm thinking we haul the car south down here to Mississippi, on Highway 61. That road goes all the way to New Orleans, you know. We need to return our equipment to that truck rental place near Tunica. I say we check for the gold there. Then we drive to Greenville and stay in a hotel there using one of our names. We hide out for a day or two and let things settle down before we head on to New Orleans. My hope is they'll be busy chasing after Eline and Albert and too busy to look for that black car."

Everyone nodded in agreement except Eline. And she said, "So, who is going to help me get Albert out of the hospital?"

Brenda said, "That would be me. I can drive an ambulance. All we have to do is get to an airport where our plane will be waiting."

Charles said, "I'll make that flight arrangement for you as soon as we are done with our meeting."

"I could use someone acting as an orderly to help me get Albert transferred from his bed onto a gurney, out of his room and put into the ambulance. I'll need the same help at an airport." Eline said.

Morty said, "Let me. I can do that then hurry back to the convention center in time to help steal the car."

Charles thought about it and said, "That'll work. Go with Brenda and help with Albert. Then high tail it back to downtown Memphis bringing the Ambulance with you."

Then Charles clapped his hand and gleefully said, "See, that's what I'm talking about."

"Where do we get the ambulance?" Eline asked.

"Don't worry." Charles said. "Leave that to my truck rental guy."

Satisfied that they had a plan, Charles laughed and said, "Okay everyone. Meeting adjourned. We have a lot to do before Saturday, the second day of the auto auction. Let's get busy!"

## Chapter: 59    (Another Assignment)

My mother in St. Martinville, Louisiana, called me to see how I was doing. I told her about the upcoming auto auction in Memphis. She does not care nor understand much about her families' fascination with cars and car racing. However, she passed along that information to my brothers.

My younger brother, Boudy Dupart, co-owns a used car lot in Lafayette with a couple of my cousins. When mom told him about the auction he immediately called me.

"Annette. Mom told me about you going to that Memphis car auction. I've been on line looking at the cars to be sold at that auction."

"Okay, and what did you find?" I asked, mildly curious.

"Well, there are some pretty high-end vehicles going through the line. But in between, there are some roadworthy cars that could be had for a good price. Some with a reserve, some without. I'm always looking for new iron for my lot. I've checked my calendar. It would be tough for me to leave the business on a week-end, but if you could be on a phone and do the bidding for my vehicles at the auction, that would be fantastic! I'll make sure you have a line of credit and are authorized to bid for me."

If I told Boudy that I was on the clock as a Federal contract employee, hunting a 'most wanted' criminal, he would just think that I was making up a silly excuse. I was trapped. He knew I was going to the auction and would see no reason why I couldn't do as he asked. I weakly said, "Okay, Boudy. I'll help."

My real role at the auction was to assist Federal agents who would be in the crowd looking for the man they knew as Perry. They had the photo I took at the airport of him, but he could look like anyone at this stage. I had seen him up close and was the one who could point him out to other agents. Then there was that mole on his face along with the unique cologne fragrance he used. I can still smell it. I sighed and wondered if I could do both tasks at the same time.

Reluctantly, I called Hop and broke the news about what Boudy asked me to do. I was surprised by his answer. "Actually, that makes a real good cover for you while you're keeping an eye out for our man."

"You mean it's okay?"

"Sure, and I'll have an eye on you, too."

"Well, that part sounds good. But who'll watch the Mustang?"

"Wolf and Florence, of course. This is a three day auction. I think the car will be okay. It's displayed on a rotating platform, and it's just a car. We're *manhunting* and need to be eyeballing everyone who comes into that auditorium. We'll have video cameras posted everywhere inside and out. And we have a team in a box suite, overlooking over the entire floor. For us, the man is the target, not the car."

I thought, *"But the car is the bait. He wants that car."* I didn't argue because I didn't have a good argument. I said, "Okay. I'll bid for my brother while eye-surfing the crowd for our suspect."

"Great! We still have two days before the Friday auction. Are you free for tonight?"

"Sure, if the offer's right." I said smiling.

## Chapter: 60    (Prepping For The Auction)

Because I would be receiving a good check from the Justice Department I figured it was time for a new look. I was tired of pony tails and messing with long black hair down my back. I wanted to look more put together like my FBI counterpart, Florence. So, I went to the beauty parlor and had my hair trimmed to shoulder length and layered. When it was done, I was very pleased with the effect. I now needed a new outfit for the car show. So, I went shopping, one of my favorite pastimes.

I used the morning to make dealer phone calls. At noon, I announce to Connie, "I'm off! While the weak stay home, the tough go shopping!" Connie laughed and Wolf's head popped out of his office. I waved and left in my Camaro vowing to leave no prisoners behind at the Wolfchase Galleria.

I had a fun time browsing through racks and racks of clothing. It was tough, making decisions that matched my ideal of what my new look should be. When my shopping was complete, I sat exhausted, sipping Bai Hao Yin Zhen tea with my eyes closed savoring the flavor at the Petals of a Peony restaurant. This was my special place, and I've enjoyed coming here on many occasions. My plan was to decompress from shopping and eat an early Chinese dinner, then go home to sort through my purchases. This was *me* time. Tonight it would be me and Hop time. But that was later.

I took another sip of tea, and you know how you can feel eyes staring at you? My eyes popped open and Jan, the photographer, was standing in front of my table. Shocked, I said, "Jan! What are you doing?"

He was wearing a loose sweatshirt over jeans. I couldn't tell for sure, but I guessed he was carrying a handgun. He said, "I came in for some take out and I saw you obviously enjoying whatever you're drinking. What is it, a cocktail?"

I sat my tea cup on its saucer and said, "No. I do not drink alcohol." I made eye contact then I saw what looked like a bulge near his back under the sweatshirt.

I waited for him to say something. Finally, seeing that I was not going to invite him to sit down he asked, "Do you mind if I join you?"

"Yeah, about that. I've already ordered and I'm meeting somebody. Now is not a good time." I said fixing my eyes on his.

This comment took him aback. He was not used to people, primarily women, turning him down. "Oh. Okay. Will you be attending the car show this weekend?" He stood there shifting from one foot to another.

"Yes, I'll be bidding on cars for my brother's used car business. I take it you'll be there with your camera shooting pictures." I said keeping my eyes on him.

"That's right. There'll be lots of good photo opportunities. Maybe I can get one in a car magazine."

"Oh, yeah? Which cars are you most interested in?"

"Oh, you know, the cool ones."

*"Weak answer,"* I thought. I asked, "Which car magazines will you query with your photos?"

"I have one or two in mind. Will you be at the show all three days?"

"I'll be in and out. Maybe I'll see you there."

Fortunately, my cellphone buzzed at just that moment. I said, "I have to take this. Nice seeing you. Enjoy your Chinese food." I turned away from him and said, "Hop! Great to hear your voice." I looked back in time to see Jan storming out of the restaurant with no food to go.

I told Hop about the encounter and explained why I thought Jan was related to Perry, the man we were after. He said, "I'll alert our agents and ask them to keep an eye on him. Wolf sent that photo he took of him to me, and we'll watch him at the auction.

I went home, unloaded my purchases onto my bed, and began to sort things and hanging them up. I purchased three days' worth of outfits. My prize purchase was a brilliant red top with flared sleeves, and I settled on an ankle length black skirt with a side split. The skirt was beautiful but functional. I could easily access my Nano from my thigh holster, if needed.

My second outfit was a burgundy skirt with split and a loose crème colored top. My last outfit, I couldn't resist. I found a smocked crop top with a high low split mini skirt in conservative grey. Boring color but it really looked good on me, and it matched my new hairdo. I found some knock-out hoop ear rings and chose a new lipstick. Maybe going to the car show to bid on cars wouldn't be that bad. I would be dressed to kill.

Speaking of which, Hop would be coming over to my place around 8:00 after a dinner meeting with local FBI personnel. I just had enough time to shower and prepare for his visit.

## Chapter: 61    (Setting Up For An Auction)


Early Friday morning Wolf and I were ready. Hop and Florence arrived at his house to follow us to the Renasant Center in downtown Memphis. Wolf suggested we take Poplar all the way downtown and skip the morning traffic jam on the freeway. Hop and Florence followed in their government issued SUV. The drive wasn't really that bad.

Chick Farrell sent a Reliant Security shadow car to follow us to our destination. I felt cocooned with a lot of people looking after my wellbeing. I refrained from using my frequent phrase, "What could possibly go wrong!" I knew the people coming after the car were capable of anything to get that car back and their belief that it held over a hundred pounds of pure gold. Wolf and I drove the Mustang, but we would ride back with Hop and Florence.

We arrived at the convention center in the Roush Mustang and using passes provided by Earl, courtesy of the Meiners Auto Auction, we drove right to the building and were escorted to our destination. Vehicles were parked everywhere. Many arrived days earlier. We drove past them and up a ramp to the second story of the building where the loading dock was located. A car friendly ramp had been constructed allowing access for cars into the main ballroom floor.

Wolf and I drove into the building. We found the place outside the ballroom and the platform where they would place our car. A workmen in coveralls was assigned to place the car on the reflecting glass platform and polish the cars exterior. We got out and watched them push the car where they wanted it. Ramps were removed and stored just on the other side of the door to the loading docks. The Jackhammer, with the hood up, was now displayed with colorful lights and looked dramatic.

Wolf looked at me and said, "Well, I guess our work is done."

I knew he was joking, but I said, "Your work is done, mine has just begun." He laughed and we went to find some coffee and a Danish.

Near the door, Morty in coveralls stared at Wolf and me. He made a cell phone call and said, "They're here and the car is in place."

"Is the storage unit for the car unloaded and ready?"

"As planned, the pickup with the car trailer will work where Ferdie left it. Other trailers and trucks are everywhere. We got here just in time. We look like everyone else who brought a car to be auctioned."

"Good. You can leave now. Go help Eline at the hospital. Tomorrow we make our move. There's nothing left to do there today."

"On my way."

Cars were displayed in every corner of the ballroom. Carpets had been removed exposing a polished concrete floor, to easily move the cars and to protect the carpet from leaking classic cars. I saw how the auction would work. Cars would be pushed in a large circle around to one end of the hall where a dais and a ramp was constructed for the cars to be auctioned. Cameras and news people were scattered around the huge room.

One man with a clipboard came over to me and said, "Hurry up, we're about to go live."

I smiled and said, "Uh, I think you have the wrong person."

"Aren't you the new member of the Channel 8 news team?"

"Fraid not! I'm here to buy cars, not talk about them."

"Oh! Sorry. You sure look the part. I'll tell the producer that he may have a good replacement if you're interested."

"I'm flattered. I'll just watch, thank you." He ran off to find his announcer so she could read a Q-card for the camera.

Wolf laughed saying, "Sure you don't want a career change?"

"You're not trying to get rid of me are you?"

"What, and miss the adventure you bring into my life? No way!"

Boudy told me that most of the cars he would be interested in would be auctioned the first day, before many of the real buyers showed up. So, I was front and center sitting on hard, uncomfortable portable bleachers waiting for the show to begin.

Boudy called, "Are you there?"

"If the camera covers the bleachers, I'm the one wearing red."

"Good, I have the numbered list of cars going through today. I'll give you the numbers. Mark them on your program for bidding. Do you have anyone to go look the cars over before they hit the auction block?"

"Wolf is here and, yes, he volunteered to do just that."

"Wonderful! What could possibly go wrong?" Boudy said.

I sighed and didn't say anything about my younger brother's comment that may have jinxed my mission.

## Chapter: 62     (Day one At The Auction)

All day long cars were being manually pushed around the ballroom. Some of them were on dolly's pushed by eager volunteers. They were pushed up a slight ramp onto the auction platform for bidding. When the bidding was done, the cars were tagged, then pushed along one wall and out of the ballroom to the storage area.

Outside, two areas were designated for distribution of cars. Those with buyers and those that failed to be sold. The sold cars were pushed down a ramp into the lower parking lot for owners to claim. It was a constant, methodical process that kept a line of cars moving along in perfect order.

On our first day, the auction went by quickly and uneventful. I bid on 10 cars for Boudy, and he won 4. Not a bad day. I went to the bidding desk and made arrangements to have the cars shipped to his car lot.

Inside the ballroom, Hop and his team of FBI agents were constantly scanning faces attending the auction. The only person that I felt was part of the gang of people coming after the car was the photographer, Jan. When he arrived today, he was visible everywhere with an attractive redheaded woman he used as prop next to a variety of cars.

The auction coordinator, Earl Trotter, came by several times to see how Wolf was doing and encouraged him to relax and enjoy the collection of cars going on the block.

When the auction closed for the day, Wolf and I hitched a ride back to Germantown. Hop drove with Wolf in the front, and Florence and I in the second row captain's chairs. During our ride, I asked Wolf if he found any cars he might bid on. He said, "There were several good looking cars in all kinds of condition. Some worth every penny they were asking at the auction, but I believe the cars at Global in Olathe were better."

Hop asked, "When this case is over, will you be able to separate yourself from the black Mustang? You seem pretty attached."

"That car is everything I imagined it to be. You bet I'll be sad to turn it over to the government. By the way, what will they do with it anyway?"

"Providing it survives this operation, and we get our man, it may go on display at Quantico along with other artifacts from FBI operations. Items with a history inspire new recruits."

While Wolf and Hop carried on a discussion about hunting pheasant in Wisconsin, I asked Florence if she had someone special in Kansas City. She smiled and said, "I've dated a couple of people I met there but my job and the hours just keep getting in the way of any real relationship." She smiled pleasantly.

I smiled back knowingly, "Thats been my case, too, for the longest time."

She smiled and nodded toward the front seat, and I said, "Well, for now. We'll see how things work out. Long distance relationships are difficult."

Hop delivered Wolf and me to Wolf's home. Hop and Florence begged off for dinner. He said he had a Zoom meeting planned with team members who worked the auction looking for their 'most wanted' person.

When we arrived at Wolf's house he waved at me and went inside to feed Roger. I drove my Camaro back to my apartment. The day had been fun, but it was time for me to remove my nice new outfit and take a shower. It would be salad and iced tea tonight for me while streaming a good mystery show.

## Chapter: 63    (Albert's Early Release)

Friday, after Morty left the car auction, Charles gave him a lift to the used truck rental place near Tunica. The truck dealer had an ambulance in good condition that Charles rented. Morty put on some scrubs and drove the ambulance to the hospital where Albert was a patient. Brenda and Eline rode with him.

Albert aka Cal Marsh was in stable condition awaiting a treatment prognosis for his brain injury. Hospital staff had been treating the pain from his brain swelling using pain medication through an IV drip. Since he could not eat solid foods, another IV provided nutrients. He was withering away.

A bullet was in his brain, but he was cognizant of what was going on around him. The news about his injury was never good. He was frustrated and afraid that he would become a permanent prisoner in a hospital room for the rest of his life.

It was mid-morning when his nurse entered the room and said, "Good news! Someone is here to take you to another hospital. I'm here to prepare you for that trip. I also have some papers to be signed for checking you out of the hospital. Do you think you can handle that?"

Albert attempted to nod his head. The movement hurt but he was more than ready to leave. He was shocked when he saw his sister, Eline, and his cousin, Morty, walk through the door. Both were wearing scrubs. Eline wore a white lab coat, a stethoscope hanging around her neck while holding a clip board with X-rays. Morty stood by patiently awaiting orders to wheel Albert out of his hospital room. Albert knew they were there to rescue him, so he kept his mouth shut but a tear escaped from his good eye.

Eline turned to him and said, "Okay, Calvin, my name is Dr. Gloria Fisher. I'm a TBI specialist hired by your parents to take you to a care facility that specializes in traumatic brain injury. Are you ready to be transported?"

Mustering all of his energy, Albert managed to blurt out, "Yes."

Hearing his voice almost made Eline cry. But she said, "This EMT with the help of your nurse will transfer you to a gurney. Your IV bottles will be attached. The hospital is providing us with additional medication and nutrient bags for your journey." She said smiling.

Worried, Albert moaned, "Guards?"

"We signed you out with a release for medical reasons. You're free to go. You're going to California."

Albert was moved from his hospital bed to the gurney, and the IVs were hooked up to the gurney. Morty and a nurse wheeled Albert out of the room, down the hall and onto an elevator. At the bottom, they pushed him to an emergency exit and transferred him onto the waiting ambulance. Eline got in the back with Albert and Morty got in the passenger door. Albert's mother, Brenda, leaned over the seat and looked back at Albert and said, "You ready to leave this pop stand?"

Albert almost choked when he tried to laugh. He was on his way to an air ambulance jet waiting at the Olive Branch Regional Airport. Albert's escape from police custody was quick, slick, and effective.

It was after the day shift, when the hospital realized that someone with fake credentials took charge of one of their patients. All hell broke loose, and questions were being asked.

Albert, his mother, and sister were on their way to a hospital in Atlanta where Albert would be checked in under Calvin Marsh, a different but similar name. Brenda would resume her role as Mrs. Marsh, the patient's mother. Eline would make a cameo appearance as a visiting physician. She checked into a nearby hotel and await Albert's condition with Brenda. If all went well she would fly to New Orleans and meet up with Charles, Dirk, Ferdie, and Morty who would be bringing the car and the gold. As the jet took off, Morty waved goodbye, got into the ambulance, and drove to the Revenant convention center for use on Saturday.

The plan was coming together. Albert would have his brain operation. The family would meet up, then take a casual boat ride or airplane trip to Aruba, five million dollars richer.

## Chapter: 64    (Sleight Of Hand)

Little did I or anyone on our team know that while Wolf, Hop, Florence, and I worked the car auction, a diabolical theft of a key witness, the son of our most wanted suspect, took place across town yesterday.

Saturday was the big day at the auto auction. Bidders arrived from every corner of the country to bid on cars they had reviewed on line. Earl reported the auction had a good first day with over a quarter of the inventory going to the early bidders. Today, the same cars, not sold from yesterday, would go through again, many with no reserve. The specialty cars that drew the most attention were held for today's auction. The Meiner Auto Auction was set to make a lot of money on auction commissions.

The Renasant Convention Center was packed to the walls with eager automotive aficionados. Today, I donned my burgundy skirt with the split, hiding my Nano, and wore the crème colored loose blouse. I slipped my auction credential over my head and attached my hoop earrings. Wolf and I both knew, if the man Perry wanted his gold, today would be the day he would make his move.

Hop wanted eyes stationed at every entrance to the ballroom. Armed with facial recognition software on their cellphones, officers and agents scanned every face knowing the man was a master of disguise. I suspected Jan was related to the man I shot. He was everywhere with his shapely redhead trailing behind. The camera flash could be seen in every corner of the room. I had to keep an eye on him because I was certain he would be a key player to take the Mustang.

Wolf, armed with facial recognition software on his phone, was instructed by Hop to move around the area outside of the ballroom scanning faces. It was assumed, because the Mustang was on display, it was safe and did not need to be watched all the time.

Cars were constantly being pushed in and out of the ballroom. So, when two men pushed a beautiful custom red 73 GTO onto the floor and set it next to the Roush Mustang display, no one paid attention. The rotating platform was turned off, and ramps were set up next to the display.

While this was going on, I was on the third row, standing in the bidding bleachers, talking on my cell phone with Boudy. He said, "Number 146. That is the one I'm really interested in."

I said, "I see it, five cars back."

"Good. How's it going with you? Are you enjoying the car auction?"

"Yes, Boudy, and happy to be working for you."

While watching the cars being pushed onto the auction dais and talking on the phone, I saw out of the corner of my eye, I saw a strange redheaded man with a bushy red mustache, standing next to me. He was studying the auction catalog of cars coming up. I smelled something familiar. It was that cologne scent that shocked my senses into high gear. My eyes widened and I turned my head, saw the mole, then suddenly felt a pinch in my left shoulder. I was about to swing my shoulder bag into the man, but suddenly felt very weak, and my knees collapsed beneath me. I fell onto the couple standing on the bleacher step below me.

People around me screamed and the man standing next to me shouted, "Now!" into his cellphone.

Alarmed bidders gathered around my body. I was numb and barely conscious when I saw the photographer's face grinning above me. He said, "Give me a hand to get her onto the gurney."

I thought, " Gurney, what gurney?" In the background, I could hear Boudy's voice shouting, "Annette, Annette! Are you there Annette?"

I was hoisted up, placed on a gurney, then hurriedly wheeled through the crowd. Auctioning temporarily halted while on the most expensive car was being actioned off. I had just been talking to Boudy, and I had no idea where my phone or shoulder bag had gone. I couldn't move a muscle.

Hop was walking around the perimeter outside of the ballroom using his cellphone scanning faces. He heard screams, and he ran into the ballroom just in time to see what appeared to be an EMT, a well-dressed red headed man in a sport coat and the photographer pushing the gurney rapidly toward an exit door. He saw my burgundy skirt and knew it was me. He shouted, "Stop! FBI!"

They ignored him and Hop spoke into his communications microphone. "All units, emergency! Three men are pushing a patient out of the ballroom. Stop them for identification, immediately."

That diversion was enough for Ferdie and Morty to push the Mustang down off the platform then push the red car onto the platform unnoticed. The two of them pushed the Mustang out of the ballroom, onto the loading dock and down the loading ramp into the parking lot.

Ferdie and Morty jumped inside and started the car using the spare key fob. They drove the Mustang out of the parking lot, down the ramp to the lower level parking area. They saw what they were looking for next to several car trailers and pickups. They drove the Mustang to the pickup truck that had an enclosed car trailer with the tailgate down to load the car. Charles stood by the trailer waving. He was signaling them to hurry.

Instead of driving the Mustang into the trailer, Ferdie drove the Mustang behind the trailer and onto a ramp that went into an orange shipping container. He got out, strapped the vehicle down, went outside, closed the container door, and put a metal seal on the lock.

Morty hurried around to the car trailer, lifted the ramp, and secured the door. He patted the trailer twice then Morty got into the truck with Charles who drove off with the truck and the trailer.

Ferdie hurried over to the side of the building and waited. Dirk, driving the ambulance with Annette inside, rushed by and out of view from the parking lot cameras. Ferdie watched while Dirk in the ambulance sped off.

Charles was pleased. Dirk had done a good job, everything was moving along as planned.

Watching from a second story landing, Wolf stood next to Hop and another agent helplessly watching as a pickup truck hauling a car trailer drove down the ramp to the first level parking lot, followed by an ambulance that did not use its siren.

Wolf turned to Hop and asked, "What just happened?"

## Chapter: 65    (The Double Bluff)

Chaos erupted around me when I collapsed on the bidding bleachers. I suddenly recognized the red headed man standing next to me as my previous abductor because of his mole and cologne. That was when I suddenly felt a sharp pinch in my left arm. Whatever he used put me down, I fell like a lead kite. The problem was, I was conscious, but I was totally incapable of doing or saying anything. My mind was screaming and nothing came out of my mouth except drool.

Hop heard the commotion and Wolf immediately rushed to where he knew I was bidding on cars. They both bumped into one another and watched while I was being hauled out of the ballroom door on a gurney by my captors. Both of them rushed after me out to the loading dock, only to see me loaded into an ambulance that sped out of the parking lot.

Hop called for backup and a BOLO for local police to look for the ambulance. Then Wolf suddenly said, "The car!"

Hop's mouth dropped and they both knew that my abduction was a well-planned diversion for the theft of the car. Sure enough when they got to the rotating display, a red Pontiac GTO was sitting in place of the Mustang. The switch had been made during the panic surrounding my collapse.

Police cars arrived at the convention center only to discover that the ambulance had already left along with a pickup hauling a car trailer. They immediately put out an all-points bulletin. They were told to concentrate on interstate and freeway traffic.

I have to admit, my second abduction was well planned. I could clearly see out the back window of the ambulance as we fled the convention center. The ambulance drove under I-40 Highway that went by the Memphis Pyramid and across the DeSoto bridge. We continued north along Main St., then turned left onto Willis and crossed the small bridge to Mud Island Peninsula. We suddenly came to a screeching stop and parked at the far end of a grocery store parking lot.

I knew I was the distraction for recovering the car and they could just as well have left me in the ambulance, but that was not in their plan. I was roughly lifted off the gurney and carried fireman style between Jan and another man to a non-descript SUV in the parking lot. I saw a pickup truck and a car trailer parked next to us. The man I knew from his smell as Perry, jumped out and trotted over to the SUV. He said to me, "Hello there wiseass. You ready for a party? Okay you guys, let's go."

I was tossed in the back seat of an SUV next to the man who had muscled me onto a gurney and then into this SUV. Jan, the photographer, and the man I knew as Perry sat in the front seat and paid no attention to me. I was seat belted in, head lolling against my hoop earrings and drooling on my pretty crème colored blouse.

This time I was worried. My cellphone was not with me so Wolf could not track me with the 'Where's Annette' app he installed on my phone a couple of years ago. And I didn't know how long I would continue to be in this condition. My hope was that cameras at the convention center and traffic cameras were tracking us. It occurred to me, I was in a different vehicle, and why did they leave the Mustang behind? That didn't make sense.

Perry was driving, He said, "That call was Ferdie. He's picked up the shipping container and loaded it onto the flatbed. He's leaving the convention center now. He said, there are cops everywhere down there but no one's paid him any attention."

The man sitting next to me said, "Charles, where are we meeting up with Ferdie?"

"That used truck lot near the casino. We'll unload the container and check out our stuff. We'll transfer the load there then go in two cars and meet up in Greenwood."

"What are we doing with her?" The man sitting next to me asked indicating me with a nod of his head.

I saw Jan's face looking back at me. With an evil grin he said,

"Oh, ik heb veel plannen met haar, nietwaar poesje?"

Now, I am not a linguist, but my brain broke down each word of the German sounding language and understood the intent of what he said. I guessed he said something like, "Oh" and "I have plans for her." I couldn't tell the rest.

Even in my incapacitated condition, I shuddered hearing his lascivious intentions.

## Chapter: 66     (The Quest For Clues)

Deputy Director Doug Simmons was on the phone with Hop. He was incredulous, "So, let me get this straight. You didn't get the man on our 'most wanted list' and you lost the Mustang you were baiting him with. On top of that you lost our FBI contract employee, Annette, for a second time? You say she was spirited out of the convention center right under your nose? Are you with me here? And at the same time, you lost the man she shot, who was in a hospital at the time with a bullet in his brain. And taken to who knows where?"

Hop swallowed hard and simply said, "Yes, Sir. I think you have it. We may have a lead on the car though."

Doug raised his voice, "What are you doing to find my contract employee? I don't give a damn about the car. You are helping this con man make a laughing stock out of the bureau! I can tell you right now, neither the Director nor I am happy."

Knowing his career was on the line Hop said, "Yes, Sir. We were blindsided. Annette was used as a diversion so they could take the car. Police have just found both the ambulance and the pickup with a car trailer that was used, not far from the convention center. We got lucky, someone was taking a family video in that parking lot. We have a description of the SUV she was taken in. The ambulance and car trailer were both empty."

"They didn't just drive off with that Mustang, did they?"

"Uh, No, Sir. The car was never in that trailer. We're reviewing video camera footage now at the convention center and searching traffic cameras to see what happened to the car. Video images show the car leaving the loading ramp and driving down to the first level parking lot. The camera angle showed the Mustang being driven into that car trailer. Where it went from there, is anyone's guess at this point."

"Not good enough, Special Agent. We're the FBI, we solve problems, we do not make more problems. Find Annette and find your most wanted man. Understood?" Simmons said irritated.

Again Hop provided a weak, "Yes, Sir." The Deputy Director hung up, and Hop gave Florence a bewildered look.

Wolf was sitting in the FBI breakout room listening to the conversation with the Deputy Director on speaker phone. He heard Hop try to explain what happened. Wolf was steamed. The same people responsible for kidnapping Annette, a just a few days ago, had done so again. He checked her 'Where's Annette' app and the phone's location was where he was, in the conference center. He sighed thinking, *"She must have dropped her phone in the building someplace. Now, he and Chick had no way to find her."*

Embarrassed, Hop ignored Wolf's inquiring stare, and he strolled over to talk to some agents. Florence saw Wolf's frustration and walked over to console him. "We were expecting something big, but not this."

Wolf didn't want to hear it. He turned to leave. Florence held his arm and said, "She's kidnapped. This is something the FBI is good at. Right now, we have no idea what direction they were going after they made the vehicle swap on Mud Island."

"Yeah, right! I bet you haven't seen hide nor hair of that smiley photographer either, have you?"

Florence looked surprised. "No we haven't, should we?"

"Annette recognized him, at least she recognized his features being the same as the man she shot in my office parking lot. He was one of them, probably a sibling."

"Well, we did manage to detain the red headed assistant that was with him. She was there when Annette collapsed on that bleacher. She's an eye witness to exactly what happened. I can confirm from video that the redheaded man with a mustache standing next to Annette helped the photographer load Annette onto a gurney which magically appeared right after she lost consciousness. The girl said she was hired the day before through a local talent agency. All she was hired to do was pose in front of cars while Jan snapped pictures. We looked her up and she checks out. She was an unwilling accomplice to the kidnapping and car theft."

"What really fries my bacon is, Annette's phone is still someplace in the building." Wolf said.

"I understand wanting to call her but surely those men took her phone." Florence said.

"That's what I'm telling you. The phone is here, in this building. I know because of a phone app she has on her phone. We call it "Where's Annette." The phone is here!" He said emphatically.

The lightbulb went on, and she said, "Well, that *is* important! Let's tell Hop."

Hop tried to avoid us until Florence said, "Hop, stop! You need to listen to this."

Annoyed and ashamed, he turned and gave Wolf an angry stare. He rudely said, "What is it?"

Before Wolf could answer, Florence told him about the cellphone in the building. She said, "We need to get our people out there to search for the phone."

"It's just a phone. The phone's here, she's not. So what?"

Wolf was now grinning. Hop asked, "What?"

"The phone has an app called 'Where's Annette', but something just clicked in my memory. In Olathe, we put a tracker on the Mustang. Look it up and find out where the car is. Annette's kidnapper and Annette will probably not be far away from that car. We need to get to that car before they discover the gold is gone. They'll just put a bullet in her out of anger."

Hop looked surprised, like he understood. "The tracker! You're right! Find the car with the tracker. I'm making that call right now. I have the code for that tracker in my billfold. Our lab should be able to track that signal in real time."

Wolf looked at the blond man who just stood there with a curl of hair creeping across his eyebrow, mouth open. He said, "Well, don't just stand there, get going!" Wolf barked.

Hop snapped out of it and said, "Yes! I'll call right now."

Florence took charge and asked the agents to begin searching for Annette's cellphone. Fifteen minutes later, a Special Agent walked into the breakout room grinning. He held the cellphone in one hand and Annettes' burgundy colored shoulder bag in the other. Another agent said, "I found that photographers camera, too. What do you want me to do with it?"

Florence took the items then thanked both. She turned to Wolf and said, "Our agents found the phone and the purse underneath the bleacher where she collapsed."

Florence slipped the phone into a plastic bag and sealed it. She winked and said, "Maybe our most wanted guy handled the phone and threw it under the bleacher along with her purse."

"Is her gun in there?" Wolf asked.

Florence shrugged and opened the burgundy shoulder bag. She looked up and said, "No gun."

Wolf said, "That could be a good thing. No gun could mean they took it, or it could mean she left it at home in favor of her Nano. Which means if she comes around, she'll be armed and very dangerous. And let me have the camera. It might come in handy."

Florence gave Wolf a flirtatious smile. She said, "You know, you're pretty savvy for a car guy."

He smiled back and said, "You're not bad yourself, for a government girl."

"Girl? I kind of like that."

"Annette first, then maybe we can find a place to enjoy an adult beverage together." Wolf said winking.

"I would like that, Wolfman." Florence said blushing.

## Chapter: 67    (The Chase Is Afoot)

Hop was studying a computer screen shared by a lab in Washington. He shouted, "Got it!" The FBI convention center breakout room erupted in cheers.

"Where's it at?" Agents kept probing.

Hop looked over his shoulder and said, "I know those roads. I was on them just a few days ago when we went to that pot farm. I wonder what his fascination is with the Blue's Highway?"

Wolf said, "It's not the Blue's Highway that fascinates our perp, it's the casinos. I bet he's holed up in one of them and he hooked up with someone who knew those pot farmers near Clarksdale. I'm sure we'll find him and his gang in one of those casino hotels."

Hop looked up in wonder. He said, "Yeah, but which one? How many are there?"

Wolf said, "There used to be a lot more but now there are six remaining. One just opened this year when the old Happy Strike Casino went bust."

"I wish I knew more about this man, where he's from and what his real name is. We can't cover six casinos. Who do we ask for? We'll just flush them out and probably lose Annette in the effort. I need some ideas." Hop said hopelessly.

Florence said, "I think Wolf is right, they're going to Tunica. We don't go to the casinos we go to where the car is at and see who comes looking for the car."

Hop said, "I'll bite! Where do you suggest?"

"It's where they were before, Highway 61. Let's get moving." Wolf said.

"Okay, if we hurry, they won't have much time to do anything before we get there." Hop said.

Florence asked, "Do we call in the Mississippi Highway Patrol to assist?"

Hop said, "Based on your last encounter with them, I think we'll leave them out of this operation. We'll inform them later, along with any local police. I think we'll rely on US Marshals to help us out."

Four FBI SUV's left the convention center in a fast moving convoy with emergency lights flashing. They headed south, toward Highway I-55 taking them to Mississippi.

Wolf and I rode in the back seat while another agent drove with Hop in the front seat. Florence rode in a car behind us. Wolf had to admit, The agent didn't let any grass grow under his car. He was hitting speeds well over 100 MPH.

On the way to Tunica, Hop used his vehicle phone app to speed dial the US Marshall's office in Memphis. He requested assistance with the apprehension of a "most wanted" suspect in Mississippi. They said they would mobilize immediately, especially when he told them a Federal employee was abducting, and they were crossing state lines. He asked them to rendezvous in the parking lot of the Key West Motel in Mississippi where I-65 meets Highway 61 near Casino Strip Blvd.

It didn't take long for Special Agent Bob to us drive past Olive Branch to the exit for Tunica. We made the exit and raced toward Highway 61. Meanwhile, Hop in the front seat, was following the progress of the tracking app of the Mustang on his laptop. He said, "The tracking device has now stopped moving."

"Where?" Wolf demanded.

"Actually, not far from the motel you mentioned. It's hard to nail down an exact spot on this app but right at Highway 61." Hop said looking up.

Wolf said, "I think the car is being transported in a truck. There's a good sized truck stop and a large lot near that intersection. It sits next to a used truck business. I've been by that place myself several times. The lot has hundreds of old used semi-trucks and trailers sitting around. Our guy may have rented one of those trucks, or maybe even the ambulance from there. He may be returning a truck. I've never met or seen the owner of that facility, but I bet that guy would do about anything for the right amount of money."

"Good. We should be there in about 10 minutes. Florence stay in contact with the US Marshalls. Tell them what we've got."

"On it!" She said.

Wolf said, "I bet they're meeting up at Wild Harry's."

Hop and Florence looked at one another with no clue as to what Wolf was talking about.

## Chapter: 68    (The Showdown at Wild Harry's)

Charles took a slow circuitous route leaving Memphis using inconspicuous streets, hoping to avoid any road blocks. Meanwhile, Dirk kept his eye on the SUV's side mirrors while talking to Ferdie on his cellphone. Morty sat in the back seat and kept a curious eye on me slumped against the passenger door opposite him.

I guess it was thirty minutes into our trip when I heard Ferdie report by speaker phone that he was leaving the convention center parking lot. He said, "Police vehicles, car trailers and pickups are everywhere. I drove the heavy duty fork lift that came with the flatbed trailer across the parking lot. I easily picked up the shipping container and put it on the flatbed trailer. Then, I used the forks to lift the forklift onto the back of the flatbed. I chained everything tight into place. Piece of cake. Then got off the trailer and started the truck and now I am leaving the parking lot. No one suspected or stopped me for anything. Everyone was looking for an ambulance and a pickup truck with a car trailer, not a semi-truck with a flatbed that held an orange shipping container." He said laughing.

Ferdie told Dirk he entered the downtown freeway system and was taking Highway 55 south toward Mississippi, driving just under the speed limit. Dirk chuckled while listening to his cousin's story.

Charles told Ferdie, "Drive to Wild Harry's Truck Stop at Bowdre, MS on Highway 61 and park next to all of the other trucks and wait."

Dirk said, "We'll all meet up there before we go to the used truck lot. How's she doing back there, Morty?"

"Still out."

I could tell, were driving on highways I had been on just a few days ago. There didn't appear to be any kind of help at hand. My body was waking from the numbness, but I was still feeling like I did not have full command of my muscles yet. I was still pretty numb. Yet, I dared not let them know. Not even moving an eyelid was my only advantage.

I'm guessing it was 30 minutes or more later when Ferdie called and announced on Dirk's phone that he was at the truck stop and parking his truck. Dirk said, "We're not far behind you, cuz. We're taking our time. We'll be there shortly. No one knows what we're driving but we're taking no chances."

Charles said, "Stay put. You'll unload the container at the used truck lot next door. I'll pay the guy for the use of the ambulance, truck, and forklift. We'll tell him the ambulance has probably been impounded by the Memphis police. Funny, when Dirk and I went to the truck lot, I saw that flatbed just sitting there and that was how I got the idea. The used truck guy told me Hispanic roofers were always renting that truck with the flatbed trailer and forklift to haul roofing materials to job sites. He gave me a good deal on it."

"He'll want that ambulance back, you know." Morty said.

"We'll pay him enough to cover the impound fee. But we can't let him see the gold. If he does, it will be the last thing he'll see." Dirk said.

Charles was happy with the way things were working out. He asked, "How's our princess doing in the back seat?"

Morty leaned over and looked me over closely. I didn't move a muscle. "She's still out of it. I don't think you'll have any problem with her. You might need a mop though, she's sitting in a puddle of spit."

In fact, I was rapidly recovering from my drug induced numb feeling. But I worked hard to remain motionless. I stopped drooling some time ago. Not being a factor in their current plans to recover the gold was my only weapon at this time.

My eyes darted around the SUV. Morty was busy looking out the side window. Charles was driving and couldn't see me in his rearview mirror. Jan or Dirk, was busy on his cell phone talking to someone named Ferdie, who somehow managed to haul the Mustang.

Our vehicle slowed down, and we turned onto another road. Then before I knew it, we suddenly pulled into a large well-lit parking lot with a lot of cars and trucks. I saw a sign that read, "Wild Harry's Truck Stop."

I thought, *"This could work out to my advantage. A public place with lots of people. Once my captors get distracted by the guy with the truck that had the Mustang, I could quickly make a break and run out of the SUV, yelling and screaming."* Then it occurred to me, I could do that only if my legs were strong enough to carry me.

Excitedly, Dirk said, "There he is!"

"I'll pull up alongside him," Charles said.

Charles rolled down his window. He grinned and Ferdie gave him a two finger salute. He said, "We made it! Let's go to the truck lot next door and unload the container. I can't wait to see that car and what's inside. Once we've done that, we're home free. Good job, Ferdie. I'm buying steak dinners for all of us tonight."

*"Damn!"* I thought. A lost opportunity. So, I continued to act like a drugged-out zombie. *"Surely, they'll focus on recovering the car and I can make my move."* In the distance, I heard thunder clouds rumbling.

## Chapter 69    (Unloading The Mustang)

I listened to the joyful banter of my captors while Charles drove away from Wild Harry's in our SUV. The semi-truck with the flatbed and orange shipping container followed us out of the truck stop parking lot. Both vehicles made a slow and deliberate turn onto Highway 61. They slowly drove a short distance then turned right again through a gated, fenced property. Trucks and trailers of all kinds and colors were lined up all over the lot. Most of them appeared to look like junk to me. I couldn't tell any difference.

Charles and Dirk got out of the SUV. Charles called back ordering Morty to stay put in the car to keep an eye on me. I definitely wasn't going anywhere until I could find an opportune moment to make my move.

Through the window and watching out of the corner of my eye, I saw Charles approach a man and shake hands. I saw a semi-truck and a flatbed trailer with an orange shipping container on the back. It was parked several yards away after Ferdie pulled into the lot. The man I took to be Ferdie, got out of that truck and set about unloading the forklift.

I heard jovial teasing, joking, and laughing in the parking lot but couldn't make out a word. I heard the noise of chains being unhooked. Then after a few moments I heard the motor of the forklift making noise moving around the lot.

My eyes shifted to the man sitting next to me. I could tell Morty was getting anxious watching the action outside. He wanted to be out in the parking lot with the big boys and not babysitting a black headed rag doll. I heard him exhale. He made a decision and opened his door. He stood outside putting his elbows on top of the SUV, watching Ferdie unload the shipping container.

Now, it was my time. I moved slowly as to not draw attention. Reaching underneath my burgundy slit skirt and using my right hand, I closed my fingers around the strap holding my Nano in it's holster. I freed the Nano and raised my gun, pointing it at the man standing outside. He was paying no attention to me. I slowly exhaled, scooted over to his side, and said in a quiet, steady voice, "One word, and it will be your last."

"Huh? What?" Morty looked down into the SUV, saw my gun, and said, "Oh!" His eyes got big, and he was about to yell, and I said, "Not a word. I can shoot faster than you can move. You'll lose at least one gonad."

I slid over to his open door and nudged him aside. I couldn't tell if he was carrying a gun or not. I took no chances and quickly frisked him. I found one and tossed it out of the way. I ordered him to sit in the rear seat.

What to do next? I thought about knocking him out, but the small Nano might only manage to injure him, and he would make a fuss. With a gun in my hand and nothing to bind him with. I made a decision.

"Get out." I demanded.

He said, "What? You just told me to sit down."

"Now I want you to get out. Be careful if you make a move I won't hesitate to shoot you. Then, I'll take up a position behind this vehicle and take out your gang members, one at a time."

Morty laughed and said, "Yeah, like you could do that."

I tilted my head, smiled, and said, "Don't test me."

Morty got out of the car and stood next to it. I turned him around intending to use him as a human shield, should his companions decide to draw weapons. The move was not really necessary because everyone's attention was on the man driving the forklift, taking his time to unload the big orange shipping container.

I heard the business owner shout over the noise, "You say, I can have that container once you take it down? What's in it?"

Charles shouted back at him, "Yes. The container will be yours."

Ferdie tilted the container on the forklift backward just enough to clear the edge of the flatbed, and he backed up with the load. He finally set the container on the ground with a heavy thump and a cloud of dust.

I heard thunder again and looked up. At this stage, no one was at all interested in me or my prisoner. I decided to stand pat and wait to see what developed. Morty was moving from foot to foot, looked like he might bolt and make a run for it. I jabbed the Nano into his kidney and said, "Don't do it, you'll lose a kidney." He relaxed and put his hands on the SUV top. I could smell something acrid, then I realized he had just peed his pants. The man just had to go to the bathroom. I sighed.

Again, louder thunder and I looked up. The sky was getting darker. Rain would soon be moving into the delta. It was spring after all, and rain is frequent during this time of year. Across the yard, I heard Dirk loudly shout over the noise, "I'll cut the seal and back the car out into the lot."

Charles said, "Good!" He cast a glance at the truck guy and said, "Then check the trunk to make sure nothing's been tampered with."

"Will do." Dirk said. Using wire cutters, Dirk cut the seal on the container. He lifted the locking mechanism and opened the doors. Even from my perspective I could see him shake his head grinning. He shouted, "Man! This is some cool car. I'll get it unstrapped and back it out, Daddy." He said in a taunting voice.

I was standing there shocked, *"Daddy? So, they are all related."*

I asked Morty, "So, is Dirk your brother?"

He shrugged, laughed, and said, "No. Ferdie and me are brothers, Dirk is a cousin."

"Come on," I asked, "Is that your real names, Morty and Ferdie, like Mickey and Minnie?"

He laughed and said, "No. We've been called that since we were kids. I'm Martin and my brother is Freddy. Charles is my uncle. His wife Brenda, was my Dad's sister. They were all in the business together with my Mom and Dad."

"Were?"

"My Dad's dead. If he were here, you'd be dead as a cockroach."

No one in the parking lot gave us the slightest glance. I said, "Nice thought. So, they were all in the business of bilking widows out of their estates, I take it?"

"My Dad always explained that it was a game. We were like Robin Hood, taking from the rich and giving to the poor."

"With your family being the poor, I take it."

I looked up when I heard the Mustang's loud engine rumble to life. The car slowly backed out of the storage container. Dirk put the car into first gear and pulled the black Mustang around to the side of the container. Ferdie and Charles cheered. The lot owner got into the spirit of things and cheered with them.

Everyone, including the used truck dealer ran over to Dirk's drivers door. Dirk turned off the engine and stepped out of the car. He was grinning. "Man, this is some car. Can I have it, Daddy?" He asked in a whiney mocking voice.

"Forget it. It's your mom's. First things first, Dirk. Open the trunk."

Using the key fob Dirk popped open the trunk and he leaned over to look inside. Something immediately stung the side of his face. He put his hand up to the wound. Then he shouted out. "Oh, my god! The trunk is full of snakes."

"What? Charles shouted out and he ran around to the trunk and peered inside then quickly stepped back. A rattlesnake immediately struck out and nearly missed Charles. He backed up again, tripped over Ferdie's foot, and fell to the ground. "What the hell have they done? They did that on purpose." Charles shouted out.

Holding his now bleeding and painful wound on his face Dirk said, "When did they do that? We were watching that car on our app almost the whole time. I saw a big one with a dozen tiny snakes."

Ferdie said, "Man, you better get to the hospital, quick."

"Huh? Nah, it's just a scratch." Dirk said.

"It's a poisonous snake bite, cousin! You'll die within hours." Ferdie yelled.

## Chapter: 70    (The Cavalry Arrives)

Holding his face, Dirk looked at Charles laying on the ground then he glanced up at me with Morty standing next to the SUV. He did a double take and said, "Hey! Morty! What's she doing out of the car?"

They all turned to look in my direction. My gun was still in Morty's kidney. He didn't say a word or move an inch.

Still holding his face, Dirk began to move toward me. Then he stumbled and fell to the ground holding his face and groaning. Charles rolled over to get up. He had murder in his eyes. He pulled a gun out of his shoulder holster and yelled, "Ferdie, go help Dirk. I'm going to put that witch down." He got on his hands and knees pointing his gun at me. I was standing behind Morty, judging the distance, aiming, ready to fire my gun.

Suddenly, four SUVs rolled through the gates of the used truck lot and skidded to a stop. Agents immediately jumped out of vehicles shouting, "FBI! FBI! Put your weapons down!"

Charles, Ferdie, Morty, Dirk, the lot owner and I were suddenly surrounded by FBI. Ferdie and Charles were thrown to the ground and disarmed. I placed my gun on top of the SUV. Then I pushed Morty ahead of me and put both hands up. Three more vehicles full of US Marshalls suddenly arrive and they lept out of their vehicles and approached wearing bullet proof vests with guns extended in front of them.

A flood of Federal agents stormed all over the used truck compound, Charles and his family members were immediately rounded up and handcuffed, including the used truck dealer. A Tunica ambulance showed up and quickly took Dirk off to a local hospital, escorted by a US Marshal to.

Wolf, Hop and Florence ran over to me. I put my arms down and Hop actually held me close and kissed me. I thought, *"I need to get kidnapped more often."*

I asked, "How did you ever find me? I didn't even have my phone with me."

Wolf with camera in hand laughed and said, "No, you didn't. Your phone and purse are in that SUV. It suddenly occurred to me that there was a tracking device on the Mustang. We tracked the car knowing that where the car was, we would find you."

Out of curiosity, several agents and Marshalls went to inspect the Roush Mustang. It didn't take long for them to realize the car was infested with poisonous snakes. One of them was smart enough to shut the trunk lid of the Jackhammer to trap the snakes inside.

The people responsible for so much hurt and torment to so many others sat on the ground next to the flatbed truck looking pretty sad. Hop said, "So, the leader's name is Charles?"

I looked at Charles sitting on the ground and asked Hop, "Should we tell him?"

Hop asked, "About what?"

"About the gold!"

Hop slowly smiled and shook his head. "What he doesn't know, won't hurt us. He still thinks the gold is hidden in that car. He thinks we're all pretty stupid. Why spoil his delusion."

I watched while Wolf was busy taking pictures of Charles, his family members, and the FBI. I said, "Valid point. You know, I didn't get his last name at first. but Morty let it slip, the name is Jensen. Morty is an ex-Marine with explosives experience. He always did what the other family members told him to do. He's your weak link. He has names, dates and places for crimes his family members committed. Isolate him and break him." I said.

"So, we caught him, the most wanted criminal on the FBI wall! I can't wait to tell the Deputy Director." Hop proudly stated.

I said, "Not so fast, Charles is just half of this crime family. The other half left with his son out of a hospital to who knows where."

"You think there's another guy out there?"

"Not a guy, his wife, Brenda, and her daughter. Morty let it slip by telling me her name. There could be more cousins. The FBI will have their hands full finding everyone in this crime family. I think she was the mastermind and is out there, like a black widow spider, she can still be trouble." I said.

"I don't think we are done with her. I shot one of her sons and Wolf caused the other one to be snake bit. Dirk may not survive. Families like this are a cult. It's not love that binds them but devotion to a common cause."

Florence asked, "What cause would that be?"

I grinned and said, "Greed and the thrill of cheating people out of their money."

## Chapter: 71    (Home Again In Germantown)

While Charles was being seated in the back of a cruiser, I asked him. "Was it all worth it, Meneer Charles?"

He did a double take then smiled saying, "That's for you to find out, poesje." He said with an evil smirk.

I said, "Dutch King cologne. That's how I recognized you." Charles just looked away.

Suddenly, thunder crackled then boomed closer and lightning lit up the sky and struck not far away. Rain began to come down in large droplets blowing in from the west. Then rain began to pour in buckets. Everyone in the used truck parking lot ran to their vehicles for cover.

US Marshalls took custody of our crime family and drove off taking them to Memphis in the rain. Since no one was shot or killed at the used truck business, Hop, Wolf, Florence, and I along with several FBI and the remaining US Marshalls, made a quick decision. We sought refuge at Wild Harry's Truck Stop diner. Inside, we sat around a collection of tables, and I retold the story of my abduction and escape to an audience of eager listeners.

Wolf was jubilant and very animated while recalling his end of the story. "As I was saying before the cloudburst, a tracking device was put into that Mustang while we were in Kansas. We were able to follow the car using a computer. We figured Annette's captor would be somewhere near that car, so here we are."

I said. "I forgot all about that tracker. So, you tracked the Mustang after it left the convention center while I was taken to Mud Island and stuffed into an SUV? The ambulance, pickup and a trailer were left behind. That must have thrown you off."

"The pickup and car trailer was a ruse meant to distract us from the flatbed trailer. When police arrived on Mud Island, the grey SUV and the pickup with the trailer were abandoned. They were all stolen property. The ambulance we found belongs to the used truck guy, next door. We really didn't know what we were looking for. All we knew was, 'follow that car'." Hop said laughing.

While the FBI and US Marshalls were busy laughing and talking with one another, I told them about a lively conversation I had with Cousin Martin, aka Marty, aka Morty, who rode in the last car with the US Marshalls to Memphis. While we waited for our captured perpetrators to be loaded into US Marshalls vehicles, he was ready to talk to anyone, who was not a person with a badge, and he spilled the beans.

"By the way, your most wanted man's real name is…'drum roll' *is* Karel Jensen. At first, I couldn't understand what Marty was telling me, then I figured it out. Charles is not German. He's a South African ex-pat. The man I shot in Wolf's parking lot is his son, Albert Jensen. His brother, Dirk Jensen, is being treated for a poisonous snake bite at a local hospital. Fredrick aka Freddy, aka Ferdie drove the truck with the Mustang in a shipping container. The Jensen's are a family of thieves. Brenda, his wife, Carla his sister-in-law, His dead brother-in-law Buck and Carla's brother a lawyer by the name of Mickelson, other cousins, and lord knows how many more were all involved with the swindles they put together over the past twenty plus years." I said.

"Were you able to find out where the wife, Brenda is?" Hop asked.

"She and her daughter Eline, took Albert out of the hospital in Memphis and went supposedly to Atlanta. Albert was to be checked into a Traumatic Brain Injury center using his alias. Who knows where they went? Brenda, has the keys to the kingdom and knows where all of the money, except for the gold, is hidden. If you hurry, you may catch up to her." I said looking at Hop.

Hop looked amazed and said, "Okay! I'll call the Deputy Director and tell him what you just told me. Thanks Annette."

"Tell Doug hello for me." I said with a smile.

"How do you know the Deputy Director, by the way?"

"Long story that took place in Baton Rouge not long ago." I said with a grin.

Looking around the restaurant, I have to say, all of those law enforcement people were a ravenous bunch when it comes to food. They ate, laughed, and enjoyed sharing stories. I was starved and ate a thick hamburger, with onions, lettuce, and tomato along with a large order of fries while slurping a strawberry milkshake. We sat and watched rain pelt cars and trucks outside.

When the rain let up, we all moved back onto the used truck parking lot where we stood in the mud dodging puddles of muddy water. Checking my now mud spattered burgundy skirt I wondered if I should dry clean it or put it in my washing machine with cold water and soap. I gave up, figuring it was a total loss.

Standing outside, I was chilled by the spring air. Hop lent me an FBI jacket to wear. A local herpetologist had been called, and he showed up in his unusual looking yellow pickup with snake decals on the side. He introduced himself as 'George the Snake Guy' from Olive Branch.

We all watched, with our breaths held, as he carefully opened the trunk of the Mustang and stood there scratching his head. He asked Wolf, "Tell me, how did the rattle snake get into the car's trunk?"

Wolf shook his head and said, "I'm not sure, really. You see, over a week ago I was on a property south of here, near Greenville. I, um, got something out of the trunk and left the trunk lid open while I did some business on the property. I nearly stepped on a rattler myself while walking around. When I was done with my business, I simply pushed the trunk lid shut and left, not checking if anything was inside."

"How long ago?" George asked.

"It's been well over a week. Surely if a snake got in there it couldn't survive that long without food or water." Hop said.

"Not true. Rattlesnakes are cold blooded creatures. They can survive for extended periods of time without food or water, especially if they're pregnant with eggs. They've been known to live in the wild for several months without food or water. They can slow down their metabolism by up to 70%. You got yourself a fine specimen there."

Hop said, "I think we would all prefer if the *specimen* and her offspring were yours, not ours. Can you get them all out?"

"I'll try, but I got to tell you those little things are sneaky, and they can crawl into any tiny crack and remain hidden."

"So you're saying someone getting into the trunk may not be safe?" Florence asked.

"That's correct. It may take some time before that car is snake free."

Hop rolled his eyes and said, "Ho-boy! I'll warn them not to get into the trunk when I send the car to Washington."

George, the snake guy, immediately brightened up. "Washington? I know a professor, who is a good friend, who lives there. He taught me everything I know."

Hop smiled and said, "I'll need his name and number."

## Chapter: 72    (Brenda Gets The News)


No one expected the man now known as Charles Jensen to confess to anything. Given his phone call, he called his shirttail in-law, Manfred Mickelson, the family lawyer, and said, "Manfred, I need your help. I'm in jail in Memphis, Tennessee."

Manfred said, "I'll notify Brenda and will be on the next plane."

When Manfred called Brenda, she exploded. "He's what? He's where? What the hell happened?"

"Charles seems to think some woman kept getting in the way spoiling his and Dirk's plans. I'll know more when I go see him. Apparently, his past is catching up with him."

"But the gold!" Brenda shouted. "What about the gold?"

"He couldn't say anything on the phone, but I take it, Dirk was bitten by a poisonous snake when he opened the trunk of some car. Morty and Ferdie were arrested along with someone who rented a truck to Charles."

"All of them are in jail? I can't believe it! How could they be so stupid? Okay, go to Memphis and try to spring him and the boys out. I'm in Switzerland with Albert who had a successful brain operation yesterday. Eline flew back to Las Vegas and is waiting for news about where to meet everyone. I'm stuck here for at least a week. Keep me posted, Manfred."

Seething with anger, she hung up and walked back into Albert's recovery room. She looked at her son who was resting in a drug induced coma. She forced herself to calm down. She couldn't think clearly in this state. She needed to focus on Albert then make a plan to fix things with her family and recover her gold. She said out loud, "Poison snakes in a car trunk. Does that mean someone discovered the gold?"

A nurse walked in and spoke in English, "Albert's vital signs are good. The doctor said we should be able to bring him out of his coma tomorrow."

Brenda looked up and said straight faced, "Sounds wonderful. Thank you."

Two days later, Manfred showed up in Memphis and met with Charles. After the meeting, Manfred went to the county court with a filing that demanded the release of his client.

The county prosecutor told him Charles was being held at the Shelby County jail. Bail was denied for him being a flight risk and he's on the FBI's 'Most Wanted' list. Manfred was presented with a litany of charges against Charles, beginning with twice committing an aggravated assault and kidnapping of a Federal employee. Then there was video footage of him shooting and killing a man in Wolf LeDuc's home while committing a burglary.

Faced with the evidence, Manfred suggested, the man in the video appeared to be Elvis Presley, not Charles Jensen and the charges were bogus. Manfred insisted that the woman in question for kidnapping, voluntarily went with Charles in an effort to entrap him for kidnapping.

While this drama was playing out at the Shelby County courthouse, Federal Prosecutors began building a strong case of murder, extortion, and theft against the entire Jensen family spanning over 25 years.

The Bonanza Boom Casino in Tunica was raided by the FBI with search warrants. Special Agents discovered a trove of false identity records stored in the casino vault under Charles Jensen's various names. They didn't find much more than that. All physical evidence collected would be added to depositions from victims across the country who were eye witnesses as proof of his crimes. Finally, the FBI began connecting DNA evidence from crime scenes of Charles' victims.

Five days after the FBI raid, Manfred called Brenda with an update. He said, "Federal Prosecutors are building a case so Charles could never be released from prison. And neither would many of our family members. But it takes time to build a complicated case of this nature. It is imperative that the Justice Department first win its case for 'flight risk' against Charles and Dirk with no bond so they would not leave the country. I think I have a good defense against the murder charge in Germantown, and they can't prove that Charles had anything to do with blowing up a woman's car. We're suggesting that as a Federal contract employee Annette Dupart used her position to entrap Charles for kidnapping. When it didn't work the first time, she set herself up again to be taken. It's all a long shot but I think I have a good chance in court."

"What about the boys? Brenda asked.

"Everything against them is circumstantial. If anything, they could be considered accessories before and after the fact. Federal prosecutors will have a tougher time making a good case against them. In the meantime, Charles has been moved to a Federal facility in Henning, Tennessee. Dirk, Morty and Ferdie are in the Federal Corrections Institute in Memphis. It's a medium security facility. They are all awaiting arraignment. I need to fly back to Buffalo for a court case. I'll return in a week or so."

"Thanks Manfred. Albert is doing better. As soon as he's released, I'll set him up in a care facility in the Caribbean. Then, I'm coming to Memphis and Eline may come, too. Maybe I can do what they were unable to do. Thanks again for the update. I know you're doing your best."

# Chapter 73     (Back To Normal)

Hop returned to Washington and Florence returned to Kansas City. Wolf and I were both disappointed to see them go. I kind of think Wolf and Florence were able to spend some special time together. I don't know for sure, Wolf would never talk about it. I know I'll miss Hop. We were finally able to work out our relationship issues.

Work in and out of Germantown has consumed most of my time through the summer. I tried to keep track of what was going on with the Jensen's legal battles. As far as I knew, they were still being held on local, State and Federal charges. The press reported that all of the Jensen family members declared they were not guilty in front of a judge. They would remain in prison until court dates could be set.

Hop called me and I listened quietly as he read a report. "A team of FBI agents scoured Atlanta searching for Charles' wife, Brenda, and their son Albert. The daughter, Eline Jensen, was like a ghost, she never existed, no record of her anywhere."

"The FBI discovered a marriage certificate for Charles and Brenda Jensen issued in New York State 26 years ago. 18 years ago, a person with Brenda's name applied for a passport. Using that name, she left the country for a trip to the Caribbean. The passport was never used again, and she never reentered the country using that passport."

"Our financial researchers in Quantico dug into bank and real estate transfer records from several of Charles victims. A pattern began to develop. Money was wired through a bank in Florida then on to the

Cayman Islands. Our people got lucky. Cayman authorities cooperated, and we discovered most of the transfers to the bank were simply pass-through transactions in small amounts. Money left the Caymans and was sent to an Aruba bank."

"Aruba? Then where did it go?" I asked.

"Aruba is a Dutch colony. Many Dutch Afrikaners sought refuge there from the British. We think this was the families final destination. The money was transferred to accounts with different names. We believe this is the home base for our international criminals."

"We think the Jensen crime family still has plenty of property and money to take care of themselves for some time. If they had recovered the five million in gold, it would have been icing on the fraud cake. We at the FBI believe that money was not the motivator for committing all of those crimes. We think they did it for the thrill of fooling victims into giving them all of their worldly possessions. Killing victims was inconsequential to them. Our profile experts will seal the case against Charles Jensen and family members where the DNA matches."

"What's happened with his son, Dirk?"

"Our snakebite guy? He's dealing with facial collapse due to muscle atrophy and a partial loss of vision in his right eye and he's suffering from a number of neurological disorders related to the snake venom. On top of everything, I'm told his injuries are extremely painful. His lawyer has threatened to sue Wolf for inhumane injuries related to keeping poisonous snakes in a car trunk."

"Right? Anyone could have put them there." I said.

"You're not confessing are you?" Hop asked.

"Wasn't me. But tell me about Morty and Ferdie?"

"The cousins lawyer asked for Martin and Freddy to be released for lack of evidence."

"They're both accessories before and after the fact in every operation the Jensen's executed since those two were in their teens. Fingerprints and DNA should prove that. Morty admitted as much to me." I said.

"Proof. That is the fly in the ointment. They aren't getting off easy. We tried to break Martin and offered to cut a deal for him, that offer is still on the table. But he's still on the hook with ATF for that fire bomb of your car in the airport and another when one of Charles victims was blown up in Florida. He may get five years with good behavior and be on parole for ten. We think he's got a lot of money stashed someplace and will probably live a comfortable life when he's free."

"Is that all?"

"No, one more thing. I am in love with you, and I miss you."

His admission shocked me. I was hoping for words like that. Now I'm faced with the reality of Hop's confession. I didn't know what to say.

"Annette, are you there?"

"Yes, I'm crying. Oh, I love you, too, Hop."

"We need to work out a plan. This cross country relationship is killing me."

"What are you suggesting?" I asked, holding my breath.

"I'm suggesting that you come to Washington and move in with me."

That did it. My relationship hopes and plans just hit a wall. I slowly said, "Move to Washington?"

"I know it's a long way from Memphis or wherever your from. But I want you here with me. We'll be able to spend more time together."

I was hurt that I was expected to sacrifice my job and my life just move to Washington, DC. He didn't ask me to marry him, just move in with him. *"Kind of selfish,"* I thought.

"Annette?"

I said, "You're right. Washington *is* a long way from here. I do love you, too. We're still building our relationship. I think we need to meet and enjoy some time together where there are no work related things going on. I've decided to put my contract employee status with the FBI on hold for a while. I enjoy my career as a CPA. This is something I worked hard to earn. I appreciate the respect I receive from the car dealers I call on. I know your job is important to you, but mine is important to me, too. Can we plan on a short vacation together, maybe soon?"

"Where? Cleveland?" Hop asked laughing.

I laughed and said, "No, how about the Indy 500?"

"I get it, car related. How about Marco Island in Florida?"

"Now, that's some place I've never been. When?"

"Let me check my calendar." Hop said.

## Chapter 74     (The Woman Wants Revenge)

Halloween is not necessarily my favorite holiday. I do enjoy watching the kiddies dress up in costume to beg for candy but the adult costumes that tend to focus on gore and blood are not my thing.

I was invited to a Halloween costume party in mid-town by fellow CPA graduates from Memphis University. I was on the alumni list and had made professional friendships with several of my former classmates. Normally, I would not have considered attending such an event, except my love life with Hop had diminished quite a bit since his return to Washington. By the end of October we never made the trip to Marco Island. We each had busy work schedules that got in the way. To be honest, I was lonely and seeking friendship. I agreed to attend the party.

I refused to dress up as Morticia and opted instead to break out my Ragin Cajun cheerleader outfit that was given to me by a former teacher. I was never a cheerleader, but I was given the outfit as a memento from the faculty who all dressed in costume to cheer me along when I was in skeet and pistol competition for the Rajin Cajuns and the US Olympic trials.

So, without a date, I dressed as a cheerleader for Louisiana University, Lafayette, and drove to the party in my Camaro. I have to admit, the food was good, party was fun, and I was able to catch up on gossip about our former instructors.

I left the party early and was walking to my Camaro, parked two blocks away when this woman dressed in black as a witch lept out from in between the cars and startled me. I wasn't scared. I said, "You had me there for a second. Looking for Dorothy? I think I saw her on the yellow brick road a block back."

She shook her head and said, "Charles said you were a wiseass."

I had to think, "Charles? You mean that crazy old man with the stinky cologne?"

She wrinkled up her nose and shouted, "Stinky? I like that fragrance!"

I was confused. *Who was this strange woman and what did she want?* I asked, "Are you one of his amorous victims?"

"No! He told me all about you. You are the one that caused our family so many problems. You and you alone are the reason he's in prison. Not only that, my two sons are suffering because of you."

"Sons? Oh, my! You must be the infamous Brenda. I've heard so much about you. I must say, you certainly dressed for the part. How's Albert doing, by the way?"

I saw the flash of anger in her eyes. She said, "Better. No thanks to you."

"And that daughter, E-line, I think." I looked left and right then said, "Where is she?"

"She's with Albert. Too bad you won't ever get to see them again."

I took her threat for real when she suddenly pulled a long ten inch knife and pointed it at me. She grinned and said, "Charles told me about your shoulder bag. Drop it! Now!"

I stared at this evil twisted woman in front of me. I dropped my shoulder bag while reaching down to unholster my Nano. She rushed the ten feet between us and was on me in a flash. I had a half a second to lift my Nano and fire. She stabbed me in my upper left arm, and I shot her again using my right. She wouldn't stop. I pushed her away and received another cut across my thigh. This time I dropped her with a bullet to her head. She fell into a pile of witch clothing on the sidewalk. I thought she was down for good, but her body jerked, and she tried to get up. This time, I kicked her hard with my sneakered foot, and she fell backwards and stopped moving.

I stood over her body holding my gun, stunned. Someone heard the gunshots and called the police. I sat down on the sidewalk put my gun in my lap and tried to stop the bleeding in my arm and leg, crying while waiting for the police to show up. I believed that my Jensen nightmare was behind me. This crazy woman made me wonder. Would the rest of them come after me and haunt me forever?

## Epilog:

Brenda came to Memphis with the hope of recovering her gold and freeing her family members from prison. Her goal was to find the gold in the Mustang and claim it. Since Charles Jensen's arrest, the Jackhammer Mustang remained in FBI custody at their storage facility in Memphis. She worked on a way to get it away from there.

Her lawyer relative, Manfred, and she presented a phony bill of sale in the name of Perry Sanchez with a claim that the Mustang was in fact hers. They demanded the release of the car. That was when she found out the gold had been discovered in the car months ago, and there may still be snakes in the trunk. This news enraged Brenda, and she vowed revenge.

FBI Lawyers laughed and told her that the bill of sale for the Mustang was invalid, and she could be charged as an accessory to Charles theft of the car in Miami. Manfred quickly managed to get her away before she could be charged.

I found out later, Brenda made several visits to Charles at the Henning prison facility. He told her about me as the woman who constantly kept showing up to prevent him from recovering the Mustang and the gold. He told her I carried a gun in my shoulder bag and was not afraid to use it. That was when Brenda decided to punish me for taking her husband, the gold, and the car.

Looking back, I was actually sorry to have shot and killed the matriarch of the Jensen crime family. I really don't think she was evil, she was just greedy. But she came after me with a ten inch butcher knife. I got cut twice and she received three bullets. Fair exchange, I thought.

The impact of the crime family on innocent victims over nearly 25 years was beyond belief. It's still unknown how many victims became ensnarled in the Jensen Family's swindles. The FBI was able to assemble a timeline of 22 known victims both alive or dead to Charles. This was the foundation of a case against Charles and his wife, Brenda, now deceased that would be presented to a grand jury.

A crook to the core, Charles Jensen receives monthly deposits up to the legal limit into his prison account from an unknown source, which makes him very popular with his fellow inmates. Unfortunately, for society, he serves as a teacher and mentor to fellow prisoners by passing along his methods and tools he used to con so many people. He is rewarded by prisoners with all kinds of prisoner payment. He managed to con the con men around him for protection and a life of prison luxury.

Hop told me that the Roush Jackhammer was finally shipped to Washington, DC. Weary of poisonous snakes, curators at the FBI museum let the car sit before exhibition. I found out later that the vehicle was deemed snake free for the public to see. The car is displayed at Quantico in a swamp diorama scene with the trunk left open and fake snakes crawling out. A sign tells the story of how the car was used to bring down and arrest a notorious man from the FBI's "Most Wanted" list.

Wolf, Ezra, and I continue to call on our car dealer customers throughout the Deep South. Our business continues to expand, and we now have eight field consultants living in five states. Wolf continues to see Miss Penlope McGruder and escort her to society functions. Ezra enjoys driving his wife Lavon around in his special Lincoln Continental. My friends, Chick, and Clarence, often enjoy dining out in the many local restaurants with Wolf and me.

I received a nice letter from Greg Simmons, the FBI Deputy Director. Enclosed was a generous stipend check for 'Services Rendered.' This time, with Chick's advice, I tucked the money away into a government bond investment known as a MUNI. It is safely growing interest for when I may need it. My hope is to one day buy a more permanent residence than the second story apartment I now live in.

This year, I finally met Hop in St. Petersburg, FL. We drove along the Gulf Coast to Sanibel Island and enjoyed a delightful time shell hunting and visiting the J.N. Ding Darling Nature Preserve. Hop is not a water person, so we did no snorkeling, fishing, boating, or swimming in the warm waters of the Gulf. Beach lounging became Hop's and my favorite pastime. Well, second most favorite. Our relationship is still touch and go.

Wolf scoured the internet to find another Mustang. He moved on from the Jackhammer and found a beautiful red Shelby GT with a white racing stripe and manual shift. It had a little over 30,000 miles on the odometer. He searched a long time for this car. Ezra kept accusing him of looking for a 'Unicorn' car. Proud of his purchase, he delights telling everyone who listens that he purchased a 'Unicorn car'.

I was shocked to learn that Olathe Police Detective, Cory Sanders, dug deeper into Steve Williams death. He was able to build a solid case against Mark Dvorak for Steve's murder. Mark was angry for being fired by Global and he sought revenge on his own when Albert provided the guns to him. His partner, Clay Bonner, was sent to the County Detention facility for aggravated assault. He remains in the AA program.

Dealing with the Jensen family as a contract employee still gives me nightmares. I'm happy traveling and working for my cousin as a CPA and dealership expert. I drove my Camaro to St. Martinville, Louisiana, and my brothers tuned the engine up for me. I love my Camaro, and I've had enough Mustang Bluz for quite a while.

End

www.ingramcontent.com/pod-product-compliance
Lightning Source LLC
Chambersburg PA
CBHW060948030726
47503CB00003B/782